NINE DAYS TO ARMAGEDDON

NINE DAYS TO ARMAGEDDON

The End Is Nigh

Mike Carter

Book Guild Publishing
Sussex, England

First published in Great Britain in 2012 by
The Book Guild Ltd
19 New Road
Brighton, BN1 1UF

Typeset in Baskerville by Ellipsis Digital Limited, Glasgow

Printed in Great Britain by
CPI Antony Rowe

A catalogue record for this book is available from The British Library.

ISBN 978 1 84624 6883

Prologue

20 August 2012
Ice cap, central Greenland

Behind him the howling wind turned into a raging jet of boiling-hot steam that shot high into the air with a terrifying roar. As he ran and skidded across the slippery ice he felt burning splashes of boiling water fall on his head and just in front of him something large suddenly fell from the sky and flopped heavily onto the ice.

When he reached it he saw that it was a body and he retched, gagging at the grotesque sight before him. Frederik, devoid of all his clothes and skin, was a carcass of browny-red flesh, cooked and boiled like a huge joint of gammon, the steaming muscle and sinew of his face frozen in a nightmarish silent scream of agony.

He vomited, again and again.

Peshawar, Pakistan

It was unbearably hot – the sun shone relentlessly, baking the dry, stony ground and heating the air like a furnace. A military canvas bag lay dusty and dishevelled, forlorn except for a scorpion, black and menacing, lying within. Nearby was an old worn sandal, encasing a mangled and bloody foot. The body, still warm but barely breathing, lay a few feet away, scorpion venom flowing through its veins as life pulsed weakly from the bloody stump. An engorged fly buzzed from the stump and alighted on the dusty canvas bag – inside, guarded by the deadly sentinel, lay another poorly built home-made bomb.

Malik Husain cursed.

'Idiots!'

Chapter 1

13 December 2012
Iceberg Alley, east of Newfoundland

Craig Macintyre hunkered down against the screaming wind. It had a bitter icy edge, barely warmed as it blew from the barren wastes of the Arctic, and carried a blizzard of sleet with every gust. Fifty metres below, huge ocean swells smashed into the base of the rig, sending spray lashing against the accommodation module and horizontally through the drilling derricks.

As an operations team leader, it was his job to ensure that nothing, absolutely nothing, stopped or slowed the relentless stream of black gold. Not even a howling gale, tempestuous seas or a looming iceberg. It was a hostile environment but he loved it. After fifteen years in the business, he understood the dangers and like every other rig man he knew of the terrible accidents that had happened in the past, almost all with the total loss of the crew – the *Alexander Kjelland* in the North Sea in 1980, the *Ocean Ranger* in Alaska in 1982, the *Piper Alpha* in the North Sea in 1988 – the list was endless.

But those were in the early days of offshore exploration and new designs had significantly improved the safety record. And *Ocean One* was one of the largest and safest oil platforms in the world, designed to withstand hundred-knot winds and thirty-metre seas. Its concrete island, on which the rig and accommodation block sat, was a massive structure designed to store oil and to withstand impact from large icebergs drifting south on the

Labrador Current from the spring and summer Arctic thaws. And, as extra insurance, sturdy support vessels constantly monitored drifting bergs and could lasso and tow away any that seemed intent on collision. With twenty-five thousand icebergs being produced each year by Greenland and Canada and several hundred of these finding their way into the North Atlantic shipping lanes, such precautions were necessary.

As the rain stung his face as he supervised his team struggling to repair a loose junction between the manifold and one of the process separators, he thought of his beautiful six-year-old daughter back home in England. He was pleased that he had bought her a puppy and he looked forward to watching them grow up together.

Suddenly, a warning siren sounded and made him jump. Two hundred and thirty-five men looked up from their work or their leisure activities, or were rudely awoken, their faces tense and anxious.

He sprinted towards the control centre, sending a blast of rain and sea spray flying into the hot and crowded room as he opened the door. Bill Watson, the offshore installation manager, Fred Paulson, the offshore operations engineer, a couple of other team leaders and a dozen other men were already there. He slammed the door shut against the howling gale and screaming siren.

Tense and expectant faces were staring at the offshore installation manager.

'Right, listen up, everyone,' Bill shouted across the crowded room. 'And pay attention because we don't have much time. The rig is in grave and imminent danger – a huge iceberg is heading our way. Where the hell it's come from, I've no idea. It's unusual to get bergs at this time of year, never mind such a monster.'

The men looked at each other and a few frowned.

'But surely this rig is designed to withstand iceberg collisions?' Craig queried. 'And, anyway, I thought that's what the support vessels were for?'

'Absolutely, Craig,' Fred answered, nodding his head vigorously, 'and it's true in ninety-nine percent of cases. But here we seem to have a one in a hundred thousand year event – a berg so big that it's off the scale. In the Antarctic it probably wouldn't be that unusual but up here it's a giant.'

'As you can imagine,' Bill continued, 'our support vessels have been frantically trying to divert the beast but it's obviously too big to lasso and too big and dangerous to try to nudge away. The US Coast Guard International Ice Patrol has over-flown it and they confirm that it's huge. Apparently, it's a tabular flat-topped berg with vertical sides and they estimate it to be almost six kilometres long, three kilometres wide and sixty metres tall.'

'Shit!' someone in the room cursed. 'That's not a berg – that's an island!'

'That's unbelievable,' Craig said, slowly shaking his head in disbelief. 'It must weigh several hundred million tonnes or more.'

It took a few moments for the news to sink in and for the shock to subside.

'How long have we got?' Craig asked, suspecting but dreading an unpleasant reply.

'The Labrador Current is running at five knots in a southerly direction,' Bill answered, 'and the wind is blowing a gale from the north so I suspect that it's moving quite fast, probably eight or nine knots. It will be here in less than six hours.'

There was a collective gasp and the room fell silent.

'We must shut down the well,' Fred continued, 'and make preparations for an emergency evacuation. One of the support vessels is racing back here and the other is shadowing the berg to see if it changes direction. The weather is atrocious and the seas are running with ten-metre swells with the occasional fifteen-metre rogue wave so it will be impossible for the support vessel to take men directly off the rig. Any rescue by helicopter is also ruled out because Newfoundland and Nova Scotia are fog-bound. I'm afraid that we will have to use our own lifeboats.'

The men in the room went deathly quiet and a few looked out of the windows at the huge white crested waves below.

'And, it will be dark soon,' Bill added unnecessarily, 'so we must work quickly to . . .'

'Hang on,' a voice in the crowd suddenly interrupted, 'can't the US Air Force bomb the berg – blow it to smithereens?'

'It's too big,' Fred replied, 'way too big. They'd need a nuclear bomb and they're not going to do that. And, anyway, in this weather, they'd never hit the damn thing.'

Craig, who suddenly grabbed a calculator from the control desk and begun punching in numbers, caught Bill's attention.

'What is it, Craig?'

'If it really is that big,' Craig answered slowly, 'and composed mainly of ice, then one-eighth is above water and seven-eighths are below. If it's sixty metres tall then there should be about four hundred metres below the water line. The Grand Banks part of the continental shelf on which we sit is three hundred and thirty metres deep so the berg could ground to a halt before it gets to us.'

He shrugged and looked round the room – there was suddenly a lot of nodding and a few smiles and brightening faces as a hint of hopefulness entered the room.

'You're right, Craig,' Bill replied, 'we had already considered that. But if you're wrong, we'd only be left with about twenty minutes as we're sitting on the very edge of the Grand Banks.'

Craig and the other men considered the chances and slowly they all nodded their agreement – they couldn't take the risk.

'Right, gentlemen,' Bill growled, 'let's get to work! We've got one derrick drilling a new well and one derrick extracting and processing oil. Get them shut down but do it safely – we don't want oil or gas spurting everywhere and we don't want any accidents. Let's go!'

As nightfall began to descend on *Ocean One*, and with the wind and sleet howling around them, Craig and his men worked feverishly under the floodlights to shut down the processing derrick. Ten thousand barrels an hour of crude oil were pumping out under immense pressure from the oil reservoir three thousand metres below in the bedrock and surging up several active wells before converging in the newly repaired manifold and the processing module. Turning these wells off while they were still under pressure was a difficult and dangerous procedure and every oilman feared a blowout from the highly inflammable gas mixed in with the oil. Over the years there had been a catalogue of disasters where leaking gas had ignited and caused devastating and deadly fires. It was every offshore oilman's worst nightmare – and especially for the crew of the *Ocean One* as they were sitting on top of a two-million-barrel concrete oil drum.

'Craig!' one of his men suddenly shouted in his ear. 'You're wanted urgently in the control room.'

Craig frowned – surely it couldn't be more urgent than what he was trying to do?

When he arrived, sodden and oily, he frowned again – his friend Sean O'Brian, the big team leader on the drilling derrick, was just leaving, his face set in an angry scowl. He looked at Craig and shook his head furiously before rushing out into the driving rain and spray.

'What is it?' Craig asked impatiently when he entered the control room, wanting to get back to his men.

Bill was shouting down the phone, his voice angry and exasperated, and it was Fred who replied.

'We've been ordered to carry on pumping and drilling. The head office technicians have run computer simulations and every time it shows the berg grounding on the sea floor almost two kilometres from here. Management don't want us to shut down as it would mean losing production for several days while all the procedures and safety checks are undergone to get back on line. Bill's almost lost his job over this.'

Craig shook his head.

'Bloody hell!' he growled. 'That's what I initially thought but then we all agreed it wasn't worth the risk. If you can have a monster berg suddenly appear against all odds why take the risk of it not grounding for some inexplicable reason? The danger to the crew and the potential ecological devastation would be catastrophic. It would be . . .'

Suddenly, Bill slammed the phone back down on its cradle.

'I don't believe it!' he shouted, jumping up and throwing his arms in the air. 'They say ignore the berg and just get on filling the storage tanks – the oil tankers are due in two days' time when this storm is forecast to ease.'

'Typical,' Craig growled, rubbing an old scar on his chin where a loose pipe chain had smashed into him, 'but it doesn't surprise me. If we lost production, even for a day, that's quite a few million dollars lost revenue. Mid-Ocean Oil might profess to be concerned with the men's health and safety and the environment but, at the end of the day, money talks.'

Bill nodded and slumped back into his chair.

'You're right, of course,' he said, his voice resigned. 'I just thought that, for once, they might see sense. Anyway, you need to get back and make sure that the extraction and processing isn't stopped. But,' he added, looking hard at Craig, 'as soon as I hear from the support vessel that the berg is less than two kilometres away and obviously not grounding then I shall sound the klaxon and everyone is to stop working and to don their immersion survival suits and prepare to board the lifeboats. Understood?'

Craig nodded and then raced back into the maelstrom outside.

It wasn't long before the klaxon sounded again. The wind, still howling and whistling through the steelwork, had lost its blizzard of sleet and a half-moon and stars appeared, disclosing a frighteningly tumultuous scene around them as heaving seas crashed against the concrete base. If they had to launch the lifeboats in that, Craig thought, God help them.

As he ran into the accommodation block to get his immersion suit he bumped into big Sean again, who was covered from head to foot in pungent-smelling oil and mud.

'We managed to get the drilling operation back on track,' he shouted at Craig, 'but we had a problem at the No. 4 wellhead so I'm worried about the drill bit overheating. We may have lost drilling mud circulation.'

Craig shrugged.

'Too late to plug it now,' he shouted back. 'Let's go!'

After donning his cumbersome survival suit, he made his way as fast as he could to the control room, men racing all round him in their orange survival suits or oily work clothes. But as he reached the control room door, something stopped him. He felt drawn to the railings at the edge of the platform, fifty metres above the raging sea. When he reached the edge of the accommodation block he looked round the corner and out to sea and his jaw fell open. There, just over a kilometre away, was a huge wall of ice – sheer, eerily white cliffs lit by the half-moon, towering sixty metres above the crashing waves.

For the first time in his life, he felt the icy talons of terror clasp his heart and squeeze as he gazed unbelievingly at the sinister ghostly colossus. At that moment, he knew they were all doomed.

Bursting into the control room, he was hit by a tense atmosphere of fear and dread. The crew of offshore platforms were a tough rational bunch used to hard work, fast living and a harsh environment. Until now, they had focused on the job in hand and ignored the demons nagging at their unconscious but now, with the klaxons screaming and men rushing to don survival suits, the demons had landed – pale clammy faces and scared wild eyes stared grimly back at him.

'Craig and Sean,' Bill shouted, as he struggled to clamber into his survival suit, 'get your teams to lifeboat No. 5. As soon as each lifeboat is full we're going to launch it. We don't have much time, maybe only about fifteen minutes. Once you've hit the water it's going to be bloody awful with huge breaking waves and a howling gale – everyone must be well strapped into their seats. The support vessels report that there is a strip of calmer water in the lee of the berg – if you can manoeuvre the lifeboat into that area then one of the support vessels will attempt to take you all on board. The helicopters are still grounded by fog so we're on our own. God help us all.'

Craig and Sean and the other team leaders raced out of the control room and headed for the muster station for each lifeboat. There were five of these on *Ocean One*, each capable of carrying fifty men; they were located close to the accommodation block ready for just such an emergency. Similar to lifeboats on cruise liners they were lowered from davits by steel cables attached to the fore and aft and maintained and operated by coxswains – but totally enclosed, with a much more solid construction and with a powerful engine.

'Doug!' Craig shouted above the wind at the second mate who was supervising the lifeboat evacuation. 'How many have boarded?'

The second mate looked down at his clipboard and frowned.

'Only one hundred and seventy-three so far,' he said. 'All the coxswains are at their helms and running through the pre-launch procedures but we've still got another sixty-two to go.' He looked through the spars and steel struts of the platform and could clearly see the huge and ominous moonlit white cliff bearing down on them. 'We're running out of time,' he added unnecessarily, his voice tinged with panic.

Craig nodded and looked at his watch. He thought that they might have about twelve minutes at most but they had to commence the launch sequence as soon as possible.

'Fill lifeboats 1 and 2 first,' he ordered, 'and get them away. I'm going back into the accommodation block to round up the slow ones. Doug, in six minutes broadcast a four-minute evacuation warning through the Tannoy. That should give . . .'

Suddenly, there was a huge explosion and a massive ball of blazing gas erupted from the main derrick and shot up into the night sky. A blast wave of hot pungent oily air hit the three men as their stunned faces stared at the orange ball of fire.

Sean looked at Craig.

'Shit!' he growled. 'Looks like No. 4 wellhead's suffered a blowout.'

Craig felt a spasm of despair. 'Then there's a good chance the manifolds into the processor could burn through . . . and the whole topside structure will be engulfed. We've got to get these lifeboats off fast. Come on, Sean.'

He raced away as fast as he could, encumbered by the survival suit, and with Sean immediately behind him. As they ran into the accommodation block Craig sent Sean to check the lower communal floors and he raced up to the first floor. He was astonished to see men in their bedrooms packing bags with their personal belongings – cash, mobile phones, cameras, clothes, pictures of their families, all kinds of rubbish – all the while the klaxon screaming its frantic call.

'Get the hell out of here!' he shouted, grabbing one of the roughnecks and pushing him out of the room. 'It's gonna blow!'

He raced up to the next level and he just couldn't believe the stupidity of some people – he found one of the crane operators idiotically trying to stuff an expensive music player and speakers into a large holdall.

'Leave it!' he shouted angrily. 'You can't take that on the lifeboat.'

He shook his head exasperated but raced on, up the stairs and onto the second floor. Here, in one room with the door closed, he found two of the Chinese cooks, still in their kitchen overalls and cowering in the corner, shaking with fear and their eyes wide with shock.

'What are you doing?' he growled. 'You need to get to the lifeboat muster stations.'

But the terrified cooks shook their heads and stared at him.

'Now!' he shouted, grabbing them by their collars and trying to haul them across the room.

Suddenly, the wailing klaxon stopped and for a few seconds there was a brief and surreal moment of calm and silence and everyone stopped and looked up. But then the Tannoy crackled to life and barked its urgent broadcast.

'Listen up!' the second mate ordered. 'The lifeboats are launching in four minutes. I repeat – the lifeboats are launching in four min . . .'

11

Suddenly, there was another massive explosion and the whole accommodation block jumped and Craig almost lost his footing. The dark bedroom window suddenly flashed a garish orange glow and he knew that the manifolds had melted and the processing module had exploded. Any moment now and the whole topside structure could become an inferno – after all, they were sitting on a two-million-barrel keg of oil.

'Shit!' he cursed, glancing for the last time at the two cowering cooks before racing out into the corridor and down to the communal areas.

Even now, men were rushing around, some heading towards the lifeboats but some stupidly heading elsewhere.

'Craig!' someone shouted at him. 'Let's go!'

Big Sean O'Brian grabbed his arm and pulled him out of the accommodation block. Immediately, they were hit by a blast of heat and the sound of explosions as the fire began to engulf the platform. As they passed the control room they could see Bill Watson standing up, gesticulating wildly and shouting down the phone. Craig started to veer in that direction but Sean tightened his grip and dragged him along the gangway. The pungent smell of burning oil swirled around them in the howling gale and when they glanced out to sea an enormous menacing wall of ice, from horizon to horizon, was eerily lit up in the silver moonlight and the flickering orange glow of the raging inferno. Huge white-crested waves smashed into the base of the platform but close to the berg the sea was calmer and he could clearly see one of the support vessels bobbing about on standby.

When they reached the lifeboat stations, Doug had already launched the first lifeboat and the second and third ones dangled precariously above the raging seas. It was a difficult task and the lives of fifty men in each boat hung on a split-second decision – one moment the lifeboats hovered just above a huge mountain of water and the next they dangled twenty metres over a deep valley. Although specially strengthened there was no way the boat and the men could survive such a plunge.

Craig could see that Doug's nerves were at breaking strain and his hand trembled as it rested on the release levers. He ordered the second mate to concentrate on filling the last two lifeboats and told Sean to watch the pattern of wave crests and troughs and count down the approach of a suitable wave.

As explosions sounded around them and the platform shuddered, Craig ignored everything, his focus concentrated on Sean. He could see Sean's head nodding rhythmically as he counted the seconds between wave trains and then suddenly his arm shot out and pointed at Craig, at the same time as he shouted, 'Release!'

Craig pulled the release levers and the fore and aft hooks of lifeboats Nos. 2 and 3 opened, sending one hundred men plunging into the water. The timing was perfect, just behind the tip of the breaking wave, and as the boats swept into the following trough their engines kicked into life and they surged away from the platform.

Suddenly, the howling wind seemed to die down and the raging sea calmed. Craig immediately knew what it meant and he looked behind him – a vast expanse of ice, sheer cliffs towering sixty metres above the sea bore down on him – an enormous island, ponderous yet unstoppable.

'Doug, get into one of the lifeboats,' he frantically shouted at the second mate. 'I'm going to launch them. You too, Sean – the seas are calmer here in the berg's lee so I don't need you.'

As the doors slammed shut he activated the launch procedure and watched as the last two lifeboats swung out from their davits and began to descend towards the dark and menacing sea below. When they were five metres from the water he pulled the release levers . . . but just at that moment a tremendous explosion ripped through the superstructure, sending a scorching blast of air across the deck and making the whole rig lurch. Lifeboat No. 4 cleanly released and plunged into the water but the stern hook of the last boat jammed as the platform jolted and the bow plunged into the sea leaving the boat dangling diagonally beneath the rig.

Frantically, he reset the lever and then pulled it again as hard as he could but the aft hook was jammed solid.

'Shit!' he swore. 'Now what?'

He looked down at the lifeboat and saw that it was swinging dangerously in the ocean swells beneath the rig, very close to the sharp edges of the concrete island. He had little choice – either he had to find a rope and abseil down to try to release the aft hook or somehow he had to cut the steel cable. Either way, he had only about three minutes before the berg struck.

And then, suddenly, he spotted a figure crossing the gangway towards him – it was big Sean O'Brian, dragging an oxyacetylene tank and equipment behind him.

'I told you to get on the lifeboat,' Craig growled, trying to sound annoyed.

'Couldn't leave you behind,' Sean replied, grinning like a maniac.

Together they clambered to the edge of the gangway beneath the aft davit and fired up the oxyacetylene cutter. Behind them the explosions and sound of collapsing derricks and super-structure grew louder and more frequent and the gangway beneath their feet shuddered. In front of them a towering wall of ice loomed up out of the darkness, pushing a surge of water before it.

Below them, the lives of thirty men hung literally in the balance and, for the first time in his adult life, Craig prayed.

'Help us, God!' he shouted to the heavens. 'Please, God, give us the strength to help these men!'

Suddenly, without warning, the oxyacetylene torch cut through the steel cable and the lifeboat's stern dropped with a tremen-dous crash into the sea and the cable whipped back dangerously close to Sean's head. They stared at the lifeboat for what seemed like ages, willing the engines to start. And, with moments to spare, it coughed into action and began to surge away from the blazing rig and the towering wall of ice.

'Come on!' Craig shouted, shielding his face from the roaring and hissing inferno. 'We need to get some height – I've got a plan.'

Sean looked at him confused but then, shrugging, chased after him, along the gangway and up to the next level. They were heading for the side closest to the approaching icy colossus and it occurred to Sean that perhaps Craig had lost his senses, over-whelmed by their terrifying predicament.

'Quick!' Craig shouted, racing up the ladder of one of the derrick cranes. 'We've got to get the arm out, away from the rig and over the sea.'

The immense vertical wall of ice towered into the night sky, rising almost twenty metres above them. Inexorably, it bore down on the platform, driven by winds and currents, a trillion kilo-grams of unyielding, implacable ice, a huge unstoppable island as large as the Isle of Wight and surging south at nine knots.

Craig dived into the crane's cab and prayed that it still had power. He punched the start button and sighed with relief as the control console lit up. Quickly, he swung the crane's arm out, pointing it directly at the encroaching iceberg, and then turned the power off.

'Come on!' he shouted, clambering around the cab and into the crane's vertical latticework tower. 'Follow me!'

Flames and explosions rocked the platform and as they climbed the heat grew more intense and the air full of fumes and acrid smoke. The fire was by now so intense that night had been turned into a lurid flickering orange day. When they reached the arm they clambered across, crawling precariously on the narrow walkway, seventy metres above the black forbidding sea, and dangerously exposed to gale force winds.

'Get ready to slide down the cable,' Craig shouted above the howling wind and roaring inferno. 'It's our only chance.'

Sean looked at the desolate iceberg and back at the blazing rig, the first hint of fear flickering across his face.

'Is this your plan?' he shouted back incredulously.

Craig grinned and, wrapping his arms and legs round the

cable, quickly slid down the ten metres to the iceberg's cold and unforgiving surface. Sean followed, dropping onto the ice just as the huge iceberg struck the rig's concrete island. There was a tremendous crash and the already weakened metal superstructure crumpled inwards, sending a huge ball of fire into the sky. Craig and Sean dived to the ground as the two-million-barrel concrete casing was sheared from the sea floor and toppled hissing into the water.

Inexorably, the immense island of ice drifted over the blazing surface oil and immediately Craig and Sean were plunged into the cold and gloomy night, their only company the silvery half-moon and the howling wind. Crouching down on all fours they looked around and then at each other. It was as wild and desolate a place as anywhere on earth and their eyes and faces said it all – fear and dread.

Chapter 2

14 December 2012
Reykjavik, Iceland

Malik had been to Iceland several times. Clearly, it was a fascinating place but he wasn't there to bathe in the hot thermal springs, trek into the rugged volcanic mountains or fish for giant cod in the freezing seas.

Indeed, Malik Husain wasn't even his real name – it was an adopted Muslim name. Born Stephen John Browning in Dewsbury, Yorkshire twenty-seven years previously, baptised and confirmed as Church of England, he was as Anglo-Saxon as they came – blue eyes, blond hair, almost six foot and with a thick Yorkshire accent.

But somewhere along the line his Christian values and spirit of nationality had deserted him and in their place was a deep-seated virulent hatred – a hatred of the immigrants who had taken over his home town; a hatred of the British government for sending him to fight useless wars in Afghanistan and Iraq and then abandoning him after a roadside bomb had robbed him of an eye, scarred his once handsome face and given him tinnitus; of the American government for starting the wars in the first place; of the local council for failing to find him a job; and of healthy people in general for treating him like an ugly disabled leper and outcast. In fact, he hated everything and everyone.

Now, though, he was going to get his own back and show

the world he wasn't just a useless piece of flotsam to be ignored or kicked about. No, he was going to get revenge. He had a plan and it had already been in operation now for three years. Everyone knew that Nostradamus and the Mayans had predicted that the world would end on the winter solstice in 2012 because of a terrible war between Islam and Christianity. Well, all he was going to do was help it along a bit – welcome to Armageddon!

'Welcome back, Mr Browning,' Frida Jonsson, the plump and buxom owner of the guesthouse, said enthusiastically, a pleasant smile on her face and a twinkle in her eye. 'I see that you're only staying for one night this time. Perhaps you could tell me all about yourself? Over a bottle of wine and a meal?'

Malik looked appraisingly at the middle-aged landlady and almost immediately said no – after all, he had important work to do. But then, on second thoughts, he realised that she might be useful to his plans – after all, she was local, would make a good cover and was expendable.

'Thank you, Frida,' he said with an engaging smile, 'that would be very nice. And call me Stephen.'

An hour later, after carefully checking his room for any surveillance devices or unusual wiring, he headed off towards the city centre. He rarely caught a taxi or bus, much preferring the anonymity of walking – that way he wouldn't need to talk to anyone or be seen closely and he could more easily detect if he was being followed. He had decided, at the very beginning three years ago, to be as nondescript and uninteresting as possible – that way he could go about his business unheeded and undetected. In the early days, he had felt the need for a full and bushy beard and a trimmed moustache in accordance with Islamic tradition but he soon realised that it attracted unwanted attention – and that could jeopardise his vital mission.

Soon he was at Hringbraut, outside the Landspitali University Hospital, and he walked straight in without talking or looking at anyone. A man dressed in a dark-grey suit is rarely questioned or noticed, and uninterrupted he made his way up to the second floor. Without knocking, he entered one of the offices.

The bespectacled white-haired Middle-Eastern man sat behind the desk looked up and smiled.

'Malik Husain,' he said softly, standing up and warmly shaking Stephen's hand, 'it's good to see you again. You are looking well.'

Stephen laughed.

'Thank you, Hashim,' he replied, equally warmly. 'And you are looking tired and overworked. But, then, you are a doctor.'

Hashim Kareem sighed, his face weary and lined.

'Yes,' he admitted, 'Iceland is paying the price for the credit crunch and its greed with years of austerity and tight budgetary constraints.'

Stephen nodded and smiled. To him, embarked on his apocalyptic mission, everyone was expendable and simply a tool to be used as part of his great plan, but he could not help but like the elderly doctor.

'Is everything ready?' he asked simply.

Hashim nodded.

'It has taken a long time,' Hashim said, 'because I did not want to arouse suspicions. But it is now ready and fully operational.'

He laughed.

'My home is almost as good as any of the operating theatres here at the hospital. If necessary, I could even perform an appendectomy or a triple heart bypass there.'

Stephen chuckled, impressed.

'But,' Hashim continued seriously, 'you must bring a theatre nurse. I cannot risk exposing our plan – there are very few Muslims here in the hospital and I am too old to try to seduce one of the non-Muslim ones!'

Stephen nodded.

'Yes, I now have two,' he replied, 'and they are both experienced theatre nurses working in busy hospitals in England. Like the rest of my team they are as zealous as I am and they have already booked their flights to Iceland.'

'Very well, Malik,' Hashim said, smiling, 'we will do our part. But now, you must go – after all, I do have patients to look after.'

'And I must fly back to Heathrow in the morning,' Malik replied. 'We don't have many days left.'

Blackpool, England

A terrible scream rent the air and Susan Macintyre jerked awake, frantically sitting up in bed, her heart racing. What was that? Lucy? She looked at the clock – 2.30 a.m.

The scream came again and this time it was clearly from Lucy's bedroom.

'Lucy!' she shouted, diving out of bed and racing down the corridor. 'I'm coming, sweetheart.'

She flicked on the light in Lucy's bedroom and gasped as she saw her daughter sitting bolt upright in bed, her hair dishevelled, her face pale and sweaty and her eyes wide open in fear and shock. Bonnie, cowering at the bottom of the bed, looked equally frightened.

'Lucy?' she gasped, rushing over and hugging her daughter. 'What's wrong? Are you ill?'

Lucy slowly shook her head and tears began to well up in her eyes and trickle down her face.

'Mummy, Mummy,' she eventually said, 'I had a terrible dream – about Daddy. It was horrible and dark with huge angry waves and giant monsters attacking his oil rig and people were dying and he had to jump and . . .'

'There, there,' her mother soothed, embracing her more closely and wiping damp straggly hair from her face. 'It was just a dream – a not very nice dream. We all have them sometimes and they don't mean anything. Daddy's fine and, anyway, you know what he's like – he likes a bit of adventure and excitement. We'll ring him in the morning, shall we?'

Lucy slowly stopped shaking and gradually, still enclosed in her mother's arms, began to drift back to sleep.

In the morning, Susan called the doctor to the house but, apart from a mild temperature and tiredness, there was nothing wrong with Lucy. Next, she telephoned the *Ocean One* oil platform, hoping to get through on the satellite link. Sometimes, atmospherics made this difficult and initially she wasn't too concerned.

But later in the day, when she had already tried several times, she started to get worried and a nagging doubt began to germinate and grow. After Lucy had asked her for the tenth time if she had managed to speak to Daddy she decided to phone the oil company's special personnel number.

'Hello, this is Susan Macintyre. My husband, Craig, is on the *Ocean One* rig but I can't seem to get through. Is there a problem with the connection?'

'Er, hold on, Mrs Macintyre,' the woman at the other end replied uncertainly, 'I'll, er, put you through to Mr Evans. He's the HR director.'

A sinking feeling in Susan's stomach suddenly erupted and her heart beat faster.

'Hello, Mrs Macintyre,' a weary-sounding voice came over the phone, 'yes, we are having trouble getting through to the *Ocean One* oil platform. It appears that a storm has swept down from the north and all communication has temporarily been disrupted. As you know, these things happen and I'm sure that everything is fine. Don't worry – if there are any problems, we'll contact you.'

Susan thanked him and put the phone down. The sinking feeling in her stomach became a hollow void – she felt uneasy and not at all comforted by the oil company. For an HR director, he sounded remarkably insincere.

Ice cap, central Greenland

Jarvik Petersen slowly sipped his coffee, warm and cosy in the small Danish wooden research station buried five metres into the snow and ice. The sun never rose at this time of year and he could see on a wall monitor that the twilight world above was a horrendous place of freezing sixty-knot winds laden with a blizzard of snow.

His old friend Frederik Larsen had been repatriated to Denmark in the summer. Jarvik had wanted to bury the body in the place where he had spent most of the last two decades and the place that he had so deeply loved – here in the ice cap, to slowly migrate to the sea with the glaciers. But his family had wanted to bury him in the little churchyard in their village of Jerup, near Frederikshavn.

Jarvik had returned to Denmark to attend the funeral, to write a report on the incident, to write a scientific paper and to recuperate. Now, back in Greenland, he looked again at the photographs of Frederik Larsen – it was gruesome viewing. It was impossible to tell that it was Frederik, so thoroughly had his skin and subcutaneous fat been cooked away. It had all happened on a cold but beautifully sunny day in the summer. And it was still as vivid and terrible as if it had happened yesterday . . .

The ice beneath his feet had suddenly shuddered and he had quickly looked at the laptop screen – large flashing red letters had frantically warned:

DANGER!
SEISMIC PROBABILITY – 100%
IMMINENT!

The pit of his stomach had lurched and his premonition demon had shouted 'Told you so!'

'Frederik!' he screamed across the lake. 'Frederik, get the hell out of there!'

Suddenly, there was another shudder and ripples began to form on the glassy lake surface; at twelve kilometres wide and fifty metres deep, it was the largest melt-water lake in Greenland.

'Shit!' he cursed. This was bad. He shouted again and this time Frederik heard him, stopping paddling long enough to smile and wave.

'Get the hell out of there!' Jarvik screamed, waving his arms frantically and running into the icy-cold water.

But it was too late. The ice shuddered more violently and an ear-splitting rumble reverberated across the ice cap as, fifty metres beyond Frederik, the surface of the water belched and a huge whirlpool formed. Within moments the whirlpool had grown to a huge gaping hole and, with a roar, water gushed like Niagara Falls into the crevasse, cascading down to the bottom of the ice, three kilometres below.

Frederik, his face suddenly panic-stricken and terrified, thrashed the paddle like a manic windmill, but the inflatable canoe, heavily laden with scientific instruments, began to be sucked backwards, slowly at first but with mounting speed towards the gaping maw of the terrible chasm.

Horrified, Jarvik had watched helpless. He was already up to his chest in freezing water and it was impossible to reach his old friend. With madly flailing arms and a long, drawn-out scream, Frederik Larsen was sucked down into the roaring mael-strom.

Jarvik had closed his eyes, his senses and mind numbed by the awful events. For two decades he and Frederik had worked together – he serious and intense, Frederik easy-going and laconic. Often in hostile environments and cramped living conditions they had formed a deep and trusting friendship and Jarvik was stunned by the shock of the sudden loss. They had taken a risk, as they had done many times before, but this time the odds had been against them.

As the water had disappeared, he was left sodden and exposed to the icy-cold Arctic air. He shivered violently and uncontrollably and it roused him from deep shock. Carefully, he made his way across the slippery ice and, grabbing the laptop, raced towards his skidoo. As he quickly discarded his sopping jacket and threw on a spare one he looked back across the gleaming icy depression where once there had been a twelve-kilometre-wide lake. Suddenly, his heart jumped and a glimmer of hope erupted out of despair – there, near the gaping maw of the crevasse, was the crumpled yellow wreck of the inflatable canoe. Could Frederik still be alive? Could he have managed to cling on desperately and even now be awaiting rescue?

Quickly, he activated the emergency rescue beacon on the skidoo, sending a distress signal back to the Danish research station, two hundred kilometres away, and grabbing another spare jacket and a coil of rope he rushed back onto the empty lake. Hope that his friend might still be alive drove him on, making him oblivious to his frozen fingers and chilled bones.

But as he neared the huge black hole he gasped at the size of it – clearly it could have swallowed a cruise liner had there been one cruising majestically on the lake and in less than an hour it had swallowed twenty billion gallons of water. The canoe, torn and crumpled, had been pierced and caught by a jagged ridge of ice and all of its contents, including his dear friend, had vanished. He peered into the gaping chasm and shuddered – what a horrible way to go, sucked into the very bowels of the ice cap. He sank to his knees, all hope gone and overwhelmed for the second time with sorrow and sadness.

But as he knelt on the edge of the hole he felt a sudden vibration through the ice. And then, suddenly, the hole began to hiss like the sound of air being forced out under pressure. He looked at it and frowned, confused. But there was no time to try to understand it – it quickly increased in strength to a roaring gale.

He stood up and began to back away, the premonition demon in his stomach awakening and once again telling him to run, as fast and as far as he could. He wasn't going to ignore it for a second time and he turned and fled. If only he hadn't ignored it the first time – poor old Frederik would not have perished and would not have made his sudden and gruesome reappearance.

Now, four months later and back in Greenland, he pondered yet again the geological processes that could have so spectacularly caused such a strange and disturbing event. He knew that Iceland, lying fifteen hundred kilometres east of the research station, was a hot spot of volcanic activity sitting as it did directly on the Mid-Atlantic Ridge. That island comprised some of the youngest rocks in the world, being created as the North American tectonic plate diverged away from the Eurasian tectonic plate and the few centimetres gap each year being filled with molten rock from the Earth's mantle. But Greenland comprised some of the oldest rocks known to man and for millions of years there had never been any hint of volcanic activity. It was strange – very strange indeed. His colleagues in the research station were as dumbfounded as he was – where the hell had super-heated steam and water suddenly come from? But he knew that there was only one way to confirm it – he had to go back and take some scientific readings and get some evidence. It could be an immense discovery and he would make sure that Frederik Larsen was given due credit and had his name forever etched into the scientific halls of fame.

Tomorrow, if the blizzard subsided, he and a small team from the research station would skidoo back to the site of the vanished melt-water lake and drop thermal sensors and cameras down the sink hole if it was still there. But this time they would be more careful and if he had so much as a hint of a premonition he would be out of there like a shot. No way did he want to be boiled alive – not even for science!

In the morning, the blizzard had blown itself out and a rare calm and crisp polar twilight, with a balmy temperature of minus twenty degrees Celsius, greeted them as they climbed from the tunnel of the research station. Jarvik had been in Greenland every year for the last twenty years but he was still moved by the sheer beauty and enormity of the land. A spectacular display of aurora borealis lit up the landscape, dancing and shimmering like fluttering curtains in flowing shades of green, red and yellow – the playful souls of Inuit children that had died at birth.

The skidoos, already loaded with equipment and provisions for five days, were quickly organised, one for each member of the remaining five-man Danish polar research team – none of them wanted to remain behind and miss this potentially exciting new discovery. They had two hundred kilometres to cover, all easy flat terrain that they had already traversed in the summer, and they expected to arrive by late afternoon the following day.

But after about eighty kilometres something strange stopped them in their tracks. The expanse of relatively smooth and flat snow and ice suddenly came to an end and instead huge jumbled ridges of ice, some rising fifty metres into the air, spread from horizon to horizon.

Jarvik scratched his head.

'That's weird,' he said to no one in particular, as the whole team dismounted and gazed in awe and confusion at the enormous jagged wall.

'It wasn't there before,' Runi Christiansen said unnecessarily.

'It's a pressure ridge,' his brother, Johann, said, slowly shaking his head in amazement. 'There shouldn't be a pressure ridge here – it makes no sense. It's not possible.'

'Not only that,' Jarvik added, pointing to his GPS. 'Look at this.'

They all crowded round and immediately there was a concerted gasp. The GPS showed that they were in the right place but not at the right altitude.

'It's not possible,' Johann repeated, still shaking his head. 'We can't be eight hundred metres higher than we should be. That's almost a kilometre.'

'We didn't notice anything on the way here,' Jarvik said, 'so either it must have been a very gradual incline or else the whole ice cap, including the research station, has lifted. That's definitely weird.'

Suddenly, there was a tremendous crash from above.

'Watch out!' Runi shouted, diving to the ground.

Jarvik looked up and saw a block of snow and ice the size of a large detached house tumbling directly towards him.

'Shit!' he cursed, simultaneously diving to the ground.

With an enormous ground-shuddering thump the five-million-tonne block crashed to the base of the pressure ridge, bounced several metres over the prostrate scientists and crashed with another thump on top of the skidoos before tumbling noisily across the ice cap.

'Shit!' Jarvik cursed again. 'That was close.'

'You can say that again,' Runi said, pointing to the flat and mangled skidoos. 'Now what?'

They surveyed the wreckage. Clearly, the skidoos were destroyed beyond repair but everything else was serviceable, albeit bent, buckled or squashed.

Jarvik considered the options. They were not equipped for an extended stay on the ice and their provisions, even rationed, would last only for ten days. Although they had cross-country skis they didn't have a sledge to carry the tents, food and spare clothes. So, they had no choice – they would have to turn back. It was disappointing but necessary.

'Strip the skidoos of the gear,' Jarvik ordered, 'and we'll camp for the night a kilometre back – after our close shave, better safe than sorry. Lucky we brought the small inflatable dingy – we can inflate it and use it to carry the tents and gear. Tomorrow, we will begin the journey back to base camp.'

Headquarters, Mid-Ocean Oil, England

David Evans was tired, irritable and fed up. For the last twenty-four hours he'd managed about two hours sleep and that had been slumped on the sofa in his office. Apart from quick and desperately needed cigarette forays, he'd been unable to leave the building and he'd lived on a succession of pizzas and black coffee. Not that that was particularly different from his normal diet but what was unusual was the absence of several pints of beer to wash it down with. Since his wife had left him five years previously his health had gone into free-fall and his waistband had gone ballistic. And now, as he waddled into yet another emergency update meeting, a pounding stress-induced headache exploded behind his eyes and forehead.

'David,' Mid-Ocean Oil's dynamic American CEO greeted, 'grab a seat and give us an update. Yours is not an easy job right now but I'm sure you're coping magnificently.'

The HR director coughed nervously and looked round the table. Apart from the CEO, who remarkably still looked smooth and polished, the other heads of departments all looked drawn and haggard – clearly the emergency was taking its toll.

'Well, er,' he began uncertainly, 'we had successfully jammed all the radio satellite links from *Ocean One* except for the one in the control room – so, we could manage the information getting out and contain the news here in the UK. Obviously, you can't stop it all because anyone can Google the weather stations in the area and all the wives know that there's a storm blowing through. But for us, that's a good thing, as it's helping to provide a cover story and none of them know about the berg.'

The CEO nodded.

'Excellent, David,' he said smoothly, 'no point in worrying the wives unnecessarily. And, obviously, we don't want any of this leaking to the press, the environmental agencies or bloody Greenpeace. Hopefully, this berg will simply sail on by and no one will be any the wiser. With oil prices so high at the moment, the last thing we want is an interruption of production or, worse, a curtailment of our offshore operations. As you are all fully aware, *Ocean One* is our most productive and profitable rig and we can't afford any downtime. With Christmas coming up, I'm sure we'd all like a decent bonus.'

'I understand that, Sir,' David said, 'but what is the current position with the rig? Is it actually out of danger yet?'

The CEO looked at David and the HR director got the distinct impression that he had overstepped the mark and that the CEO was mentally placing a big black cross against his future promotion prospects.

But eventually, the CEO smiled.

'Good question, David,' he said, 'but you can rest assured that *Ocean One* is not, and never was, in any danger. You have my word on that.'

Later, when David had returned to his office, slumped at his desk and cursed his big mouth, the phone rang.

'Hello,' he said tentatively.

'It's Mrs Macintyre here again,' a tired and worried voice said, 'can you tell me any news from . . .'

Iceberg Alley, somewhere south of Newfoundland

When Craig clambered from the snow hole they had dug the previous day, stiff and frozen, he was met by a glorious day, crisp and sunny with virtually no wind. In any other circumstances, it would have been a reasonably pleasant day but for Craig and Sean it was vital that they get rescued – they would not survive another night of freezing temperature, no water and no food. Sean, sluggish, confused and shivering uncontrollably, was already becoming hypothermic and Craig had to drag him from the snow hole and make him jump and run around to generate heat and restore circulation.

Through the crisp, white and pristine snow they trotted along, careful to avoid potential crevasses and soon they came to the edge of the iceberg. Carefully, they crawled to the very edge and peered over – it was an awesome but frightening sight. Almost sheer ice cliffs, cobalt blue in the sunshine, fell away sixty metres to a black and uninviting sea, choppy but no longer tempestuous. But, as far as their eyes could make out, there wasn't a vessel in sight – it was as though the oil platform had never existed.

'We've drifted a long way since the disaster,' Craig said, as much to himself as to Sean. 'It must be at least a hundred kilometres. I guess that we're still heading south.'

Sean nodded but said nothing, beginning to drift back into an introspective state.

'With weather like this,' Craig continued, trying to sound positive and hopeful, 'it won't be long before the search and rescue helicopters find us. And then we'll be warm and cosy in a nice hotel bar with huge tumblers of whisky and giant plates of steak and chips. You can almost taste . . .'

But a few hours later, again huddled in their snow hole, Craig's enthusiasm had evaporated and he struggled to stay awake and keep his limbs moving. He knew that if he fell asleep, he might never wake up.

Suddenly, he thought he heard the distant sound of an aeroplane engine and he dived out of the snow hole. His heart leapt as he spotted the plane, flying a few hundred metres above the sea and about a kilometre away, heading directly for the iceberg.

'Sean!' he shouted, beginning to frantically wave his arms and jump up and down. 'Get out here quick – there's a plane coming. It must be searching for us.'

Slowly and groggily, Sean clambered out of the hole but as soon as he saw the plane he launched into a manic dance and, as the plane grew larger, they hugged each other and jumped for joy.

'I think they've seen us,' Craig shouted, grinning and grasping Sean's shoulders. 'We're going to be rescued!'

But as they jumped and danced and waved, the plane, clearly one of the U.S. Coast Guard HC-130 search and rescue aircraft, flew over them and headed across the top of the iceberg. After a few moments it was lost from view and the drone of its engine faded and died.

Craig's heart sank and he looked forlornly into the distance. It hadn't seen them! How could it not see them? After all, they were wearing their Day-Glo orange immersion suits, which, against the starkly crisp white snow, must have been visible from space. We're they asleep or blind?

He looked at Sean and could see that, despite being a giant of a man, he was deflated and spent.

'Perhaps there'll be another one,' he said, half-heartedly. 'Come on – let's get back into the snow hole.'

But no sooner had they reached the opening than the sound of the plane returned, heading back across the ice towards them. It was flying low, no more than thirty metres above the ice, and its speed had slowed. Suddenly, a large cylinder fell from one of the wings and immediately it expanded and released a parachute.

'It's . . . it's . . . a life raft,' Sean mumbled.

The large orange inflatable hit the ice a few hundred metres from them and then skidded across the snow, its parachute acting as a drogue, slowing and stopping it. The HC-130 roared as it flew over them and, as it headed out to sea, it dipped its wings in acknowledgement.

'B . . . but, we're not in the water?' Sean muttered slowly, looking at the life raft and shaking his head. 'And, anyway, they'll be sending a helicopter soon so we don't need it.'

But as Craig watched the plane disappear into the distance, he immediately knew why the life raft had been dropped – up ahead, in the path of the iceberg, was a huge bank of dense fog, hundreds of metres high and stretching from horizon to horizon. Helicopters wouldn't find them in that – no, the life raft wasn't

MIKE CARTER

to prevent them from drowning, it was to prevent them from freezing. But – for how long?

New York, USA

New York was awash with a blaze of lights as garish neon bill-boards competed with cheerful flashing Christmas decorations. A dusting of snow covered the sidewalks and a gentle sprinkling fell through the crisp evening air. Office workers, hurrying home to families and dinner, mingled with Christmas shoppers and festive party-goers. And, in ever increasing numbers, nuts and fruit-cases with A-boards, proclaiming the coming of the Apocalypse, dismally wandered up and down. 'ONLY SEVEN DAYS TO ARMAGEDDON' and 'THE END IS NIGH!' competed paradoxically with store signs advertising 'ONLY EIGHT SHOPPING DAYS TO CHRISTMAS' and 'BOOK YOUR SUMMER VACATIONS NOW'.

But Jacob Goldstein wasn't interested in any of these. New York was a low-lying city of almost nine million people on the exposed eastern seaboard. It needed a treasure chest of Federal funds to design and upgrade the archaic and inadequate sea defences against global warming-induced rising sea levels and storm surges. And, as head of the Mayor's New York Coastal Defence Program, it was his responsibility to get something done about it.

But the problem was that New York's coastal defences, like most of the eastern and southern seaboards, were woefully inadequate. Years of neglect, apathy and underfunding had allowed the doom-mongers' prophecies of global warming, rising sea levels and increasing frequency and severity of Atlantic storms, to overtake the effort to protect some of the wealthiest and most vulnerable cities in the world. Competing demands – marketed as more urgent, clearly more political and arguably more glorious – channelled Federal funds away from mundane longer-term projects. National security and fighting for foreign land usurped fighting for national land – terrorists and not the elements were the enemy of the day. And, with the bailing out of the bankers and Wall Street in the recent credit crunch, Jacob felt more certain than ever that coastal defence had fallen further down the government's priority list.

The funds he received from the government's Federal Emergency Management Agency were a drop in the ocean compared to what was actually needed – what could several hundred million dollars achieve when a few billion only paid for the odd floodgate or earth dyke. All they had achieved so far was the revising of the ancient New York flood plain maps by the US Army Engineering Corps and the preparation of evacuation plans for the city. Hardly coastal defence – more like coastal retreat!

His father had been a hard-working store manager but, though he had given it his all and been a good law-abiding citizen and family man all his life, he had never had the pleasure of owning a brand-new car or travelling to exotic destinations and had died almost as poor as when he'd started. Jacob, an only child, had been determined to succeed where his father had failed and from an early age he had worked hard and slowly progressed through the administration of the Mayor's Office. And, with his wife dying from cancer a few years previously and his only son, Joseph, pursuing his own strange destiny, he had only his elderly mother, Martha, for company. Work had become his life.

Suddenly, the phone rang and Jacob cursed – he knew who it was.

'Hello, Jacob,' the softly spoken voice of Harvey Smith, the head of FEMA's global warming division, came over the phone. 'How are we progressing with the new floodplain maps?'

Jacob cursed again under his breath. Harvey Smith was a smooth and ambitious Federal administrator and he had publicly vowed that New York City would be the first American city to do detailed climate change planning and protection and now his reputation rested on achieving it. But from the outset he knew that FEMA simply didn't have the money – it was all a political game and there were so many hidden agendas that it was more complex than an Agatha Christie novel.

'Hello, Harvey,' Jacob answered pleasantly, 'the maps are coming along fine. We're working flat out but it's taking time. I don't need to tell you that New York City has nine hundred kilometres of shoreline. We've covered about fifty percent of the area, but it's a huge undertaking and we need to be thorough – after all, the previous maps are more than a hundred years old.'

Harvey laughed.

'Yes, I know,' he agreed, 'and that's why FEMA are investing such large funds in the task. If you can get me an interim report, say on Queen's or Coney Island – that would be useful. Anyway, I'm just going off to the Netherlands to learn more about the network of earth dykes there. We can have a chat when I get back.'

'No problems,' Jacob replied, thinking that the steamy delights of Amsterdam's nightlife were also no doubt on the agenda. 'I'll speak to my divisional head of mapping now. Thanks, Harvey, and goodbye.'

Jacob sat for a moment looking out of his office window in downtown Manhattan, watching the gentle snowflakes falling and the flashing neon advertising. After a while he picked up the phone again.

'Hello, Dad,' his son, Joseph, said affectionately. 'How are you?'

'Fine thanks, son,' Jacob replied. 'Long time no see, eh?'

'It wasn't that long ago, Dad. It was in the summer, wasn't it?'

Jacob laughed.

'Yes, Joseph, it was in the summer,' he said. 'The summer before last.'

'Ah, was it?' Jacob replied. 'Well, we're both rather busy and trying to fit everything in is rather difficult.'

'True, but what about . . .'

'No, Dad, I've already told you I can't make Christmas Day,' his son interrupted, a hint of irritation in his voice. 'It's after the 21 December – remember?'

Jacob frowned. Not that again . . .

The White House, Washington, USA

Theodore Jackson-Taylor, the American Secretary of State, was not renowned for his democratic approach to politics and life in general. Nor was he renowned for being charming and gentlemanly. As far as he was concerned, caution and political correctness were for 'wishy-washy' liberals and homosexuals, and a gruff Texan war veteran built like a bison wouldn't give them the time of day. His view on life was simple and gung-ho – the American way of life was the best in the world and he was going to keep it that way.

'Them Limeys have gone soft,' he was saying to the select few in the White House Oval office. 'Why we have to keep pandering to the global warming brigade beats me. Heck, they're all a bunch of scheming, self-promoting communists peddling the same old dubious pseudo-science.'

The President chuckled.

'Theodore, I don't think that you can call the British Prime Minister a dubious self-promoting communist. He's just responding to pressure groups and to his own scientific advisers. He simply phoned to see if we were happy to include global warming and carbon emissions as a priority item on the agenda of the G20 Summit meeting in Iceland.'

'You know my views, Mr President,' the Secretary of State said. 'There is as much evidence for increased carbon dioxide in the atmosphere coming from natural causes as there is from man-made causes. It's ridiculous – even Mrs Jackson-Taylor now worries about her carbon footprint when she pops down to the shops in her automobile every day or leaves the odd light bulb burning unnecessarily. It's just part of the natural evolution of the planet.

Mind you, I've no objections to someone peddling a global warming product for profit – that's capitalistic opportunity and what this country was founded upon.'

The President chuckled again.

'We should put you in charge of our renewable energy budget,' he said, 'and see if you can make it profitable. Anyway, it's now prioritised on the agenda for Iceland, so that's that.'

The Secretary of State's bull-like head nodded but he still looked unhappy.

'Theodore,' the President said, 'you look like you're about to explode or like someone's got your balls in a vice. Spit it out.'

The Secretary of State considered for a moment and finally made up his mind.

'Mr President,' he growled, 'I think we should call off the Iceland trip.'

'Because of the global warming issue?' the President asked incredulously.

'No, Mr President, because of the nuts, fruit-cases, anarchists and terrorists who think that the world is going to end on 21 December 2012 – or, actually want it to happen. They'll all be at it, at home and abroad. Paul Gates, the FBI director, tells me that they are uncovering an unprecedented number of conspiracies plotting to bring about Armageddon on that very day. And the survivalists will be mightily disappointed when they wake up on the 22 December and everything is normal. There's a good probability that some of these groups will attempt to establish their own little kingdoms in the backwoods or in some Third World country. They'll certainly have a destabilizing effect.'

The President frowned.

'What are you suggesting?' he asked.

'Well,' the Secretary of State growled, 'I don't know who decided to hold the G20 Summit meeting around Armageddon Day but he should be shot. Mr President, I think that you should stay in Washington – for your own protection and to oversee our response to any terrorist or anarchist activity.'

The President chuckled.

'Theodore, that's not like you,' he said. 'You're beginning to sound like those "wishy-washy" liberals or health and safety junkies you're always on about. Hide away in the bunker?! . . .'

The Secretary of State reddened and squirmed in his seat.

'No, Theodore,' the President continued, 'we can't do that. Otherwise, all those nuts, fruit-cases, anarchists and terrorists will have won. No, Iceland goes ahead and I will attend.'

Chapter 3

15 December 2012
Ice cap, central Greenland

The next day dawned calm, crisp and very cold. A brilliant white covering of fresh snow blazed with the reflected surreal green glow of the Northern Lights and the silvery half-moon. Jarvik stretched after climbing out of the tent and surveyed the magnificent and awesome landscape. He was always struck by man's insignificance and fragility in such a vast and powerful environment and he knew first hand that nature's fury was boundless and unpredictable. And the pressure ridge, rising like huge black teeth across the landscape, was evidence of its unpredictability and power.

Their night had been interrupted several times by loud groans and cracks from deep within the ice cap and occasionally more huge blocks of ice had landed with a frightening *crump* as they were spewed out from the pressure ridge. Wisely, they had set up camp a kilometre away from the towering wall and when he surveyed the ice sheet between the tents and the pressure ridge he was glad that he had – huge blocks of ice littered the ground, testament to an active and destructive night.

Idly, he checked the GPS. He shook his head and then the GPS – either *it* was malfunctioning or else *he* was. He could have sworn that yesterday it had shown a reading eight hundred metres higher than it should have done and now it was showing almost twelve hundred metres higher.

'Runi,' he shouted in the direction of the tent, 'can you take an altitude reading on your own GPS. I think mine's malfunctioning.'

After a moment he heard a curse from inside the tent.

'There's nothing wrong with your GPS,' Runi said, sticking his head out of the tent. 'This is definitely weird.'

'I don't understand it,' Jarvik replied, 'but it makes me nervous. I think we should . . .'

Suddenly, there was a tremendous sound of rolling thunder beyond the pressure ridge and the ice beneath their feet shuddered.

'What the heck was that?' Johann gasped, rushing out of the tent in his socks and long johns.

Moments later, they were suddenly hit by a blast of warm air and a mini blizzard of snow that violently rocked the tents.

'What the heck was THAT?' Johann repeated emphatically.

Jarvik looked at Johann and Runi and clearly they were as concerned as he was. Whatever it was, it did not bode well for the future.

'Can you smell that?' he eventually asked, sniffing the air and frowning.

Normally, the ice cap, being a clean and pristine sheet of snow and ice, had no smell apart from the cooking and unwashed body odours carried around by the explorers and scientists.

'Smells like bad eggs to me,' said Runi, wrinkling his nose.

'Yes,' Jarvik agreed, 'it's definitely sulphurous. And you know what that means, don't you?'

Johann nodded.

'But that doesn't make sense,' he said, frowning. 'This isn't Iceland – there are no volcanoes in Greenland. It's made up of the oldest rocks in the world and it doesn't have any volcanic activity.'

By now, all the scientists had gathered round and Jarvik looked at each one in turn.

'Are you sure?' he asked.

Johann was about to reply when suddenly the ice beneath their feet shuddered again and then jerked violently upwards, sending them sprawling into the fresh snow.

'Shit!' Jarvik yelled, jumping to his feet. 'Let's get the hell out of here!'

They managed to pack the tents and gear, load it into the inflatable dinghy and ski a hundred metres away when, suddenly, beyond the pressure ridge, there was a strange rushing, roaring sound and they stopped mid-stride and nervously looked back.

'What the heck was that?' Runi and Johann asked in unison.

'I don't know,' Jarvik said quickly. 'But I don't like the sound of it. I suggest we move. Now!'

They quickly turned round and began skiing as fast as they could, dragging the inflatable loaded with the gear. But they had only gone a hundred more metres when the rushing, roaring sound exploded into an enormous thunderous *crump*. Without stopping this time, they fearfully glanced over their shoulders and were horrified to see torrents of water bursting through the pressure ridge, sending immense blocks of snow and ice tumbling along cascading rivers of icy slush and water.

Quickly, Jarvik unclipped his harness and skis and raced for the inflatable dinghy.

'Get the gear out of here!' he shouted frantically, heaving scientific equipment overboard.

At first, the others stood frozen to the spot, staring aghast as a raging wall of water three metres high raced towards them.

'Move!' Jarvik screamed.

Runi was the first to respond, followed quickly by his brother and the two remaining scientists. Desperately, they emptied the small inflatable and climbed in, sat upright and squashed together, grabbing hold of any available straps.

'Hold on!' Jarvik shouted.

For a brief moment, they sat facing the rampaging wave as it roared towards them, their eyes wide with terror and their mouths open in silent screams.

'No!' Jarvik shouted. 'Get back in!'

But Magnus Haag, the youngest of the five scientists, was already sprinting away, his nerve broken by the fearful sound and sight of the raging wave.

The roaring wall, a horrible murky mixture of water, ash, mud and ice swept towards them, three metres high and as wide as the eye could see. Tongues of brown sludgy liquid surged forward in a wild and turbulent dance.

'Hang on!' Jarvik shouted again, as a fast-moving tongue of the torrent hit them.

Immediately, they were whipped away and the inflatable jumped and span like a bucking bronco. Jarvik held on with all his strength as the little raft sped across the ice cap, carried by the leading edge of the flood. For a moment he thought that they might succeed in riding ahead of the torrent but a collapsing lip of the wall caught them, flipping them over and sucking them into the brown maelstrom beneath.

In an instant, they were tumbling and turning, one moment flipping upright and the next flipping upside down. With lungs bursting, Jarvik managed to gasp for air as the raft occasionally and briefly surfaced, grimly clenching the rope and wondering how they would ever survive.

Magnus Haag, meanwhile, his legs and arms pumping mani-cally, looked round as a tongue of water swept across his feet and screamed when he saw that the flood was almost upon him. Frantically, he tried to speed up but quickly the murky water rose up his legs and he stumbled on the slippery ice, disappearing with a gurgling scream under the torrent.

As Jarvik tumbled and turned, he couldn't stop his scientific mind making a startling observation – the water was not frigidly cold as he had expected but pleasantly lukewarm. Lukewarm! How the hell, he thought, could a vast flood, a trillion gallons or more of warm water, suddenly appear on the top of a three-kilometre deep sheet of ice? But already he suspected the answer; the murky soup full of ash and mud was the only evidence he needed. There was only one place the water could come from and that was from deep down, below the ice sheet, melted by volcanic activity, a sub-glacial eruption of spouting magma from deep inside the Earth's core. The only problem was that, as every geologist knows, there were no volcanoes under Greenland.

Suddenly, the rampaging wall released the inflatable from its grip and it shot to the surface, upside down but in fast-moving calmer water. Jarvik gulped air and quickly counted the other survivors – only two other scientists were left, coughing and spluttering and attached to the raft – the brothers Johann and Runi. He raised his head as high as he could and shouted for Magnus and Gunderson – but there was no response and no heads bobbed about in the sweeping floodwater.

When they had rested and gained their breath, the three survivors managed to right the raft and climb aboard. As they desperately bailed the water out with their hands, the floodwaters washed them across the ice cap, back from where they had come. It was surreal and bizarre and they all knew it – to be rafting at fifteen knots in a tiny inflatable raft in a volcanic-induced mega-flood high up on the frozen wastes of Greenland was – simply crazy! As scientists, they found it hard to believe and they would not be surprised if the scientific world greeted their story, if they survived it, with a sceptical but sad shake of its collective head.

Heathrow, London, England

Flight PIA785 from Islamabad was into the final approaches to Heathrow Airport and the three hundred and fifty passengers had already fastened their seat belts. Over the intercom the captain ordered the crew to their landing positions and the huge Boeing 777 began to bank and lose altitude. It had been a long but smooth trip and the cabin was awash with excited chatter as passengers eagerly and happily awaited returning home or being reunited with friends and family. Children gazed with rapt aston-ishment and a little awe at the moving strings of white and red lights as convoys of cars headed into and out of the capital.

But the passenger in seat 201A did not share the excitement and happiness of his fellow passengers. Slumped beside a window, his face was pale and clammy and he had hardly stirred for most of the flight. The elderly grey-haired Punjabi gentleman next to him was worried and had almost alerted the crew – after all, the young man could have swine flu or be a terrorist. But he had done nothing, relying instead on the will of God and assuming it was simply a case of air sickness and fear of flying.

Ahmed Jayed felt awful. He had never, in his entire short life, felt so appallingly ill. He had already vomited several times, his head felt as though it was about to explode and his abdomen was hot, swollen and throbbing with excruciating pain. Over the last few hours, as the Boeing 777 had surged across the clear early-evening skies of Europe, he had drifted in and out of consciousness and in the lucid moments he had prayed fervently and begged forgiveness for the likelihood of failing his vital mission.

Beneath his jacket and shirt, blood and pus oozed from a raw and swollen wound, its glistening edges barely held together by a zigzag of surgical stitches. He had covered himself with one of the flight blankets to hide the spreading stain on his shirt but it barely stifled the unpleasant odour of gangrenous flesh.

As the plane dropped altitude and the runway lights came into view, the passenger in seat 201A began to spasm and gurgle and a dribble of blood oozed down his chin. The Punjabi gentleman looked in horror at his fellow passenger and quickly pressed the 'Attention' button.

On the ground, dressed innocuously in smart chinos and sports jacket, Malik Husain kept a discreet eye on the arrivals exit of Gate 27 at Terminal 2. Hidden behind a newspaper, he had watched as a steady stream of exhausted but happy Flight PIA785 passengers emerged and mingled joyfully with waiting relatives and friends. But, as the stream slowed to a trickle and then stopped altogether, there was no sign of Ahmed. He cursed. He had received a coded message that Ahmed had boarded the plane at Islamabad and clearly something must have happened. And, whatever it was – detained by Customs or Immigration – it was bad news.

He yawned, stretched and casually folded his newspaper and stood up. Without looking back he sauntered towards the shopping village and mingled with the crowd. He looked calm and relaxed but inwardly he was worried.

Behind him, three fluorescent green-jacketed paramedics raced out of the arrivals exit, carefully guiding a trolley laden with a deathly pale-faced young Asian man, intravenous drips and wires streaming into his arm and chest. Outside, its doors agape and its engine already running, an ambulance urgently waited.

St Francis Hospital, London, England

Abigail Townsend was excited. She had recently qualified as an autopsy technician and Professor Bellinger, head of pathology at the hospital, had finally given her the opportunity to assist him in a post-mortem examination. Not only that – this wasn't one of the run-of-the-mill geriatric deaths due to a stroke, myocardial infarction or just old age – no, this one was young and the manner of death was somewhat unusual.

Every detail of the autopsy would have to be recorded and photographed and endless tissue samples taken for later forensic testing. This, she knew, was a great test of her skills and she owed Professor Bellinger a debt of gratitude for placing so much faith in her. She was determined to show that this wasn't misplaced – she would follow the procedures by the book.

The morgue had a horrible, sickly smell – a mixture of body fluids, intestinal gases and formaldehyde – but Abigail was used to it and now she never even noticed. The room they were in was a cavernous area of stark fluorescent lighting, stainless-steel tables, sinks, freezers, large banks of stainless-steel lockers, and shelves lined with assorted equipment and pickled body parts.

Protected by a gown, rubber gloves and a surgical face mask she carefully unzipped the body bag and began taking photographs while the Professor made the usual external inspection of the corpse, dictating his observations into an overhead microphone.

'The subject is a young Asian male,' he began, 'of approximately twenty-two years of age and, as measured, is 186 centimetres tall and weighs 61 kilograms. He has brown eyes, short black hair, is clean shaven and, apart from the wound on the abdomen, has no obvious distinguishing features.'

As the Professor stood gazing analytically at the cadaver, Abigail took samples of hair and nails in case later forensic examination was necessary.

'The subject's name,' he continued, 'is Ahmed Jayed and he arrived by plane earlier this evening from Islamabad, Pakistan, and was pronounced dead on arrival at St Francis Hospital. Clearly noticeable is an abnormal extension of the abdomen, which is swollen and inflamed. It bears a horizontal wound, approximately thirteen centimetres long, on the right side of the abdomen and approximately six centimetres below the navel. It has recently been stitched, although very shoddily, and it could be the result of an appendix operation.'

Abigail bent over the corpse and took several close-up photographs of the raw and inflamed wound. Immediately, she was hit by the smell of rotting putrid flesh and she winced, but carried on taking photographs.

'We shall now begin the internal examination,' the pathologist continued, 'and I am placing a body block under the cadaver's back to stretch and push out the chest. I am going to use a standard deep Y-shaped incision.'

Abigail handed the Stryker saw to the professor and watched amazed as he quickly and deftly cut from each shoulder down to the sternum and then down to the pubic bone, releasing a cloud of bone-dust and sickly stench. When he had finished and handed the saw back to Abigail he pulled the ribs and abdomen muscles apart, exposing the heart, lungs and visceral organs.

'I am now going to eviscerate the chest cavity, starting with the heart . . .'

Suddenly, the hospital intercom erupted.

'Calling Professor Bellinger – you have an urgent telephone call in your office. Calling Prof . . .'

The pathologist frowned, looked at Abigail and shrugged.

'Take a few more photographs while I'm gone,' he said, pulling off his gloves and mask. 'But don't touch anything – I'll be back shortly.'

When he had gone, Abigail took a series of pictures of the abdominal cavity and then stood back and examined the corpse. One day, she hoped to become as proficient and famous a pathologist as Professor Bellinger and, without thinking, her analytical and enquiring mind began to mull over the likely causes of death. Professor Bellinger had already told her that he suspected a post-operative infection following the recent removal of an inflamed appendix, leading to gangrene, peritonitis, septicaemia and death. Obviously, he would be looking at the large intestine for the wound where the appendix would have been and there was no reason why Abigail couldn't do that herself – after all, she wouldn't be removing anything, just poking around a bit and taking a few more photographs.

Bending over the corpse she pulled the cold and slimy intestines to one side and immediately she spotted a long slender tube, about nine centimetres long, attached to the large intestine. She straightened up and frowned. That's strange, she thought, that's the appendix. Surely, Professor Bellinger wasn't actually wrong for a change?

Bending down again she pulled the intestines back and, suddenly, something unusual caught her eye. Carefully, she pulled the intestines away again and gasped. There, nestled in the blood and gore, was what appeared to be a very large breast implant.

Wow – that would surprise the Professor, she thought smugly.

She peered more closely at it and gave it an exploratory poke. Suddenly, a squirt of liquid erupted from a small tear where the Stryker saw had connected and it splashed across her surgical mask.

'Idiot!' she gasped, wiping her face with her sleeve.

Immediately, her nose began to run and a huge hand suddenly grabbed her chest and began to squeeze. Terrified, she gasped for breath, sinking to the floor and beginning to drool and vomit. Within moments, her eyes wide with fear and her body shuddering in violent spasms, her bladder and bowels relaxed, releasing their warm and stinking contents.

Thirty seconds later, Abigail Townsend was dead.

Tasiilaq, eastern Greenland

At the same time that Jarvik and his team were fighting for survival, the sleepy little town of Tasiilaq was unprepared for what was about to hit it. The pretty multi-coloured wooden houses scattered across the flat low-lying island were sturdy and well insulated but they were not built to withstand a glacial flood of biblical proportions . . .

Nunni Nygaard was happy. She loved her little red-painted wooden house in the little town of Tasiilaq, on the small island of Ammassalik. She wouldn't have swapped it for anything, not that she had much experience to go on, having spent all her six years in an isolated community of only six hundred houses and sixteen hundred inhabitants, just outside the Arctic Circle.

And now she had an adorable husky puppy of her own to play with, a birthday present from Dad, just before he went away on yet another one of his trips for work. She'd instantly called the fluffy bundle Miki Nanook because that's what she was – a little cutie – and in the summer she loved to gambol and play in the dirt and stalk the white nodding heads of the Arctic cotton grasses.

Even at that time of year, icebergs could be seen sailing majestically offshore, calved from glaciers on the east coast and heading south. Nunni often wondered what it would be like to have a little wooden house on one of the bergs, her own island, serenely floating towards warmer climes and adventure.

'Nunni,' she heard her mother call from the house, 'it's time to go.'

Nunni groaned – they were going to the little shop that called itself a supermarket as they did every Saturday. She hated shopping – it was so boring and Mum spent ages talking to everyone she met – which seemed to be everyone in the whole town.

But at least, as a treat, they were going to take Miki Nanook for a walk along the frozen river and on to Narsuuliartarpiip, the flower plain. There, she and Miki could run and gambol and there, her little universe could expand into a make-believe world of castles and princesses, of Hollywood and film stars, of excitement and adventure.

'Come on, Nunni,' her mother called again. 'Stop daydreaming.'

Later that day, Miki Nanook was frustrated. She wanted to play again but Nunni was being boring – after all, everyone knew that husky puppies had bundles of energy. She had already been told off by Nunni's mother for chewing a hole in the reindeer rug and now, despite her best doleful expression, she'd been ejected into the cold and draughty porch.

Inside, Nunni's mother frantically paced up and down, every minute glancing outside for signs of the ambulance. The doctor had just left, having been called away to another emergency.

She cursed. It was always the same – whenever there was something important going on, like birthdays, school prize-giving or illness, Tukku was always away. If it wasn't hunting or fishing it was guiding the tourists into the mountains or doing search and rescue training. She knew that he had to earn a living but couldn't he just get a job in the supermarket or fish processing factory?

At least, they'd see him a bit more often. And why did this have to happen now, just before Christmas?

Beside her, as she fretted about Nunni, about Tukku and about Miki, a large rucksack was already packed. If it was as the doctor suspected, an inflamed and swollen appendix, then Nunni could be in hospital for at least a week or two.

Suddenly, she heard sirens approaching and she grabbed the rucksack, the plane tickets and the passports. At least, she thought, the flight to Reykjavik was only fifty minutes. And, thankfully, the Landspitali University Hospital had a very good reputation – she was sure the doctors there would be very good.

They would look after her little Nunni.

In the fish-processing factory, Andreas Magnuson, the hard-working owner of the factory had just made contact on the radio with the *Greenland Leopardess*, at seventy-five metres long, the largest of the fishing boats on the east coast. With eastern Greenland being unusually ice free at this time of year, the fishing fleet had returned yesterday after several days away, laden with fish that needed to be brought to the factory for processing and freezing. But the *Leopardess* was a day late, the last of the boats to return to port, and already it was getting dark, though it was only early afternoon.

On the deck of the *Leopardess*, having finished clearing the nets and gear with the other three deckhands, Tukku Nygaard watched the distant lights of Tasiilaq and smiled. He was looking forward to seeing his family again and playing with Nunni and her Miki Nanook – both of them seemed to be growing up so fast and every time he came back they had changed and he felt the sadness of tender moments lost forever. But at least it was almost Christmas and he had only one more fishing trip to do this year and then he could take time off to be a father and a husband and enjoy warm hugs and cuddles before a blazing log fire and playful tumbles in the snow.

But this year, for some inexplicable reason, he felt strangely unsettled and no longer at ease with the land. Having been a seal hunter, a mountain guide and a fisherman, all arduous and dangerous occupations making a pitiful living at the best of times, he understood the seasons and he respected the tremendous power and unpredictability of the Arctic landscape.

It had all started on a hiking trip in the summer and he remembered it well. He had been sitting high up on a mountain ledge overlooking the jumbled ice of Sermilik glacier. All around him were towering peaks and jagged mountain ranges while below, down the vertiginous valley walls, the glacier tumbled into the huge iceberg-filled Sermilik fjord.

'Tukku,' a young Texan in his hiking party had called out, 'surely we're not going to eat this?'

Tukku smiled to himself. He loved to play games with the tourists and this one was his favourite.

'What!' he exclaimed, putting on a hurt and surprised voice. 'You don't like traditional Greenlandic food? It's good and nutritious, rich in vitamins and unsaturated fats – it's full of energy and good for the heart.'

Suddenly, there was a retching sound from the young Texan's girlfriend and with a shriek she spat out an offending morsel.

'Yuk, it's revolting,' she gasped, 'it's all fishy and oily and rubbery and impossible to chew.'

Tukku laughed – he couldn't keep a straight face any longer. With each hiking group he always served up a selection of traditional snacks for the first evening meal, pretending that it was the food that they would be living on for the next ten days. Almost black, tough and very chewy with an oily aftertaste they were an acquired taste – dried whale meat and blubber, half-dried cod, dried seal meat and dried seabird meat.

'OK,' he eventually said, grinning broadly, 'you win. I was only kidding – we've got beef goulash, freeze-dried I'm afraid, followed by delicious crowberries and blueberries with cream.'

Afterwards, they had all sat round the tents among the Arctic poppies and dwarf Arctic willows and listened enthralled as Tukku told tales of his hunting adventures and interesting stories of Inuit culture and history. In the distance, at the mouth of the fjord the dull roar of icebergs and growlers grinding away in the ocean swells could be heard and, in the twilight world of the never-setting summer sun, the mountains stretched dark and forbidding – the hiking group's destination for the next ten days.

Later, as they all slept and snored, exhausted from the days trekking, they were oblivious to the distant inland sounds of the creaking and cracking ice cap. Tukku had been in the mountains bordering the ice cap many times and he had become accustomed to its song – but recently, its tune had changed. He didn't know what it meant but it disturbed him. He wasn't particularly religious but it would have been easy to believe that the ancient god Kadlu was awakening – angry and vengeful.

He shivered – the land beyond was beautiful but it was also mysterious, ominous and powerful – and for the first time in his life he felt strangely uneasy hiking next to it. He had no wish to awaken a sleeping giant.

'Hello, *Greenland Leopardess*,' Andreas said into the phone, 'welcome back. Where are you now and how long do you think it will be before you can begin unloading? I assume you've got a record catch?'

'Hi, Andreas,' Captain Sven Hansen replied, laughing, 'you're always the optimist . . . You're always thinking of your profits. Well, don't forget that you still owe me a beer or two after the last record catch.'

This time it was Andreas who laughed.

'If you beat the last catch,' he said, 'I'll buy you a whole barrel of beer.'

'Well, you had better get your money out,' Sven replied, 'because we've just rounded the headland and can see Tasiilaq's lights. We should be docking in an hour.'

'Excellent,' Andreas said, 'I'll get the processing team ready. We can arrange . . . Shit! What the heck was tha . . .'

'Andreas?'

'Andreas?'

High above, the strange glacial flood from the ice cap was being channelled through the fjords, riding the glaciers and increasing in depth to fifty metres or more. Accelerating as it raced downhill and ripping out huge blocks of ice, some bigger than a house, it roared with a deafening sound that only the unleashed power of nature can achieve. Tasiilaq, nestled at the end of the fjord, didn't stand a chance – the galloping monster surged with immense destructive violence across the island and houses were instantly smashed to matchwood and boats, cars and people were swept away.

On the *Greenland Leopardess* Tukku frowned as the blinking lights of Tasiilaq suddenly disappeared, but he reasoned that a fog bank must have rolled in – not unusual in these parts.

On the bridge, the captain stared at the phone and then at the blackness where Tasiilaq's lights had been and frowned.

'Andreas?' he said, after trying to get a connection again, but finding the radio link totally dead.

He phoned his wife, the harbour master, the coastguard and the police – but every link was dead.

'Engine room,' he called down to the engineer, 'give me full speed ah . . . What the . . . ?'

Out of the bridge window his eye had caught sight of a sudden white line on the moonlit horizon. He blinked but it was still there and growing fast.

'What IS that?' he said aloud, totally baffled but rapidly feeling uneasy and scared.

Tukku, who had just walked onto the bridge, looked out of the window and gasped. Instantly, he knew that the sleeping giant had woken – Kadlu was angry.

As the glacial flood sped out to sea and spread out again it began to lose height and speed, but it was still a ten-metre-high iceberg- and debris-laden monster wave when it closed on the *Greenland Leopardess*. Horrified, the captain stared at it, frozen to the spot in shock and awe. But with seconds to spare, he suddenly jerked out of his trance, punched the ship's alarm and the emergency beacon, and grasped the wheel as hard as he could.

Apart from praying, there was nothing more that they could do.

North Pole, Arctic Ocean

Suddenly, the alarms sounded and Commander John Clayton, the grizzly old commander of the USS *Arizona*, the newest and largest nuclear submarine in the US navy, jerked awake and almost fell out of his bunk. The floor of his little cabin was tilting alarmingly and the boat rocked and rolled like a bucking bronco.

'Report!' he shouted into the intercom, frantically grabbing his trousers and shirt and trying to hold on as his belongings flew across the room.

At first, there was no response as he impatiently tapped the intercom button.

'Lieutenant Bradshaw!' he growled. 'Give me a report. What the hell's happening?'

From the intercom a breathless voice emerged.

'Commander,' the Lieutenant gasped, 'we're out of control and rising fast. We were cruising at two hundred and fifty metres and then all hell broke loose. The helmsman and planesman are fighting to gain control but, whatever it is, it's too powerful and we're surfacing bow first – we're already at one hundred and eighty metres.'

'Blow the starboard tanks and set the rudder,' the commander ordered. 'We'll try to swing out of it. I'm coming to the control room.'

Abandoning his shirt and trousers, he struggled in his shorts and singlet to clamber along the corridor, his mind racing through the operational procedures manual. They must have hit a huge up-welling or current of water but he knew from his many years as a submariner that that just did not happen.

When he arrived he immediately took in the strenuous efforts being made to control the boat but he could see they were useless – the depth gauge already showed one hundred and thirty metres and still rising fast. Tension and fear showed in the men's faces, eerily illuminated by the flashing red warning lights. They all knew the danger – after all, they were beneath the Arctic ice, in places several metres thick.

'Sparks,' he growled at the radar man, 'what's the ice thickness here?'

The radar man quickly scanned his dials.

'Four metres,' he replied, his voice tense and his face fearful.

'Shit!' Clayton cursed, before punching the weapon's control intercom. 'Torpedo room, load and arm tubes 1 and 2 as fast as you can. And tell me when you're ready to fire.'

He looked up and saw Lieutenant Bradshaw watching him and he shrugged – what else could they do? The hull was made of especially hardened steel and designed to resist pressure down to three hundred and ten metres but a collision with a solid sheet of ice at the speed they were travelling could easily rupture the hull. And that would endanger all one hundred and fifty-two of them.

'Seventy metres,' the diving officer said, nervously watching the depth gauge dials. 'Sixty metres . . .'

'Come on,' Lieutenant Bradshaw hissed, 'if we don't fire soon the concussion could kill . . .'

Suddenly, the weapons control intercom crackled.

'Torpedoes armed and read . . .'

'Fire!' Clayton growled impatiently.

The weapons control panel flashed from green to red as tubes 1 and 2 disgorged their sleek seven-metre-long torpedoes. They didn't have to wait long before there were two almost simultaneous explosions and the boat shuddered violently and the hull reverberated with an ear-splitting *crump*.

Suddenly, another alarm sounded and new warning lights began to flash frantically.

'Damage Control!' Clayton growled. 'Report!'

Lieutenant Bradshaw studied the damage control panel and cursed.

'One of the pressurised steam pipes in the water reactor has blown,' he gasped, his voice difficult to hear in the raucous screams of the alarms.

Commander Clayton cursed inwardly – somewhere in the nuclear reactor superheated water under immense pressure would be blasting out and anyone in the vicinity would be boiled alive. They had protective steam suits for the repair gang but there was no time for that now as the bow sped towards the ice.

'Thirty metres!' the diving control officer intoned. Twenty-five . . . twenty . . . fifteen . . .'

President Oppenheimer was just about to leave the Oval Office for an important domestic health care meeting when his phone rang.

'Oppenheimer,' he said simply.

'Mr President,' the gruff, Texan voice of the Secretary of State said, 'we have a problem . . .'

Blackpool, England

Susan Macintyre put the phone down and frowned. All day now she had been unable to contact Craig and every time she called Mid-Ocean Oil their hollow reassurances only deepened her unease. She had already spoken to Janet Watson, the offshore installation manager's wife, and she too was concerned and felt as though they were being fobbed off. It just wasn't good enough but what could they do, other than camping outside Mid-Ocean Oil's offices?

And, to make things worse, Lucy had slept badly, woken almost every hour by disturbing dreams in which her father battled giant waves and huge monsters. She had woken screaming so often that Susan had brought her into her own bed but it had made little difference and now they were both tired and irritable.

At least it would soon be the school holidays and Christmas, and, as a special treat, she had promised to take Lucy into Blackpool to see the illuminations, play in the amusements and venture up the Tower. Lucy had jumped for joy at the news and she had spent the whole day excitedly telling Bonnie all about their forthcoming adventures.

Susan didn't have the heart to tell her that Bonnie couldn't go because, sadly, dogs weren't actually allowed up Blackpool Tower.

Tasiilaq, eastern Greenland

With the ship's alarms wailing and Sven and Tukku staring horrified through the bridge window, the huge wall of water hit the bow of the *Greenland Leopardess*. For a fraction of a second, time seemed to freeze and in that brief moment Tukku saw a huge block of ice, starkly white in the black water and the size of a car, heading straight for the bridge.

'Watch out!' he managed to shout, diving to the floor as the ship slammed into the wave with a tremendous juddering crash.

Sven, desperately gripping the wheel, frozen to the spot, watched as the block of ice headed directly for him, smashing into the bridge and shattering the toughened glass windows and steel frame. Unstoppable, it ploughed through the bridge, crashing into the steering console, ripping it from its mountings and bulldozing it and the captain through the back of the bridge and into oblivion.

A deluge of black icy water poured into the bridge and Tukku was picked up and dragged backwards as the glacial flood swept over the *Greenland Leopardess*. In the freezing inky water he frantically grasped anything he could, desperately trying to cling on, his lungs bursting for air. As the water poured over him, he knew

NINE DAYS TO ARMAGEDDON

that if he lost his grip he would instantly be swept away to his peril in the dark and lonely night.

For what seemed like an eternity the bow of the *Greenland Leopardess* began to rise up through the floodwaters, shaking and juddering as she shed water and ice. Tukku, with lungs screaming for a gasp of air, and hands numb and barely able to hold on any longer, suddenly felt the water recede from his head and desperately he gulped for air. Frozen and shivering uncontrollably, he clambered to his feet, groping uncertainly around the shattered and devastated bridge. By the weak silvery light of the half-moon he could just make out the havoc the wave had wrought and the wreckage the wave had left in its wake. The whole of the front and rear of the bridge was smashed open, the navigation and steering consoles were gone, and there was no sign of the captain.

The ship had clearly lost all its lighting and power and it wallowed, low in the water, in the turbulent seas. He knew that they were about a kilometre from land but no welcoming lights shone from Tasiilaq and, with the bridge destroyed, it was impossible to send a mayday call.

Through the gloom he carefully felt his way down the steps at the back of the bridge and found that the door to the cabins and galley had been burst open and everything was drenched. Even if he could get down to the engine room, he knew nothing about large diesel turbine engines and there was no way that he could get them started unless he could find the engineer. He didn't know how long he had before the *Greenland Leopardess* succumbed to the waves – she was already beginning to list to port and he guessed that she had been holed by one of the blocks of ice.

Fumbling just inside the doorway, he found one of the emergency waterproof torches and unclipping it he carefully made his way through the sodden corridor to look for the rest of the crew. Inside the galley he gasped as he found Ingar Magnusson, the cook and general deckhand, crumpled against the wall, his forehead

)rofusely and his head bent sideways at an unnatural

.g his way to the engine room steps he could descend
ietre – oily water sloshed backwards and forwards as the
led. Floating face down was Ingar's older brother and
r, Davidson – clearly dead.
ckly, he searched the cabins, but there was no sign of Erik
i or Serl Larsen and he guessed that they must both have
washed overboard along with the captain. Out of a crew
x he was the only one lucky enough to be alive but, unless
quickly got into an immersion suit and launched one of the
atable life rafts, he knew he would be next. The *Greenland
pardess* was settling lower and lower into the water.
Finding the emergency locker he struggled into one of the suits
nd then raced back towards the exit as oily water gurgled from
ne engine room and spilled into the galley. Already, the port stanchions were awash and quickly he made his way forward round
the aft side, struggling to maintain balance as the 75-metre-long
boat began tipping over. Frantically, he grabbed the straps of the
aft life raft and snapped open the retaining bolts, releasing the
life raft from its container and automatically activating its gas
bottles to inflate the tubes. As the life raft quickly took shape,
water began to flood round his feet and hurriedly he dived inside.
Trapped air hissed and bubbled out of the hull and the *Greenland
Leopardess* began to slip beneath the black and icy Arctic waters.

Tukku prayed – prayed that the fragile life raft would not snag
or rip on the ship's stanchions or trawling equipment, and prayed
that someone, somewhere, would come to his rescue.

10 Downing Street, London, England

'Prime Minister,' the voice of the PM's principal private secretary came over the intercom, 'I have Sir David Appleby here.'
The Prime Minister sighed. He quite liked his Chief Scientific

Adviser but he always seemed to talk in riddles. Or, perhaps science was like that – full of conflicting and ever-changing theories and mathematical models that one day sounded ever-so plausible and the next totally debunked.

'Thank you, John. Send him through.'

The PM rose from his paper strewn desk, stretched and walked over to a small drinks cabinet. He glanced at his watch – 7.30 p.m. – a perfect time for a mellow hand-bottled malt whisky from Speyside after a hard day's work.

'Sir David,' he greeted the scientist, being careful not to groan on spotting an armful of scientific papers. 'Scotch?'

Sir David nodded and sat down in the casual meeting area, spreading out his papers onto the coffee table.

'We've got a new model, Prime Minister,' he began, swapping a bundle of scientific papers for the drink.

The PM inwardly groaned and put the papers on his desk.

'I assume that it's a revision of the global warming models,' he said. 'Is it good news?' he added optimistically.

Sir David shook his head.

'Sadly not, Prime Minister,' he replied, savouring the whisky and settling into the sofa. 'You remember the Lithotropic Gaseous Conversion model?'

The Prime Minister nodded, although he wasn't sure which of the myriad of models this specific one was.

'Well,' the scientist continued, 'new reiterations of the model using recent data to tweak the biosynthetic conversion ratios show that there could be an even faster acceleration of the permafrost decay than originally thought and that the carbon stored away in the soil has been underestimated. Although we knew that the southern tundra could melt, and is, in fact, melting, the new thermal profile assumptions imply that even the permafrost of the northern tundra could melt and that the carbon dioxide stored away there would then be released into the atmosphere.'

The scientist paused and took another sip of his whisky.

'As you know, the permafrost is supposed to be permanent – all the way down for a hundred metres or more and occupying almost a quarter of the surface area of the northern hemisphere. The amount of carbon stored in the frozen soil was massively underestimated by the previous models and when this is released into the atmosphere it will accelerate atmospheric warming and have a huge destabilising effect on our climate.'

The Prime Minister frowned.

'How long?' he asked simply, dreading but suspecting a depressing reply.

Sir David flicked through some of the papers and selected a complex multi-coloured graph.

'Obviously, Prime Minister,' he replied, 'there are several potential scenarios but the most likely, and the one gaining the most consensus at my department, is that the permafrost will be totally gone, not in the hundred years or so as previously thought, but in about ten years. This will increase the rate of global warming by a factor of 2.3.'

The Prime Minister frowned again. The expression 'no news is good news' was so apt for climate change. It was a never-ending series of depressing doomsday stories and he was convinced that the scientists revelled in the opportunity for headline-grabbing apocalyptic prophecies. Sometimes he couldn't help but feel that mankind was already in an irrevocable downward spiral of cataclysmic proportions and at other, albeit brief times, he felt optimistic about man's ability to reform and halt the downward spiral.

'Thank you, Sir David,' he said eventually. 'I will read the report you have given me as a matter of urgency.'

When the scientist had left, his principal private secretary popped his head round the door.

'I'm off home now, Prime Minister,' he said, 'but just wanted to let you know that I've made all the arrangements now for your attendance at the G20 Summit meeting in Iceland. You'll be in

NINE DAYS TO ARMAGEDDON

Reykjavik from the 20 to 22 December – it's already in your diary.'

'Thank you, John, and goodnight.'

Metropolitan Police headquarters, London, England

Superintendent Jamie McDougal was tired. It had been a long day and at almost 11 p.m. he had done yet another fourteen-hour day. It never ceased to amaze him that at this time of year, with Christmas approaching and all the Christian values of goodwill and charity to all men, that the capital's streets were even more infested with crime and criminals than normal. Shoplifting, pickpocketing, handbag snatching, mugging, drug dealing, credit card fraud – take your pick. And everyone was so busy rushing around getting ready for Christmas and engrossed in a mania of present buying that they made easy targets – some people were so naive or blasé that they seemed almost willing victims. And the paperwork it generated was mountainous.

But just as he turned his computer off, stood up and closed his briefcase, the telephone rang.

'Inspector Cassidy here, Sir,' a breathless voice said, his words almost lost in a cacophony of sirens and shouted voices. 'Sorry to bother you so late, but we have a 101 Code Red incident.'

The superintendent instantly became alert, losing his tiredness and immediately ready for decisiveness and action.

'Where?' he barked.

'At St Francis Hospital, Hammersmith – in the morgue,' the inspector replied. 'We've got seven dead and one seriously injured. Whatever it is, we're trying to contain it. We've cordoned off the hospital and designated it a Hot Zone and we've set up decont-amination areas and special shower tents. All the emergency medical personnel, scientists, police and army units are in full NBC protective suits.'

'Who are the dead and how did they die?' Jamie McDougal asked.

'We think we've got a Professor Bellinger, head of pathology at the hospital,' Inspector Cassidy replied, 'an Abigail Townsend, who was an autopsy technician, a hospital cleaner, two police constables and two of the three paramedics who were all called to the emergency. Apparently, an autopsy of a young Asian man was in progress and something must have gone terribly wrong. And get this – the NBC boys have recovered something rather odd from the body.'

'Something odd?' the superintendent queried, frowning. 'Was it a bomb?'

'No, Sir,' the inspector continued, 'there wasn't an explosion. They've found what appears to be a large breast implant imbedded in the abdomen. It was obviously put there in a botched operation because the young man died of septicaemia and gangrene. He'd apparently just flown in from Islamabad, Pakistan.'

'Good God!' the superintendent growled. 'Whatever next?'

'It appears that somehow during the autopsy,' the inspector continued, 'the implant was punctured, releasing an extremely toxic substance. The experts don't think it's biological as it's too fast-acting and so devastatingly virulent. They think it's chemical such as a nerve agent – and the most deadly nerve agent of all is sarin.'

'Good God, man!' Jamie McDougal exploded. 'Are you serious? That's the nerve agent terrorists released on the Tokyo subway in 1995 – killed seven commuters and injured several thousand more. It's terrifying.'

'Yes, Sir. But what worries me is that it was being carried inside the man's body in a large breast implant bag. Clearly, he was simply transporting the poison and this wasn't the intended delivery system or the intended target. At room temperature, sarin is a clear and odourless liquid but it is a much more potent terrorist weapon of mass destruction in a gas or aerosol form since only a few molecules inhaled can cause paralysis and death. In Japan,

the death rate could have been much, much worse if the terrorists had dispersed the sarin more effectively.'

'Good God!' the superintendent exclaimed again. 'This is our
worst fears come true – another terrorist attack on the capital.
There could be dozens, perhaps hundreds, of terrorists in the
city preparing to unleash death and mayhem. And,' he growled,
'just before Christmas too.'

'Yes, Sir,' Inspector Cassidy agreed. 'We've instigated the 101
Code Red response at the hospital and surrounding streets, but
as you know lots of specialists running around in full NBC protective suits cordoning off areas and setting up emergency decont-
amination zones and showers tends to make people nervous. Given
the immediate and potentially devastating threat, we need a city-
wide response – but only the Prime Minister can give that.'

'Right, I'll contact him now,' Superintendent Jamie McDougal
said. 'Where are you setting up the Emergency Response Room?'

'At Hammersmith police station, Sir.'

'Right, as soon as I've spoken to the PM, I'm on my way over.'

Sandringham House, Norfolk, England

'Prime Minister!' the PM's principal private secretary shouted
through the bedroom door. 'Sir, you have an urgent call coming
through on the telephone.'

The PM rubbed sleep from his eyes and looked at the clock.
It was five minutes to midnight and he'd only just dropped off
to sleep – couldn't it wait? After all, it had been a very late night
discussing politics and world affairs with the Queen and the Home
Secretary and there had been an awful lot of whiskies. And then
there had been the terrifying news from Superintendent Jamie
McDougal. Admittedly, he had privately been afraid of another
terrorist plot on London but he'd never expected something quite
like this.

'Who is it?' he finally managed to mumble.

'It's the President, Sir,' his secretary replied.

'The President?' the PM mumbled, his still-sleepy brain thinking it was a senior company or committee executive.

'Yes, Sir – the American President. He says it's urgent.'

The Prime Minister jumped out of bed and put on his glasses. Why on earth was the President of the United States of America phoning him so late in the day?

'Hello, Matthew,' the President greeted, 'sorry to disturb your beauty sleep but we have a bit of a situation and we may need your help.'

'Yes, hello, Mr President,' the PM greeted the world's most powerful man. 'What sort of a situation?'

'One of our submarines,' the President began, 'the USS *Arizona*, the newest and largest nuclear submarine in our navy, has been damaged by the ice in the North Pole. Apparently, it was cruising at depth when it hit what is believed to be a huge up-welling of current that forced it to the surface out of control and at speed. The ice in that area is quite thick but with the commander's brilliant quick thinking they managed to punch a hole through it with torpedoes and reach the surface. Unfortunately, the hull sustained a number of leaks and the forward weapons compartments were breached. There's five men drowned and several are seriously injured. They've managed to contain the flooding by closing off those compartments but the ship is totally immobilised.'

'I'm sorry to hear that, Mr President,' the PM said. 'We'll do whatever we can – what do you need?'

'Well, we've dispatched our emergency response teams,' the President said, 'but it will be some time before they can get there. I understand that the British ship the *Polar Explorer* is currently cruising with scientists and tourists close to Franz Josef Land. Apparently, it's a substantial icebreaker and is closest to the submarine and there is a doctor and a helicopter on board. I was hoping that you could divert the ship to offer assistance – otherwise some of the injured crew may die.'

'Of course, we'll assist,' the PM agreed. 'I'll get on it straight away.'

'There's one more thing, Matthew,' the President added after a moment's pause.

'Go on,' the PM prompted.

'Well,' the President said hesitantly, 'it may not be without danger. We also lost some men who were overcome by fumes when they opened the hatches. Apparently, the submarine is in the midst of a plume of toxic smoke and gases. My advisors tell me that satellite images suggest a massive underwater volcano has suddenly erupted. The tremendous weight of the water at that depth has absorbed most of the ash cloud but they believe that a plume of gas, probably carbon dioxide and carbon monoxide, is rising to the surface. My scientists are astonished by what is happening but clearly we need to get those men out of there . . . And, the submarine, if possible.'

The Prime Minister thought for a moment. Clearly, there was a significant risk and he could only *ask* the *Polar Explorer* to voluntarily steam into danger. After all, it was full of scientists and tourists and not the armed services or emergency rescue personnel.

'Don't worry, Mr President,' he finally said, 'we'll do what we can.'

'Thank you, Matthew,' the President said gratefully. 'I'll see you in Iceland soon. This is going to be an important meeting for the G20 – we have a lot of important issues to resolve.'

Chapter 4

16 December 2012
Ice cap, central Greenland

'Anyway, thank God you're alive,' Gunnar Pattersen, the director of the Danish Geological Society said over the satellite link.

'Only just,' Jarvik replied, his voice full of exhaustion and grief. 'I'm terribly sorry to have to tell you but Magnus and Gunderson have perished and Johann is badly frostbitten. We were swept away by a sudden and weirdly warm glacial flood and it must have carried us for seventy kilometres, fortunately back towards the research station, but then we had to trek the final ten kilometres in sodden clothes. We're lucky to be alive but I think Johann will lose most of his fingers and Runi might lose a couple of toes. Whatever's happening under this ice cap is bizarre and, admittedly, a bit frightening, but geologically it's immensely exciting.'

'Yes . . . and it's also devastating,' the director said. 'God, poor Magnus and Gunderson – that's shocking news. They both had families. But you were fortunately on the edge of the flood because it appears to have swept across part of the eastern half of the ice cap. It's destroyed several small towns and villages on the east coast – totally wiped them away. We've no idea yet of the loss of life but it must be in the thousands. On some parts of the ice cap the flood must have been several metres deep and when it spilled down the fjords it became a torrent fifty to a hundred metres deep . . . more violent than any river on earth.'

'What I don't understand,' Jarvik said, 'is, even with sudden and unexpected geothermal or volcanic activity, how the ice cap can have risen by twelve hundred metres and created trillions of gallons of melt-water. Even if melt-water lakes were draining down to the base at a phenomenal rate they would only raise the ice cap by a few metres or . . .'

'It's worse than that,' Gunnar interrupted. 'You were on the edge of the upheaval. Satellite GPS data indicates an increase in height to the north of where you are of two thousand metres or more.'

'Christ!' Jarvik gasped. 'That's two kilometres! Nothing can do that so fast. Not even a volcanic eruption or tectonic plate movement.'

'Well,' Gunnar added, 'every seismometer around the globe is detecting unusual seismic activity beneath the ice cap so something's obviously happening. The UK Climate Research Group are suggesting that man-made global warming has melted the ice cap to such a degree that its weight is no longer sufficient to force down the crust of the Greenland Plate and it's begun to rise. I've spoken to Sir David Appleby, the UK's Chief Scientific Adviser, and he believes that our continued pumping out of carbon dioxide has tipped the balance and the Greenland ice cap will melt in a couple of years and raise worldwide sea levels by seven to eight metres. He says the glacial flood you witnessed proves it.'

'Rubbish!' Jarvik exploded. 'The ice is still three kilometres thick and, although the melt-water is admittedly increasing each year, there's no way the ice has lost that much mass. Even with the glaciers calving into the sea faster than they're replenished, it will be several decades before there's significant loss. And tectonic plate movement, even in active regions such as the Mid-Atlantic Ridge, is only a few centimetres a year. No, there must be something else and we need to find out.'

'Yes, we do,' the director agreed, 'but not you. You and your team have done a fantastic job and you've suffered enough. With Frederik, Magnus and Gunderson all dead and Runi and Johann injured out of your team of six, it's clearly been a heroic struggle and it's time to come home. I'm sending a plane from Iceland to pick you all up. Johann and Runi clearly need urgent medical attention, otherwise gangrene may set in. And we don't want that, do we?'

'But, Gunnar, you can't,' Jarvik pleaded. 'I need to follow this through – it could be the greatest geological discovery of this century. Please – for Frederik's sake. And for Magnus's and for Gunderson's sake. They all risked and ultimately gave their lives for this research. We should honour their memories and allow me to continue where they started.'

'No, I'm sorry, Jarvik,' the director said after a brief pause, 'but you need a rest. I'm sending in another team on the same plane coming to pick you up. They'll be better equipped and will be fresh and strong. It's a harsh environment up there and this is a vitally important investigation, so some of the team are flying in from England, some from Canada and some from Norway.'

'Jesus, Gunnar, how can you?' Jarvik exploded. 'Greenland is a Danish jurisdiction and this is our discovery. Frederik and I have spent twenty years here and now you're about to hand it over to the Norwegians.'

'Sorry, Jarvik, but they have the expertise and equipment,' Gunnar said, beginning to sound annoyed, 'and the Danish Geological Society has made its mind up. You're coming home, Jarvik, for a well-earned rest. The plane is due tomorrow at noon so I suggest you spend the rest of today recuperating and getting ready for your evacuation.'

For a moment there was silence, neither man speaking. Eventually, it was Jarvik who broke the icy spell.

'Very well,' he said half-heartedly, 'we'll be ready.'

Landspitali University Hospital, Reykjavik, Iceland

Gilda Nygaard waited quietly beside Nunni's bed, outwardly content and relaxed but inwardly deeply worried and sad. Nunni's appendectomy appeared to have gone well and they were waiting for the surgeon to visit for the post-operative examination. Nunni was overjoyed that it was all over and, apart from missing Miki Nanook, a sore stomach and revolting hospital food, she was enjoying being the centre of attention and the luxury of lying in bed all day reading comics and books.

Gilda had not told her about the devastating news from Greenland. She couldn't bear to think about telling her of the complete destruction of their little town, Tasiilaq, the total loss of their home, their friends, all the houses and shops, and, of course, Miki Nanook. Only seven months old and such a loyal and happy-go-lucky ball of fur and energy! . . . Nunni would be absolutely heart-broken. And all wiped out in a matter of seconds by a freak flood – how could such a terrible thing happen?

And still there was no news from Tukku. Search and rescue missions had failed to find any of the fishing fleet and the more time went on the more likely . . . But she didn't want to think about it – it was just too horrible to contemplate.

'Mrs Nygaard, good morning,' a kindly looking white-haired bespectacled doctor said. 'And how is our little patient today?'

'Hungry,' Nunni replied.

Dr Hashim laughed.

'Well, that's a good sign,' he said. 'And, just between you and me,' he added conspiratorially, 'I agree that the food here is awful. Let me see if I can get you something different – how about pizza?'

'Wow! That would be great,' Nunni said, smiling broadly. 'And thank you for making me better, Doctor.'

'My pleasure,' he said, 'and now, can I have a look at your tummy? Make sure that everything is fine.'

Nunni allowed herself to be examined and the doctor nodded his satisfaction. The wound was surprisingly small, very neat and adeptly stitched together. He almost said that she would soon be able to go home, but thankfully, at the last moment, he remembered that she didn't actually have a home to go back to.

'Mrs Nygaard,' he said softly, taking Gilda to one side, 'I'm very sorry to hear about the terrible news from Greenland. It's just so absolutely dreadful and devastating. If I can do anything to help, please let me know. But, rest assured, I will make sure that Nunni gets the best food and attention she can – she'll be well looked after in here and she should certainly recover very quickly.'

Later that day, back in the little guesthouse owned by Frida Jonsson, Gilda fled to her room and collapsed onto the bed, sobbing uncontrollably with pent-up wretchedness and grief.

North Pole, Arctic Ocean

The *Polar Explorer* had left Franz Josef Land far behind and steadily it ploughed through the ice. Captain Crowder was pleased with his progress and fortunately the ice was much thinner this year. He'd spent most of his career on icebreakers and he remembered some years when the ice was almost ten metres thick and impossible to break. But this year it averaged only about four metres and in places was only one or two metres thick, easily within the operating threshold of the *Polar Explorer*. If this was the effect of global warming, he mused wryly, then he and his ship would be out of work in a few years' time.

On the bow, cocooned in bright-red padded down jackets, scientists and adventurous tourists watched through the powerful spotlights as the heavy reinforced bow cracked open the ice with reassuring effortlessness.

John Howard, one of the adventurous tourists, was glad that he had voted to go to the aid of the stricken American submarine. After all, not only might they be saving lives but it added more adventure, more excitement to the trip. At sixty-two, after spending a lifetime plodding away as an accountant, slowly rising through the ranks and supporting and providing for his family and his pension, he was desperate to get out and see the world

– to taste adventure and excitement and, occasionally, to experience a little danger. John could see that the captain was steering
the ship towards the Northern Lights but still there was no sign
of the submarine.

Margaret Howard, four years his junior, was, however, unfortunately not of the same mind and she was still in their cabin
reading one of her romantic novels. She preferred to laze around
in a plush hotel or endlessly traipse around all and any shops.
And that is why she had insisted that they go to Paris next year
and why she had voted not to go to the aid of the Americans –
after all, who needed even more adventure and excitement, not
to mention putting all their lives at risk. She didn't care even if
the Prime Minister himself had asked them – after all, she'd never
voted for him in the first place.

An open lead, devoid of ice, lay ahead and from a lookout
post high above the bridge came a shout.

'Whales! Whales ahead, off the starboard bow!'

There was sudden excitement among the throng of scientists
and tourists and they rushed to the starboard side, craning their
necks or peering through binoculars, hoping to see the giant
mammals breaking the surface and blowing their characteristic
fountains.

'Look!' one of the scientists shouted excitedly. 'Those black
ones are bowhead whales with babies . . . and look, there's a pod
of belugas . . . Beautiful creatures, just like large white dolphins.'

John considered racing down to the cabin to fetch Margaret
but immediately realised that he might miss the spectacle and
equally that she might not be interested anyway.

But as the *Polar Explorer* slowed as it entered the open water,
his excitement quickly began to evaporate – clearly something
was wrong. Instead of gracefully gliding across the surface, some
of the whales were thrashing about spasmodically and some were
barely moving, their huge fins and flukes listlessly flapping the
water.

Groans of dismay and sadness rose from the crowd of onlookers as they neared the whales. It was obvious that the beautiful beasts were distressed and maybe close to death; large patches of raw blistering flesh covered many of them, starkly red against black-and-white skin.

'Oh my God!' one of the female tourists cried, tears beginning to moisten her eyes. 'This is awful. The poor creatures, they're suffering so horribly – it's heart-breaking. Can't we do something?'

But there was nothing that they could do and the *Polar Explorer* slowly steamed through the pod of dying beasts, the decks silent and melancholy, a mournful funeral cortège among the bleak Arctic ice. John closed his eyes and sadly shook his head. This wasn't the adventure and excitement he'd been hoping for.

On the bridge, Captain Crowder watched the spectacle and frowned. He didn't like it – there was something definitely strange happening in the Arctic this year and it made him uneasy. And the only response he was getting from the submarine was the regular automatic emergency transmission from its EPIRB. Either their radio was dead or else they were.

'Prepare the helicopter,' he ordered the first mate. 'Let's find that sub.'

Cambridge University, England

Hunched in front of a bank of computer monitors and surrounded by reams of scientific data printouts and reports, Dr Joanna Turnbull gasped.

She was an unlikely-looking scientist, with long blonde hair and a model's beauty and slim figure, but she had wanted to be a scientist ever since she had been twelve years old – to carry out research and to teach at a university. And, what better place than at the Environmental and Geological Research Unit at Cambridge – it was her dream job.

She looked at the latest printout – it was the fourth time she had run her computer simulation and it was the fourth time that the results had come back the same. Inwardly, she had expected it but it was still a shock nevertheless. It was her mathematical model and, admittedly, perhaps a trifle complex, but it had had to absorb gigabytes of information and data – surface and sub-surface water temperature readings of the Arctic Ocean, carbon dioxide and carbon monoxide concentrations of the water, ice and air in the Arctic, seismic readings, weather patterns, Arctic ice thickness . . . years of historic data. Naturally, with a consensus view that global warming was induced by mankind's voracious burning of fossil fuels, she had expected the model to project the ultimate demise of the Arctic ice but in years . . . not in days!

But what was strange was that over the ten-year period of the model, there was an almost insignificant correlation between carbon dioxide levels, water temperature and ice thickness . . . until now, that is. For some reason, the correlation for the last few months was completely perfect – as precise a fit as you could possibly get. And it coincided with huge changes in the data – the readings had simply gone ballistic!

It was something she had been working on for months now and, finally, she had sufficient proof. Something was happening and it was happening fast. And, whatever it was, it was going to be big and it was going to be catastrophic!

She picked up the phone and dialled a government number.

'Hello, I'd like to speak to Sir David Appleby, please. It's urgent.'

Headquarters, Mid-Ocean Oil, England

Susan Macintyre was glad that she had left Lucy and Bonnie with friends back in Blackpool. It had been a long drive in cold wintry conditions to the headquarters of Mid-Ocean Oil and it had been almost as long a wait in the large opulent boardroom seated with dozens of other wives and relatives. She was getting increasingly impatient with the oil company and clearly so were many of the other wives.

'I think it's disgusting,' Janet Watson hissed for the umpteenth time. 'They make a fortune out of our men and this is how they treat us. One cup of coffee and no information in almost two hours . . . It's completely inconsiderate and tactless. I'm going to ask Bill to change oil companies after . . .'

Suddenly, the large mahogany door at the end of the room opened and two businessmen entered: one tall, lean and smartly dressed and clearly the senior of the two, and the other, short, fat and scruffy.

'Good day, ladies and gentlemen,' the taller man greeted them in a distinctive American accent. 'I'm John Houston, the CEO of Mid-Ocean Oil, and this is David Evans, who, as some of you may already know, is our HR director. You all know that a storm has been raging along the east coast of Canada and that we have had difficulty contacting *Ocean One*. Well, we've finally established communications and it does appear as though there has been a bit of a problem.'

There were several gasps and Susan's heart missed a beat – all along she felt as though they had been fobbed off and a feeling of dread enveloped her. She looked closely at the distinguished-looking man and decided that she didn't like or trust him. He seemed to have worked just a little bit too hard on the polished look and she instinctively knew that his jet-black hair greying at the temples and the ski-slope tan were from bottles and his immaculate suit was from Savile Row. She thought his words would be as hollow as he was.

'Unexpectedly,' the CEO continued, 'a rather large iceberg appeared out of the storm and, because it looked like it might threaten the platform, we made sure that there was an orderly evacuation of the rig onto the lifeboats.'

This time there were even more gasps throughout the room and many faces clearly registered shock and horror.

'Tell us what's happening!' one of the women at the back of the room shouted.

'Are our men all right?' another shouted, standing up and waving her arms.

'Has the iceberg crashed into the rig?' another shouted. 'Is it . . .'

The CEO raised his hands in the air and gestured for calm.

'The danger has passed,' he said quickly. 'We have two support vessels in position and they are taking the men off the lifeboats. Once everyone is on board they'll head for St John's, Newfoundland, and disembark all the men who will then be able to fly home for a well-deserved rest.'

This time there were sighs of relief and some of the women began chattering away, excitedly discussing the men's homecoming.

The CEO looked at the HR director.

'I'm sure we can give the men an extra week's holiday, can't we, David?' he said, smiling generously.

On cue, David nodded.

'Yes, yes,' he agreed, trying to sound positive and enthusiastic despite knowing that, with the loss of the company's largest oil platform – a fact the CEO had carefully managed to avoid divulging – many of the men would soon be made redundant.

'Excellent, excellent,' the CEO enthused. 'And now that we are back in contact we'll let you know as soon as the men arrive in Newfoundland.'

He looked round the room and smiled, sincerely and openly.

'You can rest assured, ladies and gentlemen, that Mid-Ocean Oil has the comfort and safety of its men above all else.'

As they were led out of the room, everyone relieved and happy that their men were safe and coming home, Susan grabbed hold of Janet's arm and steered her into a ladies toilet.

'I don't trust them, do you?' she whispered, looking in the cubicles to make sure no one else was present. 'Especially that CEO – he reminds me of a politician – condescending and full of false sincerity and platitudes.'

Janet laughed.

'Yes, I know what you mean,' she agreed, putting on a strange accent. '*White man, he speaks with forked tongue.*'

This time, Susan laughed.

'But that fat chap, the HR director,' she said, being serious, 'he seems more normal and he didn't look very happy with what the CEO was saying. I think we should have a private word with him.'

Janet looked at Susan and realised that she was being serious. 'What, now?'

Susan nodded. 'Yes, now,' she said. 'I'm not going home until I'm satisfied that our men are all right. All we have to do is find his office and barge in. He'll be so surprised and unprepared that he might actually tell the truth.'

Janet looked at her again and enthusiastically nodded.

'Come on!' she growled. 'Let's go get the fat one.'

Peshawar, Pakistan

Malik didn't want to be in Peshawar – it wasn't part of the plan. He should have been in Iceland, making final preparations for the beginning of the Apocalypse; or in London, ensuring the transits went smoothly; or in New York, overseeing the diversionary operation. Yes, there were lots of places that he could more usefully be than in hot, crowded, dusty and polluted Peshawar.

And, although he had been here several times before, it was impossible for him to blend in – every characteristic screamed Westerner in garish neon lights – blue eyes, blond hair, and six foot height – and when he opened his mouth out came a pathetic smattering of Urdu in a broad Yorkshire accent. Tourists didn't come to the ancient city of Peshawar, situated as it was near the Khyber Pass and the main link into Afghanistan – no, only refugees, spies, terrorists, aid workers, journalists and more refugees. And that is why he was now climbing out of the fourth taxi that morning, having spent two hours meandering around the bustling city to throw off any unwanted followers.

After stepping out of the taxi he quickly slipped down a narrow side street into the old quarter, its hot air filled with the pungent smells of cumin, coriander, chillies, turmeric and almonds as households prepared their midday meals. After rounding a sharp corner, he sidestepped into a dark and nondescript courtyard and quickly tapped on an old and scruffy wooden door, its faded sign proudly proclaiming 'International Spice Exporters'. Above him, on the roof, he sensed movement and he looked up to show his face.

For a moment, nothing happened and momentarily he felt uncharacteristically alone and vulnerable. But then the door creaked open and a hand beckoned him through.

Inside, his nose was immediately assailed, not by pleasant aromatic smells of exotic spices, but by a sickly stench of filth, squalor and decay. Inwardly, he groaned and cursed – someone would pay dearly for this.

'My dear Malik,' Abdul Hamid, the portly owner of the small warehouse greeted him profusely. 'This is a most unexpected but pleasant honour. Come in. Come in and let's have some nice sweet green tea.'

He followed Abdul through into the next room, which, once his eyes had become accustomed to the gloom, he realised was the main storage shed. But there were no hessian sacks filled with spices . . . No, instead there were a few groaning heaps of filthy blankets, mounds of dirty unwashed dishes, swarms of flies and, in the dark corners, the scurrying sound of rats and cockroaches. And – the indescribable stench of rotting food and flesh.

Malik bent down and examined one of the groaning heaps. A young, frightened man gazed back at him, barely conscious but clearly in pain. Malik threw back the blanket and was immediately hit by the foul stench of infected flesh, urine and excrement.

'What have you done?' he screamed, jumping to his feet and grabbing the grubby warehouse owner by the shirt. 'Where are the nurses? Where are the cleaners? You are paid a small fortune in gold to look after these men. You told me this place was disinfested and disinfected daily and so clean that you could eat your dinner off the floor. Look at it – it's a foul, stinking, festering cesspit!'

'B-b-but, it's not my fault,' Abdul babbled, trying to cower away. 'It's the cleaners. Yes, the cleaners – they're lazy and greedy and stupid and . . .'

Malik growled and with the speed and accuracy that came from army training he whipped his elbow round and caught the warehouse owner a sharp crack across his cheekbone, felling him to the floor.

'These men are sacrificing their lives for the great cause,' he screamed at the cowering wretch, 'and you treat them not as warriors or soldiers but as dirt, like a stupid man would treat a lame camel. They've just had operations, expensive operations, and you're meant to be providing a clean and healthy place for their recovery. Don't you realise that they're due to fly out to London tomorrow?'

Abdul, scrabbling on the filthy floor away from Malik, rubbed his grimy hand across his bloodied face and broken nose and looked imploringly at the big Westerner.

'I'll get new cleaners and new nurses,' he mumbled. 'I'll sack the old ones. No, I'll beat them, I'll . . .'

'Liar!' Malik shouted, aiming a kick at the scoundrel's head. 'You're a greedy, filthy cheat!'

He was unbelievably angry and annoyed. He had spent three years putting in place his operation and this fool was going to ruin it for his own personal greed. Quickly, he counted the groaning heaps – six of the fifteen operatives were probably too ill to travel and one or two close to death. With Jayed in London almost certainly having succumbed to an infection in this lousy place, he might lose half of his operatives for the main event.

From his pocket he took out one of the many mobile phones he carried and dialled a local number.

'Mohammed, its Malik. I'm at the warehouse and we have a problem. I need a medical team and a response team. And,' he added, looking directly at Abdul, 'I've got a new recruit for you – he's keen to show his zeal for the cause. He'd make an ideal suicide bomber.'

Later that day, as Malik waited at the hotel reception to check out, he got the shock of his life.

'Stephen!' a man's voice suddenly called. 'Stephen John Browning!'

Malik froze. 'No!' he screamed inwardly, not now, not so late in the end game. His adrenalin started pumping, activating his body's fight or flight response. No, that was no good – stay calm, he urged himself, stay calm.

'It is you, I'm sure it is,' the voice continued.

Malik didn't recognise the voice but, as he was the only Westerner in the queue and everyone was looking at him, he had no choice. He turned and saw a plump, ruddy-faced Englishman in khaki chinos and jacket striding towards him. 'Bugger!' he thought.

'Captain Wainright, isn't it?' he said, vaguely remembering the 'Rupert' from the intelligence section of his division in Afghanistan – it wasn't easy as in three years he had morphed from a fit soldier into a fat civilian.

'Just plain Charles Wainright now,' the ex-captain said, beaming and clearly pleased to see another Englishman in Peshawar. 'How the devil are you? You did a brave deed back there in Helmand, trying to pull that American soldier to safety. You got the Military Cross for it, if I remember rightly.'

And, Malik thought bitterly – a glass eye, a scarred face, tinnitus and unemployment.

'I'm attached to the British Embassy in Islamabad,' the annoying ex-captain continued. 'I'm up here for a few days with the consul. How about you?'

'Oh, you know, import and export, that sort of thing,' Malik replied as naturally as he could. 'I'm in Peshawar to buy some spices for a British company. Just been inspecting the wholesalers.'

'That's interesting,' Wainright said enthusiastically. 'I might be able to help. Have lots of contacts here, if you know what I mean. Have you got your card?'

Malik looked at him confused.

'My card?'

'Yes, yes, you know – your business card that you salesmen are always handing out hoping to drum up business.'

'Ah,' Malik replied, thinking fast, 'I've run out, I'm afraid. It's been a busy trip. Anyway, what do you do at the embassy?'

Wainright smiled and winked.

'Can't tell you, it's on a need-to-know basis,' he said, tapping his nose conspiratorially. 'But, between you and me, I spend a lot of time listening and watching. And,' he added, laughing, 'writing endless intel reports.'

'Ah,' Malik said simply, smiling and nodding his head knowingly. Shit! he thought, that's all I need. 'Look,' he said out loud, 'why don't we have a drink and chat about old times?'

'Excellent idea,' Wainright agreed enthusiastically. 'We can have some spicy snacks with it . . . I'm famished and you can tell me all about your import and export business.'

'Excellent, but instead let me buy you lunch,' Malik agreed. 'I know a very tasty curry house not far from here and I'm friendly with the owner. Let me just make a phone call and he'll send a car for us.'

Wainright nodded readily – the idea of a few beers, a curry and a free lunch seemed the perfect way to spend the day.

Malik got one of his phones out and phoned a familiar number.

'Mohammed,' he said, 'it's Malik again. I need a car at the hotel. And,' he added, whispering, 'I have someone here who is surplus to requirements. He needs to disappear.'

Sadly, Charles Wainright never got to enjoy his free lunch.

Adirondack Mountains, New York County, USA

Mary Dewey-Bell was a small, prematurely grey-haired God-fearing woman who went to church as regular as clockwork every Sunday morning. Her husband Ned had been killed in Vietnam two years after they had been married and he'd barely had time to see his two baby sons. Tom, and the slightly elder Billy, had grown up to be strapping God-fearing young men before they were blown to smithereens – Tom in Iraq and Billy in Afghanistan. The lives of three God-fearing young men obliterated futilely in three God-forsaken countries.

And, as the good Bible said – *an eye for an eye and a tooth for a tooth*. It was only right, it was only just. The three wonderful men in her life had been callously taken from her and it was her right to seek revenge, to mete out God's justice. It had taken quite a while to come to such a firm but righteous decision, but she had been helped by another wonderful young man, a man who had helped her to crystallise her mind and formulate her plan. At the time of Billy's death, he had been a soldier with the British armed forces in Afghanistan and he had been blown up by a secondary bomb as he had tried to drag Billy to safety. To her, Stephen John Browning was a hero and another reason for seeking an eye for an eye and a tooth for a tooth – not only had the bomb badly scarred his face and given him tinnitus but it had literally taken an eye.

And now, Operation Righteousness, as he had called it, was God's justice and she was God's servant to ensure that rightful retribution was delivered and, as Stephen had planned, was delivered on Righteousness Day, in five days' time. And who better to deliver this retribution than three God-fearing young men from the three countries where her own God-fearing young men had been smitten – Jakbar Mulla, a devout Muslim from Afghanistan; Ali Pasha, a devout Muslim from Iraq; and Nguyen Phan, a devout Buddhist from Vietnam. And now, after two years working with her on her small farm in the wild and rugged recesses of the Adirondack Mountains in New York County, they had become part of her family, her surrogate sons.

And when her mobile phone buzzed with a text message that simply said, '*An eye for an eye*', she knew that it was time to act.

And, one minute later, when a text message from the same

source arrived on Jakbar's phone, simply saying '*Armageddon*', the Afghan also knew that it was time to act.

In the county sheriff's office in Downy Beck, one hundred and fifty kilometres from Mrs Dewey-Bell's desolate farmstead, Deputy John Banks looked at the incident report for the fifth time. He didn't really know Mary but from what he'd heard she was a sweet, if rather odd, little old lady and an ardent churchgoer at that. But what seemed strange to his unsophisticated but practical mind was the brief mention from the post office of regular parcels from Detroit of quite large quantities of chemicals. What she wanted with canisters of aluminium, magnesium and iron oxide powders was anyone's guess. He had asked his father-in-law, a cattle rancher on the lower slopes of the Adirondacks, if they were used for pest control or for fertilizers but he hadn't heard of them being used in farming.

Unfortunately, the sheriff thought that his deputy was wasting his time and had told him to stop playing the FBI agent and get down to some proper police work, like traffic violations and weekend drunkenness.

Deputy Banks sighed and closed the report. Oh well, he thought, shaking his head slowly, forget his gut feelings and get on with the mundane police work. After all, Mrs Dewey-Bell was a sweet old lady.

Washington, USA

'Ye Gods!' Theodore Jackson-Taylor shouted angrily, thumping the table and jumping to his feet. 'You're telling me that you've been monitoring this information for the last ten years and this year there has been a dramatic rise but it's only now that you've decided to tell me?'

Paul Gates, the youthful bespectacled deputy director of the

FBI, squirmed and glanced nervously around the table, looking for support from the other security chiefs.

'W-well,' he began uncertainly, 'there has, admittedly been an increase but, county by county, it didn't seem significant and . . .'

'Didn't seem significant!' the Secretary of State exploded. 'Didn't seem significant! You're telling me that the theft of nine hundred and fifty kilograms of explosives from quarries and demolition firms in the last year didn't seem significant?'

'W-well,' the deputy director of the FBI continued, his face flushing and perspiring, 'individually, these amounts weren't particularly noticeable and it's only recently that my analysts have compiled all the historic data and looked at the trends. Getting all the information together from all the security agencies around the country has . . .'

'God damn it!' the Secretary of State shouted, thumping the table again, 'my old grandmother could have done that and she's eighty-two. All you had to do was join the dots!'

Paul Gates opened his mouth to speak again but thought better of it. He knew they had failed and it would forever be a stain on his reputation and credibility. After all, six to nine percent increases in annual explosive thefts jumping to a massive one hundred and twenty percent increase in the last year was something that his department should have spotted much, much earlier. But, as always, it was human error – unimaginably vast computing power was still only as good as its weakest link and couldn't make up for failings in communication and inter-agency rivalries.

'But what worries me,' Bob Gould, head of the homeland security division of the National Guard, said, 'is what exactly does it mean? Does it mean, for example, that, with the approach of the prophesied doomsday scenario, that every survivalist, criminal and crank throughout the country is getting ready for the big day or, more worryingly, is it the work of one or two groups stockpiling huge arsenals? And, if so, why?'

'That's the big question, ain't it?' Theodore growled. 'We need to get all the dots joined up, and,' he added with emphasis, looking directly at Paul Gates, 'I mean *all* the dots. Whatever it takes, even if you all have to work 24/7. And, until this bloody Armageddon day has come and gone, I want a briefing meeting every morning at 0500 hours sh-'

Suddenly, the phone rang.

The Secretary of State looked at it and frowned.

'Yes, Mr President?' he said, looking at his watch and knowing that it must be something very urgent to warrant the President phoning him so early.

'Theodore,' the President said breathlessly, 'I've just come off the phone with the British Prime Minister and he told me that he's just issued a Code Red alert for London. Apparently, there's been a chemical attack in London and a few people have been killed. It seems to be the deadly nerve agent used in Tokyo a few years ago. They suspect that there might be multiple releases and have mobilised all their emergency and anti-terrorist units. You need to speak to a Superintendent Jamie McDougal of the Metropolitan Police. He will fill you in with the details in case something similar is being planned over here.'

Chapter 5

17 December 2012
Ice cap, central Greenland

Olaf Sigmundsen, the big and bluff expedition leader from Norway, watched the lights of the DeHavilland Twin Otter lift from the ice amid swirls of powdery snow and rise into the twilight gloom of the Arctic winter's day. Slowly, he shook his head and frowned.

Apart from some broken-down equipment and rubbish from the Danish research station, the plane was returning empty – Jarvik and the two Christiansen brothers had vanished. Mind you, Olaf thought to himself, it didn't surprise him, having met Jarvik on a couple of occasions and knowing his reputation for stubbornness and single-minded determination. But to drag the two injured younger scientists along with him was insane – clearly, not only was he putting his own life in jeopardy but he was also risking theirs.

And, more annoyingly, he had a head start. With a potentially far-reaching discovery that could amaze the world and bring fame and glory to the finder it was the holy grail of every scientist. And he was determined that Olaf Sigmundsen would be credited with that discovery – certainly not Jarvik Petersen.

As the Northern Lights danced and swirled in a dazzling display of colour, Olaf made his mind up to leave as soon as everything was unpacked and loaded onto the skidoos rather than losing time settling into the research station. After all, Jarvik had at least a day's head start and every minute counted.

'Olaf!' Pierre LeBlanc, the gangly Canadian scientist shouted. 'Have you seen the altimeter reading on the GPS?'

Olaf absently shook his head, his mind absorbed by the challenge ahead.

'It's crazy!' Pierre gasped, tapping the GPS in case it was faulty. 'I've got a reading of six thousand metres! The ice here is supposed to be three thousand metres thick. What the hell's going on?'

Olaf snapped out of his trance and grabbed the GPS.

'That's not possible,' he growled. 'Let me have a look.'

He stared at the GPS, tapped it, turned it off, reset it and stared at it again. Six thousand and sixty-eight metres! Impossible! He had been told by Gunnar Pattersen only two days before that it was two thousand metres higher than expected and now, all of a sudden, it was three thousand metres higher. How could the ice cap, a vast area of two million square kilometres, increase in thickness by a kilometre in two days? That was just impossible. Something very strange was happening and the more he thought about it the more he was determined to be the man to discover it. And, without meaning to, he grinned.

'Come on, you guys!' he shouted across at his team of scientists labouring to unload and sort out their tonnes of equipment. 'Get a move on – I want to get going as soon as possible. You've got two hours to get this mess sorted and loaded on the skidoos. There's science to do and discoveries to be made!'

Two hundred kilometres to the north, a lone skidoo and heavily laden trailer sped through the twilight gloom, its three fur-clad occupants coated with a layer of snow and rime.

The glacial flood had breached the pressure ridge in several places and this time they managed to negotiate a path through and were now approaching the coordinates where the melt-water lake, and Frederik Larsen, had disappeared.

Jarvik, driving the skidoo, was frozen and exhausted, his breath barely able to escape the icicle-encrusted facemask. With his goggles opaque with frost and swirling snow drifting across the ice in the gusting wind, his visibility was severely limited. But he would not stop until he reached his destination, driven on relentlessly by the knowledge that a multinational expedition was on its way and might already be closing the gap. This was a discovery that was rightfully his and Frederik's and there was no way that he was going to be usurped.

Behind him, huddled precariously on the two-man skidoo, Runi and Johann were frozen to the bone and, after almost sixteen hours of non-stop travel, were desperate to stop, get the tent up, devour a hot meal and curl up into a warm sleeping bag. But Jarvik had pursued his quest unremittingly, and now they were seriously beginning to wonder if they had made the right decision. Both were badly frostbitten and in the first stages of hypothermia and were in need of urgent medical attention – fame and glory were one thing but at what price?

Jarvik struggled to keep his eyes open and more than once he had caught himself nodding off, jerking awake just in time to control the skidoo. And as his tired and sore eyes began to droop again, he suddenly spotted something different in the terrain ahead. He tried wiping his frosted goggles with a sleeve but it made little difference and he lifted them away from his eyes, exposing them to the icy blasts. And then he saw it – a shadow darker than the twilight lay just ahead and instinctively he knew what it meant – the ice had suddenly vanished.

He slammed the brakes on but the heavy machine skidded through the snow, charging headlong to a cliff edge.

'Jump!' he shouted, but his frozen mask muffled his voice and Runi and Johann barely stirred.

Frantically, he swung the skidoo to the left and immediately the heavily laden trailer jack-knifed and flipped over, sending the skidoo tumbling out of control. Jarvik and Runi were thrown off, landing heavily in the snow, but Johann's foot got trapped in the skidoo's half-track and he was flipped beneath the heavy machine as it rolled over him. He screamed as it landed with a bone-crunching *crump*.

Jarvik and Runi clambered to their feet and ran over to him. And as they bent down to pull the skidoo off him, Jarvik gasped – they had managed to stop precariously within a metre of the cliff edge. He hadn't spotted it sooner because it was hidden by cloud that was drifting level with the ice and gently undulating as though it was alive. As he struggled to lift the heavy machine, Runi dragged his brother from underneath and away from the edge.

Johann was still conscious and groaning in pain; from the unnatural angle of his foot, his leg was clearly broken.

'We've got to get him into the tent,' Runi shouted, 'and get him warm; otherwise he'll die of shock.'

Jarvik nodded and rushed over to the trailer, its back-end hanging in space. As he fumbled with the straps he couldn't help but peer over the edge and into the strange cloud. Instantly, he froze – as the cloud writhed and drifted, he got a momentary vision of hell. Beneath him, the ice cap fell away, down three kilometres of almost vertical cliff face, a fissure of unimaginable size and at the very bottom, a yellow-and-orange steaming and bubbling river of molten lava. The void was so vast that he felt he was toppling over and into space and he had to grab the trailer for support.

'What the..!' is all he could say.

Landspitali University Hospital, Reykjavik, Iceland

Gilda Nygaard was exhausted. She hadn't slept all night and must have cried non-stop for twenty hours. And then, when she thought she couldn't cry anymore, Nunni accidentally saw the terrible news on television and promptly burst into tears, setting Gilda off again. Hugging each other on the hospital bed, they had shared their sorrow and anguish – distraught at the devastating potential loss of a loving husband and father, their innocent and loving puppy, their friends, their home and the little town that they had all grown up in.

Nunni had sobbed and rocked in her mother's arms, but mercifully, after a while, had fallen into an exhausted sleep. Gilda, still holding her daughter's hand, had slumped into the chair next to the bed and now she stared through red-rimmed eyes at the floor, her gaze inward and unfocused. She lost track of time as the day drifted by in a dream, a horrible, cold and despairing dream, and at first she didn't realise that someone was talking to her.

'. . . Mrs Nygaard,' Dr Hashim whispered. 'Mrs Nygaard, I have some news for you. It's good news.'

Gilda jerked out of her trance and looked at the doctor. She smiled politely, thinking that he was going to tell her that Nunni was recovering well and could soon leave the hospital.

'They've found your husband,' he said, smiling. 'He's alive.'

Gilda stared at him – was this still part of the dream?

'Tukku?' she mumbled. 'Tukku's alive?'

Dr Hashim nodded.

'Yes, he's alive,' he said. 'He had a miraculous escape from the sinking trawler and was found in a partially deflated life raft two kilometres from the ruins of Tasiilaq. Apparently, he's badly frostbitten and hypothermic and he's being brought here with three other injured patients – the only survivors, I'm afraid, from your town.'

'He's alive? Alive!' Gilda shouted, jumping to her feet. 'It's a miracle!'

'Mum?' Nunni whispered, sitting up suddenly and staring at her mother. 'Is Dad alive? Is it true?'

Dr Hashim grinned and nodded.

Nunni jumped out of bed and ignoring her stitches hugged her mother and then the doctor.

'And he's coming here?' she asked unbelievingly. 'To Landspitali University Hospital?'

Dr Hashim grinned and nodded again.

Gilda could not believe it – their Tukku had risen from the dead. It had been inconceivable that anyone could have survived such a catastrophic event and, against all odds, he had been saved, spared the death and destruction wrought on so many innocent and helpless people by the glacial flood. And now, he was coming to the very same hospital as Nunni – it was a miracle!

'And I've got some more news for you,' Dr Hashim continued, laughing and acting conspiratorially, 'but you'll have to wait here – I won't be a moment.'

Gilda and Nunni looked at each other, overjoyed and unable to contain their happiness and excitement. Gilda grabbed her daughter's hands and together they danced and laughed around the bed until eventually Nunni groaned from her sore and tender stitches.

And when Dr Hashim returned, little Nunni had another shock. Bewildered, bedraggled, limping badly and with a hang-dog expression, Miki Nanook came into the room. As soon as she saw Nunni, she gave a yelp of excitement and hobbled as fast as she could over to her. Nunni gasped and, crouching down, hugged and kissed her, tears of joy streaming down her cheeks as she sobbed with happiness.

Gilda smiled at Dr Hashim and kissed him on the cheek.

'Thank you, Dr Hashim! You have been so kind.'

'She's lucky to be alive,' the doctor replied, a little embarrassed. 'She was found among all the driftwood several hundred metres from the shore – frozen and petrified. We've X-rayed her leg and it's not broken, only badly sprained. But remember that this is a hospital and pets are not allowed. So, keep her hidden otherwise I'll get my knuckles rapped.'

Gilda looked at her daughter who now had her Miki Nanook and her father back and her heart leapt with joy. This was better than she could ever, ever have hoped for.

'Thank you, Dr Hashim,' she said again. 'You are a good man.'

Dr Hashim was exhausted and he was sitting slumped at his desk in his office, his glasses off and his eyes closed. It had been a long and tiring day with an endless stream of operations, consultations, patient rounds, trainee doctor mentoring and, of course,

NINE DAYS TO ARMAGEDDON

mounds of forms and paperwork to complete. And now all he wanted to do was to go home and fall asleep.

But first, he had one more important job to do. He looked at his watch and it said 9.03 p.m. – it was time. From his pocket he took out a small key and used it to open the desk drawer. Inside, it was empty apart from a mobile phone and he took it out and switched it on. It had a single message, received three minutes previously – '*The angels have landed*'.

He nodded, slowly and seriously – Malik's nurses had arrived in Iceland. Tomorrow the prophecy would begin.

Metropolitan Police Headquarters, London, England

Superintendent Jamie McDougal looked at the report and then at Inspector Cassidy.

'You're telling me,' he eventually said, slowly shaking his head in disbelief, 'that, despite a city-wide Code Red alert and every available counter-terrorism agent involved in the operation, you have no more information than when the search started?'

'Well, that's not strictly true,' the inspector replied quickly, 'we have confirmed that the toxic liquid was sarin and that Ahmed Jayed wasn't his real name. He had a forged passport and obviously travelled from Islamabad, having bought a ticket with cash. Whether or not he was a British citizen we couldn't say and none of the other passengers on the plane knew him. Naturally, we've rigorously screened all of them and none appear to have any terrorist connections or fundamental extremist inclinations.'

Superintendent Jamie McDougal slowly shook his head again. This was clearly not good. In fact, it was becoming something of a disaster and later that day he had to brief the Prime Minister. Who knew what plot was being hatched at that very moment in the country's capital? Clearly this Jayed, whoever he was, was not acting alone. Sarin was a difficult and dangerous nerve agent to produce and someone must have operated on him as well –

it could only have been funded and organised by one of the terrorist networks and al-Qaeda was clearly top of the list. Someone, somewhere, knew what was going on and with Christmas fast approaching – an obvious target for extreme Islamic fundamentalists – they were running out of time. If sarin was used in London on Christmas Eve, in a busy shopping mall or on the Underground as had been used in Tokyo, then hundreds, perhaps thousands, might be killed or maimed. It was imperative that they uncover the plot and find the terrorists behind it. But what if . . .

Suddenly, the telephone rang.

'McDougal,' he barked, annoyed that his train of thought had been disrupted.

'Superintendent,' an American voice bellowed down the phone, 'Theodore Jackson-Taylor here. The President asked me to give you a call.'

Jamie McDougal winced – he had been expecting the call but he had been hoping for something useful to say.

'Theodore,' he said, indicating for Cassidy to pick up the extension, 'yes, I've been expecting you. We've got a Code Red alert here – let me give you details of . . .'

'No need,' the Secretary of State interrupted, 'I'm being kept informed already.'

Jamie McDougal frowned and looked at Cassidy, who shrugged.

'I'm phoning to give *you* some information,' the Secretary of State continued. 'It's from Peshawar, in Pakistan, a real hotbed of gun-running, terrorism, drug smuggling and God knows . . .'

'Yes, indeed,' the superintendent agreed. 'In fact, we've just heard our head of intelligence in the region has disappeared. He was escorting the British consul in Peshawar but seems to have vanished.'

'Naturally, we've been keeping a close eye on Peshawar,' the Secretary of State continued, 'because of its proximity to the mountain passes into Afghanistan and its use by the Taliban. Well, this morning a man called Abdul Hamid gave himself up to the police station. He was lucky – they almost shot him – he was wearing a bomber's suicide vest. Apparently, he'd been ordered to detonate the bomb inside the police station . . . could have murdered dozens of policemen. Thankfully, he didn't want to be a martyr and instead started babbling on about a terrorist operation involving the nerve agent sarin. Took the police into the backstreets and showed them a warehouse for the export of exotic spices. Only, it wasn't exotic spices the policemen found – it was two corpses like your Ahmed Jayed, both dead from an infection and blood poisoning and with newly stitched abdominal wounds. The police have cordoned off the area and are waiting for specialists from Islamabad.'

'That's a fantastic lead,' Jamie McDougal said, impressed. 'That certainly sounds like part of the same operation. But are the three dead terrorists *all* of the operation or are there more? For us, that's a vital question.'

'Unfortunately,' the Secretary of State growled, 'they were the tail-end. This Abdul, whose job, apparently, was to look after them, said that fifteen volunteers had undergone the operation, of which nine had boarded planes to London last week, two left for London yesterday and two left today. You may be able to intercept the last two.'

The superintendent and inspector looked at each other and the inspector put the phone down and raced out of the room.

'And another thing,' the Secretary of State continued, 'this Abdul gave the police another important lead. The man in charge of this terrorist operation is named Malik Husain and he was seen there, in Peshawar, yesterday but has since vanished. But get this – he's not Asian, he's Caucasian, from England!'

'Christ!' the superintendent cursed – another home-grown Islamic fundamentalist. What was wrong with this country?

'I can't tell you the source,' the Secretary of State continued, 'except to say that it's very reliable. Apparently, Malik is on his way to London.'

Iceberg Alley, somewhere off the east coast of America

The life raft had been a godsend – it had literally saved their lives. As the fog bank had rolled across the iceberg it had obliterated the sun and the temperature had plummeted. The snow hole had protected them from the wind but, without any insulated flooring, it had gradually stolen their body heat. The double walls of the life raft were a massive improvement and the emergency rations had fuelled their starving bodies and lifted their spirits.

But now, on the fourth day on the iceberg, with the constant cold and damp invading their bodies and insufficient food to generate any more body heat, their core temperatures were beginning to slump further into a hypothermic state and Sean had sunk into a lethargic apathy. He was so weak, listless and confused that he had taken off his gloves in his delirium and, before Craig had noticed, his fingers had blackened and swollen. In the rare lucid moments, he talked of the gloriously long sunny days of his youth, fishing and surfing in Cornwall, a free and happy-go-lucky spirit.

Craig knew that his friend was already in the third and final stage of hypothermia and that, unless they were rescued soon, he would fall into a coma. Death would be close behind.

'I'm going to see if I can find some food,' he said to his barely conscious friend. 'I may be able to catch a seabird or something.'

From the life raft's emergency gear, he took out the small coil of fishing line and the knife and climbed out into the swirling mist. It was damp and cold outside and he immediately began shivering uncontrollably.

'I'll have to keep moving,' he mumbled to himself, 'otherwise I'll freeze and that won't help poor old Sean.'

The iceberg was vast and desolate and, apart from Craig's boots crunching on the snow and the odd creak and groan underfoot, completely silent. In places, the wind had whipped away the covering snow revealing a treacherously glassy layer and, without skis or crampons, he slipped and slid his way across the ice. But at least he felt safer here – on the snow-covered areas, who knew when there might be a slender and precarious snow bridge crossing a deep and frightening chasm? To fall into a crevasse was a primal fear – to suddenly plummet into a bottomless, black void was as nightmarish an ending as any on earth.

But after several hours wandering around the iceberg and two abortive attempts to capture an injured petrel, the weak light had begun to fade from the sky and he decided it was prudent to head back to the life raft. But that was easier said than done. When he looked round, the landscape he could see through gaps in the shifting mist was a whitewash of sameness – it was impossible to tell where he had come from and to where he should go. He knew that he wouldn't survive a night in the open and, for a brief moment, panic almost surfaced before his logical pragmatism took over. He tied the fishing line to an icy outcrop, chose a direction and set off.

But he didn't get far before a snow bridge collapsed beneath him.

'Argh!' he involuntarily cried as he fell through and into the void.

But almost immediately he hit a snow ledge three metres below and, crashing into a snowdrift, he ended up with his head dangling over the edge of the pitch black chasm. Winded, he lay for a moment to catch his breath and he could feel a deep and sinister chill rising up the crevasse from the bowels of the iceberg. He shivered – what a frightening place, he thought.

Rising to his feet he saw that the snow bridge widened further on and that there was something on it.

He gasped – what the . . . !

Rising from the snow ledge, its nose buried into it, was a wooden sledge. And at the back, a trailer, smashed against the crevasse wall and pinioning the driver. As he reached it in the descending gloom, it was an eerie sight – the Inuit driver, frozen solid and his face a mask of panic and pain, stared demonically at Craig.

Craig shook his head slowly and sadly. Hopefully, he thought, this poor hunter had died a quick death and had not been trapped here alive and in despair. It was impossible to tell how long he had been there, but it could have been years, maybe centuries – clearly, he had fallen into the crevasse somewhere in Greenland and as the glacier had been pushed to the sea and calved off as this giant iceberg, he had sailed south – a strange ending to his fate.

When Craig glanced beyond the sledge and down into the crevasse, he gasped again. Dangling in harnesses below, six frozen huskies, a sorrowful tableau that made him wince. Poor faithful dogs, he thought, what a terrible ending.

But he couldn't stay long – the light was fading fast and he was beginning to shiver uncontrollably. Using the life raft's knife he quickly cut the ropes holding the trailer's cargo together and began prizing open the frozen canvas covering the hunter's possessions. Beneath were layers of fur blankets and leather sacks of frozen whale and seal meat – the bedding and provisions of the unfortunate Inuit hunter. Grabbing some of the sacks and folding one of the stiff fur blankets round his body, he clambered up and over the trailer and back onto the surface. At least they now had some food and a blanket for warmth – if only he could find his way back to the life raft.

Paris, France

It had been a long trip from Islamabad and Malik was exhausted. For security purposes he liked to vary the route and had purposely avoided flying back directly to Heathrow. Instead, he'd taken flight PIA-721 to Paris where, on arrival, he'd been picked up by a couple of Moroccan-born associates in their battered old Renault van full of jars of Moroccan olives and spices and smelling heavily of Turkish cigarettes.

Despite his telling them to slow down, they had driven with wild abandon and flamboyant rude gesticulations, and at any moment Malik had expected to be pulled over by the notorious French traffic police. Not that he cared about a potential on-the-spot traffic fine – no, it was the potential discovery of two hundred kilograms of Semtex explosives hidden away in the jars of olives and spices that made him nervous. Destined for the iconic clock tower, Big Ben, and the Houses of Parliament in London, his plan was not necessarily to kill or maim, but to inflict a painful dent to the British national pride. Welcome to Armageddon!

It was almost four hours by the time they reached Calais and he was pleased to leave the smelly rickety old van and jabbering occupants. Of course, it was only for a short respite – as a precaution he would board the SeaFrance ferry to Dover as a passenger and then re-join the van after it had cleared Customs. It was unlikely that the explosives would be detected but, at this crucial stage in his plan, he couldn't afford to take any chances.

He had very little luggage and he managed to board the ferry without mishap. The cursory check of the forged passport given to him by the Moroccans didn't show anything unusual and certainly not his regular visits to Pakistan. And, if anyone asked any questions, he had a forged outward ferry ticket dated the same day and several bottles of red wine and brandy – he looked no different from the thousands of English day-trippers taking advantage of the vastly different tax rates on alcohol imposed by the UK and French governments.

Unfortunately, as it was nearing Christmas, the ferry was packed full of boisterous, verging on rowdy, Brits eager to compare their booze booty and, in some cases, to start drinking it before the ferry had even left the port. But, though he couldn't relax and doze in a quiet corner, he did take advantage of the camaraderie and blend in with a jovial group of foot passengers, mingling with them on disembarkation. As they surged towards Customs, happily gossiping and joking, he mentally began to run through the next stage of his operation – apart from the hiccups in Islamabad, it had all gone according to plan and he began to congratulate himself on a . . .

'Sir, would you mind stepping over here for a moment?'

Malik pretended not to hear and, laughing at one of the day-tripper's jokes, carried on shuffling along with the crowd.

'Sorry, Sir,' the Customs officer repeated, at the same time grabbing his arm. 'I'd just like to ask you a few questions.'

Malik glanced at the Customs man and laughed again – after all, he was just one of the day-trippers and with not a care in the world. But then he glanced further down and noticed a Springer Spaniel eagerly sniffing at his shoes. Damn, he cursed inwardly – he had no drugs because he never used them. Stupid dog!

'This way, please.'

Malik followed the Customs officer to one side and tried to look as nonchalant as possible.

'Sir, you may have noticed,' the customs officer continued politely, 'that our sniffer dog has detected something on your shoes or trousers. It may be nothing,' he added, looking hard into Malik's eyes, 'but Sadie here is one of our most experienced drug detection dogs.'

Malik thought fast – he had no drugs and hadn't been anywhere near drugs so he . . . oh no – not the Moroccans! They'd probably been smoking cannabis in the van and Malik could easily have stepped on a discarded joint. Damn!

'Can I see your passport, please?'

Malik smiled and, making a show of waving goodbye to his day-tripper 'friends', he handed over the bogus passport. As it was a European Union passport it showed trips only outside Europe and there were only two immigration stamps – both for innocuous and fictitious trips to America.

The Customs officer scanned the passport and nodded non-committally.

'And, the purpose of your visit to France?'

Since Malik was carrying a day-sack and a clinking bag of bottles of wine and brandy, the purpose of his visit was obvious, but years of travelling had taught him to play along with the apparently puerile questioning.

'Just been to Calais for the day to get some nice wines and have a jolly day out,' he replied casually, handing over his ferry tickets.

The Customs officer nodded and indicated for Malik to hand over the bags. It didn't take long for the inspection and even Sadie showed little interest in them.

'Hmm, they seem to be OK,' the Customs man said eventually, a trace of disappointment in his voice.

Malik began repacking the bags and held out his hand for the return of the passport.

'But, in view of the sniffer dog's interest earlier on,' the customs officer continued, 'I'm afraid we'll need to run a few more checks. And, I'm afraid, we will need to do a strip search.'

Malik growled to himself. Apart from the indignity, he wasn't too bothered about the strip search but, if they delved deeper into his identity, who knew what they could find?

He shrugged and followed the Customs man down the corridor and into a small office. It was empty apart from a desk, filing cabinets and stacks of immigration forms.

'If you would just wait here a mom . . .'

But he never got the chance to finish his sentence – Malik had smashed his fist into the man's face and knocked him senseless. Quickly he closed the door and, rummaging through the desk drawers, found a lighter. After pouring a bottle of brandy over the desk and the stack of immigration forms, he set light to it and watched as a smoky fire quickly took hold. Grabbing his passport and bags he strolled out of the office and into the corridor and, for good measure, smashed his fist into the fire alarm.

As the raucous sirens started screeching he entered the disembarkation hall again and joined the tail-end of the foot passengers, their mood suddenly turning from jollity to anxiety and then to fear and panic.

'Fire!' Malik shouted, adding to the mayhem. 'Run!'

Outside, he found the old Renault van waiting and quickly he climbed aboard.

'Let's go!' he growled. 'To London – and to Armageddon!'

North Pole, Arctic Ocean

'There she is!' the helicopter pilot shouted excitedly into the radio. 'Her bow and conning tower are pushing through the ice. I'm going lower to get a closer look.'

On the bridge of the *Polar Explorer*, Captain Crowder watched the helicopter's lights through his binoculars. His sense of unease had not diminished and, if anything, seemed to be growing stronger.

'Take it easy,' he ordered the pilot. 'Just take it nice and steady.'

'Will do,' the pilot called back, 'but I think I can see some men on the ice. I'm going lower.'

The captain watched as the helicopter began to lose altitude, ready to recall the pilot if anything went wrong.

'Oh my God!' the pilot suddenly gasped. 'They're dead . . . it's bodies I can see . . . must be dozens of them . . . all slumped over in the ice.'

'What?' the captain asked, his heart sinking. 'How many are there?'

'Must be forty or fif . . .'

Without warning, the pilot erupted into a coughing fit – it became more and more violent and over the radio they could clearly hear his desperate gasps for breath. And then his gasps became horrible choking and gurgling sounds.

'Get out of there!' Crowder shouted frantically. 'Stuart? Stuart?'

But it was too late. Horrified, he watched as the helicopter spiralled out of control and plummeted into the ice. He lowered his binoculars and closed his eyes as a ball of flames shot up into the night sky. The pilot had only been with him for two seasons but he was a damn good, hardworking, friendly man and in a split second his life had been taken. Whatever was happening here it was extremely dangerous and he couldn't risk anyone else's lives.

'Get the rib ready,' he ordered the first mate. 'I'm going to have a look myself.'

'Sir?' the first mate queried. 'Why not send me and a couple of volunteers?'

'And, put some diving equipment in,' the captain added, ignoring the first mate's suggestion. 'I have a strange feeling that I might need it.'

An hour later, he nudged the rib through the black sea of the open leads. In the shimmering glow of the Northern Lights and silver moon he could make out the dark silhouette of the conning tower and, close by, a black pall of smoke from the burnt helicopter.

And, there was something else – an acrid, sulphurous smell was in the air and it seemed to be getting stronger as he neared the submarine. Perturbed, he shut down the rib's motor but instead of a sudden silence there was a strange bubbling and splashing sound all around him. He pointed the rib's searchlight into the water and gasped – it was alive like a giant witch's cauldron, spouting and pumping puffs of yellowy-grey smoke into the air. His eyes and throat began to burn and he struggled for breath, choking and coughing in pain. Frantically, he grabbed the mouthpiece and mask of the diving equipment and quickly opened the valve of the oxygen tank, releasing a stream of pure and cool air that he desperately gulped down.

When he had recovered sufficiently, he peered over the edge again and shone the searchlight straight into the water – he was astonished to see huge silvery bubbles rising from the depths and exploding at the surface. This was bad, he thought, very, very bad. He didn't need to be a scientist to realise that he was sitting directly over an underwater volcano. Who knew what it would do next? He would have to be quick.

He started the motor again and raced through the open leads, ignoring the danger of ripping open the buoyancy cells on the sharp edges of the pack ice. As he reached the thicker ice near the submarine he stopped and, jamming the anchor into the ice, carefully scrambled out of the rib, dragging the heavy diving equipment behind him. It was like entering a mystical world where the starkly black shape of the conning tower drifted in and out of the yellow-grey mist and the only sound was the bubbling sea and the crunch of his own footsteps.

As he neared the submarine he saw the corpses – dozens of them scattered around – and when he looked more closely he could see that they had died an agonising, asphyxiated death.

The bulbous bow of the submarine rose majestically through the ice but along one side was a long gash of jagged metal, torn open like a flimsy tin can, exposing pipes and wires and inner workings. Dragging the heavy oxygen tank behind him he clambered up to the conning tower, the tank clanking loudly against the hull.

He cursed – the hatch was closed. He slumped down, breathing heavily, and wondered what to do next. He had only another twenty minutes of oxygen left and . . .

Suddenly, he heard a metallic banging beneath him and he jumped to his feet and grabbed the oxygen tank. Carefully, he tapped it three times against the conning tower and listened.

CLANG! CLANG! CLANG! a reply quickly came back.

They were alive! Some of the men were still alive!

Back on the *Polar Explorer*, John Howard was having a hard time. He had returned to the cabin to keep Margaret company but she had spent the last hour berating him for dragging her to this godforsaken and dangerous place – if he really loved her he would have taken her to the shopping malls of New York.

John, who had seen the helicopter crash and the brave captain head off alone into the twilight world, was struggling to contain his contempt and anger. Could she think of nobody apart from herself? Were the lives of the helicopter pilot, the captain and the crew of the submarine totally meaningless? And, did he, her husband of thirty-two years, mean just as little to her?

'Margaret,' he said carefully, through gritted teeth, 'there are far more important things than . . .'

Suddenly, the *Polar Explorer* lurched violently to one side and John fell heavily across the cabin, cracking his head on a wooden coffee table.

'Argh!' he groaned, trying to pull himself off the floor.

Margaret stared at him, her eyes wide with fear.

Suddenly, the ship lurched even more violently and began to shake and judder and the ship's alarm bells burst into a raucous screech.

Margaret, her hands hysterically grasping her hair, screamed.

'We're sinking!' she screamed. 'We're going down! We're all going to die!'

New York, USA

Jacob Goldstein had never been to the top of the Statue of Liberty and since September 11, 2001, not many other people had either. It never ceased to amaze and sadden him how tiny minorities always seemed to ruin it for the majority, whether they were health and safety fanatics, environmentalists, global warming enthusiasts, criminals, terrorists, weirdos or lunatics. Why did they have to spoil everyone else's freedom?

A million people a year visited Liberty Island and every last one of them would have liked to have attempted the arduous climb up the three hundred and fifty-four steps from the entrance, through the engineering marvel of the spiral staircase, and up to the observation platform within the head, ninety metres above sea level. From the twenty-five windows in its crown they would be rewarded with spectacular views of Manhattan, Staten Island, Governors Island, the George Washington Bridge, New York, New Jersey – the list was endless.

But for some, it was more than just a tourist attraction – to some, it was a dream. The Statue of Liberty was more than just a statue – she was an iconic lady who represented the freedom of tens of millions of immigrants who had sought a new start in a land of opportunity, far removed from the poverty and tyranny of their homeland.

And one of those immigrants, despite her advanced age of eighty-five, still vividly recalled the tyranny and horror of her homeland and the day, sixty-six years earlier, on 21 December 1946, that she had sailed as a pale and debilitated young woman into New York harbour and gazed, with tears in her eyes, on the symbol of hope and freedom. To Martha Goldstein, mother of Jacob and survivor of Auschwitz, this was the Promised Land and this lady, this Statue of Liberty, was her friend and saviour. And, before she died, there was one more thing that she needed to do, and that was to pay homage to Lady Liberty and gaze through her eyes across the land of freedom.

And Jacob had promised that she would – after all, he was head of the New York City flood defence programme and, apart from this very private and personal affair, he would never abuse his position. But without that authority no one, apart from main-tenance men, was allowed into the statue itself and security was very tight – from the fast police boats that patrolled the harbour to the bag searches at the ferry terminal and the armed uniformed and plain-clothed security officers who patrolled Liberty Island itself. Such was her iconic status, not just in America but throughout the world, that Lady Liberty needed round-the-clock protection.

But Jacob wasn't sure that Martha was fit enough and he wanted to see for himself how difficult the climb was. And now, having stepped onto Liberty Island off the crowded ferry from

Battery Park, Manhattan, he made his way to the base and entered through the massive walls of what once had been Fort Wood. After trudging up the one hundred and eighty-six steps of the pedestal with hundreds of excited schoolchildren and tourists, he reached the base of the statue, the limit of public admittance, and quietly introduced himself to the security guards. They were expecting him and, having unlocked the doors, one of them led the way up the spiral staircase to the crown. It was a long climb – would Martha be able to do it?

One of the tourists left behind, more observant than the rest, smiled to himself as he continued to video the statue's architectural and engineering wonders. He was probably the only one who had noticed, and filmed, a certain civic dignitary passing into the secure area and he nodded with satisfaction.

Time to go, Jakbar Mulla thought to himself – he had seen enough. But, in only four days' time, he would be back.

Chapter 6

The Prime Minister greeted the government's Chief Scientific Adviser. 'Come in, Sir David. I'm glad that you could make it – I know how busy you are. I think you know Dr Joanna Turnbull, don't you?'

Joanna Turnbull smiled and nodded.

Sir David looked at her and frowned.

'I thought I was here to brief you for the forthcoming G20 Summit in Iceland, Prime Minister,' he said, his tone wary and piqued, 'not for a theoretical discussion. Do we really need Dr Turnbull?'

The Prime Minister looked at Sir David Appleby and he realised that he had become more than just the government's chief scientist – he had become a Czar of the global warming movement, a kind of high priest of carbon emissions. It occurred to him that those on the committee of the Global Task Force for Climate Change had almost become like the priests of the Aztecs or the Grand Inquisitors of the Spanish Inquisition – untouchable and unquestionable.

'Yes, that's true,' he replied, 'but I wanted to ensure that I was up to date with all the facts and all the various theories surrounding global warming. After all, nothing is black and white and there are, er, opposing views on this subject. Dr Turnbull's Environmental and Geological Research Unit at Cambridge might not follow the consensus view but it is always useful to get both sides of the story.'

The Chief Scientific Adviser nodded but didn't look convinced.

'Well, Prime Minister,' he began, ignoring the Cambridge scientist, 'the evidence for the thawing and melting of the Arctic ice is overwhelming. This year, especially, has seen an unprecedented warming of the Arctic Ocean and never before have the extremities of the north polar ice been so restricted.'

'And you think it's the man-made carbon dioxide?' the PM asked.

'Undoubtedly,' Sir David responded firmly. 'It's no different from the Himalayan and Alpine glaciers melting and retreating.'

'What about these reports of volcanic activity under the Arctic?' Dr Turnbull asked. 'Don't they contribute to the ice melting and the CO^2 emissions?'

'Huh,' Sir David scoffed, 'that's just pure speculation by all those pseudo-scientists desperate to discredit what we all know to be fact – that man is driving the global warming engine.'

Joanna, sadly familiar with the arrogant attitude of some senior male scientists from the Civil Service, ignored the barbed comment and opened a folder in front of her.

'There is a ridge, Prime Minister,' she began, 'called the Gakkel Ridge in the Arctic Ocean which is eighteen hundred kilometres long – it's a divergent tectonic plate boundary between the North American and Eurasian Plates, running across the Arctic Ocean all the way from northern Greenland to Siberia. As the two plates move away from each other they generate volcanic activity and, indeed, there have been some huge volcanic eruptions in the region recently. These must have released tremendous volumes of carbon dioxide and contributed to the thermal heating of the Arctic waters.'

'Well, the ridge may have become volcanically more active,' Sir David agreed reluctantly, 'but it's far too deep, almost four kilometres down, and the weight and pressure of water above prevents any serious eruptions. It's just not possible for steam and gases to reach the surface.'

The Prime Minister nodded and frowned.

'Does this ridge go near the North Pole?' he asked.

Sir David looked at the PM quizzically.

'Yes, as a matter of fact, it does. It passes very close to the North Pole. Why do you ask?'

'Oh, nothing,' the PM replied, although he couldn't help wondering if there was some connection between this Gakkel Ridge and a damaged American nuclear submarine. And, it also occurred to him that he had asked for the icebreaker to divert to the aid of the submarine.

'In Greenland, Prime Minister,' Sir David continued, 'there's been an unprecedented glacial flood – it's killed hundreds – and without doubt it's been caused by the catastrophic release of stored summer melt-water from the ice cap. And, as you know, Prime Minister, if the Greenland ice cap melts then sea levels will rise by several metres and drown hundreds of towns and cities, transforming the landscape and making hundreds of millions of people homeless, destroying crops and . . .'

Suddenly, the telephone rang.

'Sorry, Prime Minister,' his principal private secretary said, 'I have an urgent call from Superintendent Jamie McDougal of the Metropolitan Police.'

The PM stood up and apologised to Sir David and Dr Turnbull, ushering them out of the room.

'Superintendent,' he said, 'go ahead.'

'Sir,' Jamie McDougal began, his voice breathless and hard to hear over police sirens, 'we've got an incident at Heathrow. We'd been forewarned that a flight from Islamabad might be carrying two terrorists similar to the one at St Francis Hospital and we'd instructed the captain to taxi the plane to a secure containment area. Our information was obviously correct, but unfortunately the two terrorists suspected something was amiss and now they're threatening to blow up the plane.'

The PM closed his eyes and shook his head slowly – this had the makings of a terrible, terrible disaster.

'How many passengers?' he asked simply.

'We're not sure, as yet,' Jamie McDougal replied, 'but it's a Boeing 777 so it could potentially have three to four hundred passengers and crew on board. Apparently, two young Asian men jumped out of their seats shouting and screaming and before anyone could react they had ripped open their shirts, wrenched open stitched wounds and each pulled out a package. They then held them together and screamed that they would detonate them and kill everyone on board.'

'Oh my God!' the PM gasped. 'They're fanatics! What possesses them to do that? Surgically implanted bombs? And what do they want?'

'We don't know yet what they're after,' the superintendent replied, 'but if they're part of the same plot as the St Francis Hospital terrorist, which seems likely, then the plane itself may not be their target. The Americans believe that they're part of quite a large sarin nerve agent plot and they all seem to be heading for London. We could storm the plane but what worries me is that they've put two packages together. If one is a breast implant full of sarin and the other is an explosive device, with PETN or Semtex, then a cloud of sarin mist could sweep down the plane and kill everyone inside.'

'Oh my God!' the PM gasped again. 'They're lunatics!'

Blackpool, England

Bonnie was a happy carefree dog – what more could a seven-month-old podgy Labrador puppy want? At home he had a warm cosy bed, mountains of delicious food and, of course, kind and loving owners. But, best of all, he had miles and miles of beach to run and gambol on, dig holes in, splash in the sea and play chase with the seagulls.

While Lucy screamed and giggled as she raced after him, her trainers and skirt getting sodden and sandy, Susan looked out to sea, forlorn and melancholy. Out there, somewhere across the cold and cruel Atlantic Ocean was her husband – warm and safe in a support vessel and heading towards Newfoundland or perhaps already perished in the burning rig or black stormy seas. The HR director of Mid-Ocean Oil, under relentless questioning by Susan and Janet, had finally admitted that there had been a terrible accident and the crew had had to scramble to abandon a blazing platform before it exploded or was smashed to smithereens by a giant rogue iceberg. And, finally, he admitted that the oil company had no idea how many men had escaped.

Suddenly, her mobile phone rang and frantically she grabbed it, desperately hoping that it was Craig, phoning to say that he was on his way home. But it wasn't.

'Susan,' a tearful voice said, 'it's Janet. I've just heard from some of the other women and they've been in contact with their husbands.'

For a moment, the phone went silent apart from a couple of gasping sobs and the sound of a nose being blown.

'Apparently, some of the men are in hospital,' Janet eventually continued, 'with hypothermia, burns or broken bones, but at least they're alive. There's dozens still missing and the weather is closing in – something about a massive fog bank hampering the search and rescue operations. With each passing hour the chances of more men being found is, is . . .'

Long drawn-out sobs burst from the phone again and Susan closed her eyes as tears began to fall down her cheeks. Had Bill and Craig perished in the burning rig? Or drowned in the icy seas? Would Lucy be left fatherless? And how would she tell her? And how would she survive, without the warmth and support of her husband?

'Janet,' she eventually managed to say, trying to pull herself together as Lucy and Bonnie came bounding up, laughing and giggling, 'we must remain strong and continue to believe that not all is lost. They could be in a life raft, or something, and be found and rescued. Hope Janet – and, maybe, pray.'

New York City, USA

Joan Abbot was lost. She stood in the corridor on the third floor of City Hall humming 'I wish I was in Dixie' and staring at the sign emblazoned on the glass doors:

FLOOD MANAGEMENT DEPARTMENT
Head: Jacob Goldstein

She was sure that she had visited this office a few moments ago but her mind had gone blank and she couldn't even imagine why she would need flood management advice. But perhaps that wasn't surprising considering her advanced age of ninety-two and the onset of Alzheimer's several years previously. She might still be sprightly and still vividly remember when she worked at City Hall in the typing pool more than thirty years previously but she couldn't remember what she'd done thirty minutes ago. But, then, she wasn't to know that major refurbishments a decade previously had disbanded the typing pool and created the Flood Management Department in its place. So she was actually in the right place but a generation or more too late – almost as if a time machine had transported her to the future.

'I'm sure I put my coat in here,' she mumbled to herself, not realising that she had actually forgotten to put a coat on in the morning.

She opened the door and purposefully stepped into the reception area of Jacob's department.

'Can I help you?' the bored young receptionist snapped, irritated at being disturbed in the middle of booking an online skiing holiday.

'Er, yes,' Joan replied, desperately trying to remember why she'd come into the office and glancing round the room for inspiration. 'Aha,' she finally said as she spotted a fur coat hanging on the coat rack. 'There you are, you naughty ermine.'

The receptionist looked at her and slowly shook her head. What was it with old people, she thought, that made them so annoying?

'Aha,' Joan said again, 'and that must be my walking stick. Goodbye – I'll be back tomorrow to finish that report I've been typing.'

'Stupid old fool,' the receptionist snarled, seeing the 'time out' message that had just flashed up on the screen.

Outside City Hall, a dusty, ramshackle pickup truck waited on the double yellow lines, a spare wheel with a flat tyre and a hydraulic jack lying in the road and two young men crouching down beside it smoking and chatting.

'She's been ages,' Jakbar Mulla said impatiently to the passenger in the truck's cab. 'Perhaps she's got lost or died or something?'

The little old lady beside him looked at her companion and shook her head.

'Be patient, Jakbar,' Mary Dewey-Bell said. 'After all, she's old and needs a walking stick so she's not going to be sprinting around City Hall. Just remember, when she does come out, grab her quickly and efficiently – we don't want to damage her. Not yet, anyway.'

Ten minutes later an elderly lady in an ermine fur coat and a walking stick emerged from City Hall, still merrily humming 'I wish I was in Dixie'.

'That's her,' Mary Dewey-Bell growled, tapping on the windscreen to alert Ali Pasha and Nguyen Phan.

Thirty seconds later, Joan Abbot found herself being roughly bundled into a roll of carpet and tossed unceremoniously into the back of the pickup truck.

'It's been lovely to see you again, Martha,' Jacob said gently to his mother as he led her out of his office and into the department's reception area. 'So I'll pick you up on Friday morning and we can go over to the Statue of Liberty. I've arranged for our access to the upper levels of the statue so you'll be able to reach the top and gaze out across Hudson Bay and across to Ellis Island. It will be quite an occasion for you, after all these years.'

Martha nodded, her eyes focused somewhere in the distant past. 'Yes,' she eventually said, 'I remember Ellis Island so well. That's where all my fellow immigrants from Germany were processed and allowed entry into America. I couldn't keep my eyes off Lady Liberty. She is a powerful symbol and I realised then that I was finally free.'

Jacob nodded and, though he had heard the story countless times, he was always moved by it.

'But we must take it carefully up those stairs,' he said, 'it's a long way to the statue's head. And, talking about being careful, you need to put your coat on – it's freezing out there. Er,' he added, looking at the empty coat stand, 'where exactly did you put it, Martha?'

'Hmm,' Martha replied, eyeing the empty coat stand. 'I'm sure that I put it there.'

'Trixie,' Jacob called out to his receptionist, 'have you seen Martha's coat and walking stick?'

Trixie looked at Jacob, then at Martha and finally at the offending coat stand.

'No, no,' she replied, quickly looking back to the computer screen. 'Are you sure she had one?'

Jacob looked at Martha.

Martha, who didn't suffer from Alzheimer's and knew very well that she had come wearing her favourite ermine coat, smiled.

'Oh, probably not,' she replied, not wishing to get the young receptionist into trouble. 'Anyway, Jacob, you can accompany me downstairs and call me a taxi. That way, I won't need my coat and walking stick.'

Prudence Island, New England, USA

Old Man Williams didn't like the 'newcomers'. They were new, there were too many of them and they were an odd bunch.

Until a year ago, Prudence Island had been a perfect hideaway from the hustle and bustle of the modern American way of life, tucked away as it was in the middle of Narragansett Bay, several kilometres from the mainland. Fifteen square kilometres and home to one hundred residents, it boasted a few houses, a post office, a general store and a lighthouse and its only link to the outside world was a daily ferry service, the telephone and the television.

Unfortunately, in summer, the population could swell tenfold as holiday homers and tourists visited for their annual vacation but in winter, apart from a bit of farming, nothing much happened in sleepy Prudence and only the raucous squawks of the seagulls and the mournful song of the foghorn kept the residents company.

And that's the way Old Man Williams liked it and, except for leaving to do his duty fighting the Nazis in his early twenties and a triple heart bypass in his late seventies, he had spent every day of his eighty-two years in that small oasis. He sometimes said, although he couldn't prove it, that he was descended from Roger Williams, the founder of Rhode Island, who had bought the island off the Narragansett Indians, way back in 1637.

Like almost every other day, Old Man Williams could be found on the large T-shaped wharf on the south end of the island, fishing for his dinner, watching the seals lazing about on the rocks or watching the world go by. In the summer, the wharf, which had been built by the US navy to service a Second World War ammunition storage facility, was irritatingly busy with small boats coming over from the mainland, but in the winter only the daily ferry disturbed his peace.

That is, until the 'newcomers' had arrived. Now, even in winter they were busy going backwards and forwards to the mainland, frightening the fish away and cluttering up the wharf with huge mounds of crates and boxes.

They had started to arrive in springtime, having apparently bought one of the few farms on the island and, bizarrely, a handful of the ammunition bunkers left behind by the US navy. Speculation among the spartan winter population was almost as widespread and varied as the residents themselves, ranging from the innocuous mushroom growing or fine wine storage, all the way to naked dancing and satanic worship.

Finally, the truth had emerged after a damaged parcel at the post office had spilled out all its contents and Jake Short, the inquisitive postmaster, had 'accidentally' read some of the magazines and pamphlets. Apparently, the 'newcomers' were a sect of Messianic Jews, though until Jake had done some more snooping the residents were none the wiser. But eventually Jake had put two and two together and came up with his theory that they were waiting for the biblical Apocalypse and the reappearance of Yeshua, or the Messiah – known to everyone else as Jesus. The purchase of the farm, the underground bunkers and the importing of huge amounts of goods were irrefutable evidence.

Old Man Williams couldn't care less what they believed in – he had no quarrel with the Jews, having seen first-hand how they had suffered under the Nazis – but he wasn't so sure about the arsenal of weapons they appeared to be bringing in. And these weren't little rabbit or vermin guns either. No, this group meant business and, whatever was coming, they were getting ready for it on a massive scale.

Deep inside one of the bunkers, Joseph Goldstein put the phone down and frowned. He was in a bit of a dilemma. His father had just asked him if he would help accompany Martha when Jacob took her up the Statue of Liberty. Normally, Joseph would have jumped at the chance for he loved his kind, old grandmother – but not on 21 December. That was THE day – the day of the Second Coming of the Messiah and the final cataclysmic battle with Satan on the Plains of Megiddo. Everyone knew that, but if they chose to ignore it and not to protect and defend themselves, then that was their choice. Joseph and his small sect of ninety-three Messianic Jews would survive the Apocalypse and would emerge safely from their bunkers on Prudence Island, to farm the land and to prosper. They would be ready for the New Dawn.

Adirondack Mountains, New York County, USA

There can't be many people in America with relatives, friends or business connections in a hot and dusty old city called Peshawar thousands of kilometres away, next to the Khyber Pass and near the border between Afghanistan and Pakistan. And the chances of it happening when narrowed down to the Adirondack Mountains in New York County were miniscule. But there was a certain symmetry – both were wild, both were rugged and both were remote.

So when Paul Gates had received a call from the FBI's Mobile Phone Monitoring Division to say that the surveillance software had identified unusual traffic between these two unlikely places, his interest was aroused. And when they told him that the connection had been two cryptic texts within a minute of each other – one simply saying '*An eye for an eye*' and the other even more simply saying '*Armageddon*' – his interest immediately turned to suspicion.

And that is why, two days later, he was crouched, cold and uncomfortable, behind a rock high up in the windy Adirondack Mountains watching a scruffy collection of huts that called itself a farm.

'Eyrie's Nest, this is Eagle 2,' the deputy director's intercom suddenly burst into life. 'We're now in position at the rear of the property and everything is quiet. I repeat – there is no movement.'

'Eyrie's Nest, this is Eagle 1. We are now in position at the front of the property and the target is quiet. We can see into an open shed that could have been used for vehicles but it is empty. There are no dogs or chickens or any other animals and it looks deserted.'

Paul Gates looked at his watch – 13.23 hours – and then

scanned the farm through his binoculars. He could see his agents and heavily armed National Guard units scattered around the buildings, crouching behind rocks and bushes or lying prone behind sniper rifles. If this was a terrorist cell of fundamental extremists, who knew what they were capable of – blowing themselves and anyone else to kingdom come was certainly high on a list of possible outcomes.

'Eagle 1 and Eagle 2,' he replied, 'move in as planned at 13.30 hours. But exercise extreme caution. We need to preserve any evidence and we don't want any unnecessary loss of life. Remember, there could still be someone hiding in there and it's unlikely to be like your little old granny.'

He looked at his watch again and it flicked to 13.29 hours. He hoped that this operation would produce enough leads to track down a terrorist network if there was one – but he doubted it. International religious terrorists tended to be organised, clever and crafty; unlike the home-grown deranged idiots with their own festering grudges who tended to act alone, illogically and at random. And, with the widely heralded Armageddon Day just round the corner, there would be no shortage of those.

At the appointed time he watched his men rise from their positions and stalk forward, weapons at the ready, expressions tense and alert. Eagle 1 reached the veranda of the main shack and spread out, two men beside each window and six by the door. At a command from the FBI agent leading the unit, they donned gas masks and after smashing the windows threw stun and tear gas grenades inside. Immediately, there were short, sharp explosions and clouds of gas began to billow out of the windows and, exploiting the element of shock and awe, the National Guardsmen smashed the door in with a short heavy battering ram and burst inside.

Suddenly, the deputy director's intercom crackled into life again.

'Sir, it's Deputy John Banks from the county sheriff's office in Downy Beck. I've got some information on that farm in the Adirondacks. It's owned by a Mary Dewey-Bell, an old lady and a regular churchgoer – used to drive to church every Sunday in a battered old pickup truck. It must have taken her about three hours each way. Apparently, she had a few Asian men working for her on the farm but we've no information on those guys as they kept themselves to themselves.'

'Hmm, could be cheap labour,' Paul Gates said, peering intently through his binoculars. 'But I can't imagine what they did in this run-down old place.'

'There *is* something rather odd,' the deputy sheriff continued. 'The post office in Downy Beck apparently received a regular supply of parcels for a Mrs Bell and these were always picked up by one of her farmhands. We've traced the senders and these were just normal manufacturing companies in Detroit, but what Mrs Bell wanted with canisters of aluminium, magnesium and iron oxide powders beats me. They're not used in pest control as far as . . .'

'What!' the FBI deputy director suddenly shouted. 'Did you say aluminium, iron oxide and magnesium?'

'Er, yes, Sir, regular deliveries every . . .'

'Shit!' Paul Gates growled, flicking the intercom back to his units on the ground. 'Eagle 1 and Eagle 2 – get the hell out of there! It could be a . . .'

Suddenly, there was a huge explosion and the shack disintegrated into a fiery fireball, shaking the ground and blasting a shockwave of energy and splintered wood over the deputy director. A billowing mushroom cloud of orange flames and smoke shot into the air and the sound rumbled like thunder down the mountainside.

'Sir?' the deputy sheriff asked tentatively. 'What the heck was that?

Paul Gates, blood streaming down his face, stared in horror at the remains of the farm. A few blazing timbers and a large smouldering crater in the ground were all that remained and scattered among the boulders, groaning and writhing in agony, were the remains of Eagle 1 and Eagle 2.

'Help,' the shocked deputy director mumbled into the intercom, 'we need help. Officers down, Code 10-00, Code 10-00, officers down! We need paramedics, we need . . .'

North Pole, Arctic Ocean

Three kilometres below the ice near the North Pole, in a frigid world of immense pressure, cold and darkness, a violent scene from Dante's Inferno was being enacted. Along Gakkel Ridge, a red snaking fissure, a kilometre wide and a thousand kilometres long, had split the Arctic seabed and fountains of red-hot magma and gas violently spewed from a necklace of submarine volcanoes, blasting lava a kilometre or more up into the sea. Pyroclastic flows, barely dulled by the water's oppressive pressure, exploded from the fissure and rolled at immense speed along the sea floor. Huge lumps of orange molten lava, as big as houses, spewed from the fissure, turning black and exploding in the freezing water to rain as glassy lumps hundreds of kilometres all around.

Silvery bubbles of carbon dioxide and carbon monoxide, escaping as a curtain of gas along the fissure's length, shot through the water, expanding a thousand-fold as they rose from the depths and exploding at the surface in massive geysers of foam, three kilometres above.

Lying on the seabed, in the frigid black water and covered in a layer of volcanic debris, lay the *Polar Explorer*, desolate and incongruous. And in one of the cabins, two of the passengers floated – John and Margaret Howard, hand in hand, reconciled and together in their final moments.

More than three kilometres above, in the twilight winter world of the Northern Lights, a USAF AWACS aircraft, searching for the USS *Arizona*, came across the giant undulating necklace of waterspouts.

'Holy Cow! Will you look at that,' the co-pilot gasped. 'I've never seen anything like it. What the heck is it?'

119

The pilot, Lieutenant John Lawrence, looked out of the cockpit window and just gawped. It was like something from a disaster movie – a surreal image of computer-generated natural forces gone wild – huge, incredible and utterly unbelievable.

'Hank,' he eventually shouted behind him to the navigator, 'make sure you get a good record of this. I'm taking us closer.'

Unseen among the ice floes, a lone submarine waited for rescue. The remnants of its crew, thirty-four survivors from the original one hundred and fifty two, had been bolstered by another – an erstwhile rescuer turned rescued. Captain Crowder, late of the *Polar Explorer* and now its only survivor, had been pulled to the tenuous safety of the submarine, with only minutes to spare in his oxygen cylinder. Around them, covering a huge expanse of the Arctic Ocean, a cloud of carbon dioxide and carbon monoxide, heavier than air and born from the bowels of the Earth, lay deadly and invisible, ready to ensnare the unwary.

As the USAF AWACS banked towards the spouting geysers and lost altitude, Lieutenant Lawrence radioed his airbase.

'You won't believe this,' he said, trying but failing to contain his astonishment, 'but as far as the eye can see there's a huge string of geysers bursting from the sea. We're flying over the Gakkel Ridge but there's no sign of the Arizona, only this amazing view of . . .'

Suddenly, the two engines on the port side coughed, spluttered and died.

The air traffic controller back at the airbase waited a moment and then called back.

'USAF AWACS 143, please come in. Do you have a problem?'

As the plane continued to lose altitude and fly deeper into the suffocating cloud, the starboard engines were starved of oxygen and they too misfired, spluttered and died.

'Mayday! Mayday!' Lieutenant Lawrence suddenly came back onto the radio. 'We're going down. We've lost all engines and are ditching. We're at longitude . . .'

Suddenly, the radio went silent.

'USAF AWACS 143, come in,' the air traffic controller said, trying to keep his voice calm and controlled. 'Come in, USAF AWACS 143. Come in. Please report . . .'

Reykjavik, Iceland

Hotel Majestic Borealis was a large, modern and plush hotel close to Reykjavik's business and city centre. It had been built at the height of Iceland's economic and financial boom and had been lavished with such opulent and spacious rooms, restaurants, conference facilities and leisure areas that it had rapidly become Iceland's premier hotel for business travellers. If you wanted to hold a meeting, from a handful of people to more than three hundred, then there was a choice of several state-of-the-art audio-visual and computer-networked rooms available. And with first-class à la carte banqueting facilities, the hotel was often frequented by large international companies or trade bodies hosting executive meetings or conferences.

And that is why Frida Jonsson was so happy. Not only had she been asked out to dinner by a strong, handsome man but he had brought her to the Hotel Majestic Borealis – the only five-star hotel in Iceland. And, of course, she had made a special effort, shopping for a nice outfit in the morning and having her hair done in the afternoon. Mind you, it hadn't been cheap so she hoped he appreciated it.

Stephen John Browning, pouring a glass of champagne for Frida and sparkling water for himself, gazed appreciatively over at his companion. Of course, she wasn't his type and he had other things on his mind but he had to admit that she knew how to enhance and display her curvaceous charms and, annoyingly, he felt his loins stirring. But no, he thought sternly, he had a job to do and she was, after all, only there to provide him with a natural reason for being in the hotel.

Suddenly, his mobile phone beeped, notifying him of an incoming text. He read it – it simply said: '*Winter is here*'. He gave Frida a sweet smile and apologised that he had an urgent telephone call to make and that he would only be a few minutes.

Unhurriedly, he strode out of the restaurant, turned left as though heading for the toilets but veered onto the stairwell, ascended to the first floor, strode along the corridor past rows of bedrooms and then descended back to the ground floor. In that way, he had avoided the lobby and the prying eyes on reception and arrived at the complex of conference rooms. He quickly found Suite 4A, a small conference room with seating for twenty people, and sent a text reply: '*Spring is coming*'.

Moments later, the door was unlocked from inside and Malik stepped quickly through.

'Hello, Patrick,' Malik said warmly.

'Hello, Stephen,' Patrick O'Keefe replied, grinning and quickly closing the door. 'I'd offer you a whisky but I know you Muslims don't drink.'

Malik looked at his old friend and chuckled.

'You haven't changed a bit,' he said, 'apart from that scruffy old beard and those nerdy glasses.'

This time Patrick chuckled.

'It's all part of the image,' he said. 'I'm the IT and conference technical manager now. Nobody bothers looking at a geek. You can get away with anything – especially if you're disabled.'

Malik nodded.

'That's true,' he said. 'And how is you're leg now? The last time you were in quite a lot of pain.'

'It's still a bit sore,' Patrick replied, rubbing his thigh. 'I never really got used to the prosthetic limb.'

Patrick O'Keefe was about the same age as Stephen John Browning. They served together in Iraq and Afghanistan and Patrick had lost the whole of his right leg, and almost his life, when a snatch Land Rover had driven over a mine in Helmand province. Invalided back into the UK he had found it impossible to get a job and, despite having a family with two young children, the council had refused to find him accommodation. Apparently, he'd left the army voluntarily and technically made himself homeless, and the council, treating him more like a third-rate citizen rather than a returning war hero, had put him at the back of the housing queue, behind the single mothers, the worthless, the villains and the immigrants. When his wife left him and took the children back to Ireland that's when he'd almost drunk himself to death. Until, of course, Stephen had bumped into him.

'Is everything ready here?' Stephen asked.

Patrick nodded and grinned.

'Everything is set,' he replied. 'Don't worry. I have waited a long time for this.'

Abeye Umgalla grinned at her friend Elli Salumptu, as she saw the operating theatre – it was far more professional than she had expected. She had expected it to be more like the grubby rooms in the provincial hospital in her home town in Ethiopia, not like the Birmingham City General where they both worked. Although it must have once been a simple house, the whole of the ground floor had been turned into a large, well-equipped operating theatre, gleaming with stainless-steel tables and surgical instruments, autoclaves, anaesthetic equipment, heart monitors, scrub-up areas . . . everything. And upstairs, the bedrooms had been converted into hospital wards, with sufficient beds for fifteen patients.

'You look pleased,' Hashim said, watching the two young nurses who had just arrived from England and nodding his head with satisfaction as he saw how professionally they inspected his preparations. 'But now I think that you must rest. Tomorrow we have a busy day – we have ten operations to get through. And,' he added, nodding his head solemnly, 'we must be even more careful than usual.'

Gilda Nygaard jerked awake and peered at the ceiling in the gloom. She wasn't positive but she thought a loud bang in the room above had disturbed her. Suddenly, she heard the clatter of a bottle falling on the floor and then a high-pitched giggle.

And then a muffled woman's voice.

'Mr Browning! What sort of woman do you think I am?'

And then another high-pitched giggle.

Gilda looked at the clock – 1.30 a.m. Frida Jonsson! And, I thought you were such a homely woman.

Slowly, she shook her head and then tried to get back to sleep again.

Ice cap, central Greenland

Jarvik couldn't sleep and instead he laboured alone to set up the satellite phone equipment. His mind was as active as the groaning and trembling ice beneath him and the groaning Johann beside him. He was astonished by what he had seen – volcanic activity beneath Greenland was unheard of and to experience a glacial flood and then find a huge fissure full of oozing magma was unbelievable. Here, the Earth's crust was supposed to be older than anywhere else on the planet and there was no geological evidence for tectonic plate movement, certainly not like the Pacific Ring of Fire. Although Iceland, which was only three hundred kilometres from eastern Greenland, was a hot spot of volcanic and geothermal activity, there were no plate boundaries beneath Greenland. Or were there?

And, just as worrying – how was the ice cap actually rising? It wasn't increasing in thickness – if anything it had been melting – so it could rise only by being pushed up from below. But, by three kilometres or more? Geological events of such magnitude could only arise when tectonic plates crashed into each other or drifted away from each other. If the Earth's crust had suddenly become unstable here, who knew what might happen.

And, what a fantastic, Nobel Prize-winning discovery.

As his mind gloried on the accolades to come, and as he powered up the phone and connected to an orbiting satellite, it rang. He stared at it and frowned.

'Hello?' he said tentatively.

'Jarvik,' a crackly voice said, 'it's Olaf. Don't hang up. I've got something urgent to tell you.'

'I'm busy,' Jarvik snapped, instantly annoyed.

'Look, I just wanted to warn you,' Olaf said quickly. 'You might be in terrible danger.'

'Humph!' Jarvik scoffed. 'You just want to frighten me away because you want to discover it all for yourself. Well, that's not going to . . .'

'Listen!' Olaf suddenly growled. 'I don't care what you do but you and your team should be aware that our seismometers are going mad. They're picking up violent tremors deep in the Earth's crust. Not only are there multiple waves of increasing amplitude but there's no single epicentre – the earthquakes seem to stretch in a line from north-western Greenland all the way to south-eastern Greenland. And it passes just north of where I am. Jarvik, you must be right above it!'

For a while, the phone went silent.

'Jarvik? Jarvik, are you still there?'

'What Richter scale readings are you getting?' Jarvik finally responded.

'They're crazy,' Olaf replied. 'They started off at magnitude 7.2 but within just a few hours rose to magnitude 8 . . . and recently we've recorded a couple at 9.2 – that's the same as the Anchorage earthquake in 1964. Something odd is happening beneath the ice and I don't like it.'

For a moment, the phone went silent again.

'Well, there's nothing happening here,' Jarvik eventually replied. 'Your instruments must be faulty. Could be the cold. Anyway, I've found nothing so we're heading back – you might as well do the same.'

'But that's not possible,' Olaf began, 'not with all the seismic activity. It just isn't possible that . . . Jarvik . . . Jarvik? Are you still there?'

But Jarvik had switched the phone off and was frantically unloading his video equipment. He didn't think for a minute that Olaf would fall for his ruse so he had to act quickly if he was going to get the news of his discovery to the outside world before his rival. He needed to get all the equipment set up for satellite streaming as he captured the incredible images of this unbelievably massive fissure in the Earth's crust. When those pictures hit the worldwide news networks he would be . . .

Suddenly, he heard the sound of a skidoo engine and when he looked round he saw the snowmobile racing south, Runi at the controls and Johann strapped to the trailer, clouds of powder snow billowing behind them.

Jarvik cursed. Let them go, he thought – he didn't need them. If they didn't want to be part of a momentous discovery, then that was their loss. He still had the tent, the equipment and some food, and soon his name would be making history.

As he assembled the satellite antenna and transmitter equipment, he began to hum, happily and unconsciously, the Danish national anthem. This would teach that Gunnar Patterson, he thought. What right did an armchair geologist have telling Jarvik to leave the field and go home? Just as he was on the verge of a historic discovery.

He would show him.

The Earth's core

Deep in the Earth's core, a cancer festered and grew. For millions of years, it had slowly risen from the hot molten core and expanded as it sought to escape – to reach the Earth's crust.

In a time before Pangaea, in the Devonian epoch four hundred million years ago, when primitive fish ruled the seas and insects ruled the land, huge and terrible upheavals shaped the Earth. In the northern hemisphere, Laurentia, later to become North America, bore the brunt of cataclysmic collisions with Baltica, its European neighbour. At the collision zone, the Earth's crust deformed and buckled and a huge subduction trench formed, pushing down giant slabs of oceanic crust into the Earth's mantle. Such was the enormity of the cataclysmic upheavals that a slab the size of Australia was pushed deep through the mantle, three thousand kilometres to the outer layers of the core. Here, in an alien world of enormous temperatures and pressures, it began to fester, heating up and expanding for millions of years. Composed of less dense rock than the iron-rich core, it began to float above the molten metal and push its way back through the mantle, rising ever faster as the pressure decreased.

By the time man jumped ahead in the evolutionary race and strode away from his quadruped ancestors, the ancient slab was already pushing against the Earth's crust, lifting and cracking it like a malignant tumour bursting through the skin. And now, barely detected by man and hidden beneath Greenland's massive ice cap and the desolate Arctic seas, it prepared to burst forth into the modern world, taking its rightful place again as part of the Earth's crust.

Chapter 7

19 December 2012
Atlantic Ocean, eight hundred kilometres east of Cape Cod, USA

'Holy cow!' Frank Mulholland, the deck supervisor on the deep-sea trawler *Lucky Lady*, shouted excitedly. 'We're going to be rich!'

Five days out from Halifax, Nova Scotia, the net had caught another huge load of cod and the winches creaked and groaned with the strain.

'A couple of days more,' he continued happily, 'and the holds will be stuffed to the brim and we can all go home and celebrate.'

The deckhands cheered and punched the air.

'How much will I get?' Lanky Pete asked, already dreaming of riches beyond belief.

'Loads, Lanky,' Frank replied, slapping the young and scrawny deckhand on the back. 'Easily enough for new tyres and a paint job for that rusty old Mustang of yours.'

On the bridge, Seamus O'Reilly, the captain and owner of the *Lucky Lady*, allowed himself a brief smile as he watched the bulging net rise from the water. It was about time they had some luck but he needed a lot more trips like this to pay off the bank loan on the boat. Mind you, it was an eerie place this – a bit like the Bermuda Triangle, he imagined – glassy smooth seas with a long gentle swell; the air as still as a summer's day; a cold, damp and dense fog, drifting and wafting like a living beast; and the only sound, the rumble of the engine, the clanking of the gear and the boat's melancholy automatic foghorn.

It had been like this for days and he was exhausted. Barely able to sleep and constantly having to check on the radar – they were on the main route from New York to Europe and were a sitting duck if one of the huge cargo or cruise ships emerged from the gloom. They wouldn't stand a chance and out here, in the midst of a vast impenetrable fog bank, they would be lost in moments.

So when the regular beeping of the radar suddenly changed, someone walked over his grave and his blood went cold. He quickly looked at the radar screen – its pale-green circular display showed something appearing at the top of the screen, moving in from the north and heading south. It wasn't the normal single bright *blip* of another ship – no, this was huge, a bright-green *blob*, gradually filling the top of the screen.

'What the . . .' he growled, tapping the screen to check if it was faulty.

The blob moved slowly south, growing and filling the top third of the screen. He estimated that it must have been moving at three or four knots and he could only think that for some reason a whole flotilla of boats was heading his way. He opened the side window and peered into the grey murk. He couldn't see anything and only the *Lucky Lady*'s foghorn, clanking winch and idling engine emerged from the gloom. It was eerie – without a doubt.

'Hey, Frank,' he shouted down at his deck supervisor, 'can you hear anything unusual out there?'

Frank stopped working, midway in hauling the bulging net on board, looked at Seamus quizzically, cocked his ear to one side and then shrugged.

'Get that net emptied and stowed quickly,' Seamus shouted back. 'The radar's picking something up and I want to be ready to move.'

He looked back at the radar screen and gasped – the top half had been overrun and flashing warning lights screamed *COLLISION IMMINENT* at him. He was a seasoned trawler captain and yet panic began to overtake him. In all his years he had never seen anything like it – it must be huge, at least several kilometres across and moving twice as fast as he'd first thought.

Frantically, he switched the foghorn from automatic to manual and activated it every few seconds. The deckhands quickly looked up at the bridge, saw the grim and panic-stricken face of the captain, and feverishly began to pull the net on board.

Suddenly, as Seamus strained to see though the swirling mist, it momentarily lifted, revealing an unbelievable sight – a hundred metres from the *Lucky Lady*, a vast wall of ice bore down on them. For a few seconds, time seemed to stand still and, horrified, he stared at it, as though a ghostly phantom had materialised. His finger hovered, frozen, over the foghorn button and the sudden silence added to the eerie scene.

'Cut the net!' he suddenly screamed, jerking from his stupor. 'For God's sake, cut the net!'

Frantically, he pushed the throttle forward and pulled the wheel over hard to port. For a few precious seconds nothing happened as the big diesel engines built up power, but slowly the *Lucky Lady* began to accelerate and turn away from the approaching icy megalith.

But it was too late. Beneath the water lurked the bulk of the iceberg and unseen knobbly outcrops caught the bow, tearing the hull open as easily as a beer can. A surge of freezing, menacing water flooded into the engine room and immediately the engines stalled and the trawler began to list.

Seamus grabbed the radio but only had time for a silent scream as the vast ice wall crashed into the boat and pushed her down, beneath the waves. The *Lucky Lady*, and all her crew, vanished – sucked down into a dark and lonely icy grave.

'Did you hear that?' Craig said, as much to himself as to the almost comatose figure huddled beside him. 'Sounded like a foghorn. We must be near land.'

Hurriedly, he unwrapped the emergency blankets and Inuit fur from around them and forced his frozen and stiff limbs to crawl out of the life raft. Dense fog still surrounded them but he could distinctly hear the sound of a foghorn. He tried to calculate where they could be – with the Labrador Current and wind pushing them from five to nine knots for two, or was it three, days they could have travelled almost one thousand kilometres, and since the current moved south-westerly they could easily be close to Nova Scotia or even Boston. He knew that icebergs had occasionally been spotted as far south as New York so he knew it was possible – if only this damn fog would lift.

Slowly, he stretched his petrified limbs and began to hobble to the edge of *Ocean Two*, the name he had bestowed on the iceberg in honour of the lost oil platform, their friends and their colleagues. When he reached the edge of their island, he carefully peered over and tried to penetrate the grey murk – but he could see nothing. They must be close to land as the foghorn seemed to be just below them and he gripped the ice in preparation for a violent impact.

But then the foghorn stopped and there was no impact.

His mind, numb and befuddled with hypothermia, was confused. What had happened to the land? It couldn't have just vanished. All this time he had tried to remain strong, especially for Sean, but now he broke down and began to sob. After all this time, having survived the exploding oil rig, an iceberg collision and days marooned in freezing temperatures, perhaps they really were doomed. Doomed to sail on this giant island, heading south to warmer climes, their dead and frozen bodies eventually slipping into the sea as *Ocean Two* shrank and finally joined its predecessor, *Ocean One*.

And, he would never, ever, see Susan, Lucy and Bonnie ever again.

La Palma, Canary Islands

Through the gently swaying palm trees David Evans idly watched the waves crashing against the black sand of the beach and dreamily narrowed his eyes as he took another swig of ice-cold San Miguel and a bite of pizza. This was the life, he mused, chilling out in the sunshine in a beach-side bar watching the world go by.

Not that Puerto de Naos, nestled on the west coast of La Palma, saw much of the world – no, it was renowned for its peace, tranquillity and lack of tourists. And that is exactly why the HR director had chosen it. He needed to think – to think about his job at Mid-Ocean Oil and whether or not that was the type of employer that he really wanted to work for. He knew that he was no moral angel but what they had done was downright dishonest and ruthless – they had callously put profits before people.

After being confronted by two of the wives of the *Ocean One*'s crew, and realising halfway through the heated discussion that his spouting of the party line was a disgraceful tissue of lies, he had stopped, told them the truth and then gone sick. And that's why, two days later, he was recuperating in the sun in the Canary Islands.

Beneath huge volcanic cliffs and surrounded by luxuriant banana plantations, palm and dragon trees, Puerto de Naos was a beautiful oasis away from the stresses and disillusionments of the modern world. And La Palma, rising almost seven kilometres from the sea floor, was a jewel in the Atlantic Ocean.

For David Evans, this was a defining moment. Fat, unfit, ethically dubious, depressed and rapidly approaching his fortieth birthday, he felt he was at a crossroads. He could carry on as he was and die early and exploited or he could rise like a phoenix from the ashes of failure and soar into a new beginning, to a new David Evans – thinner, healthier, more ethical and happier. He looked at the beer and the greasy pizza in front of him and pushed them away. Yes – he would start the transformation right away.

'*Por favor,*' he called out to the proprietor, 'could you tell me the best places to hike around here and see the island?'

'Aha, you have come to the best place for hiking,' the proprietor enthused. 'La Palma is a famous walking island. And from Puerto de Naos you can catch a tour up to the volcanoes you see behind you. And there you can walk along the famous volcanic ridge, the Cumbre Vieja, almost two thousand metres high and eighteen kilometres long. It is a beautiful walk with fantastic views of the island and sea, through the pine woods and up the ridge where you go from one volcano to another, each more impressive than the last. But take care,' the proprietor added conspiratorially, 'not to disturb the sleeping giant within.'

The HR director laughed but then frowned when he realised that the proprietor was being serious.

'You have not heard the story?' the proprietor asked incredulously. 'The story about the Cumbre Vieja monster? It is a terrible tale – a tale of fear, of trepidation, of destruction and of death.'

David Evans looked at the proprietor's solemn expression and the hairs on the back of his neck stood up – is that why few tourists visited La Palma, he thought.

'It all happened in 1949,' the café owner continued, 'when three volcanoes – San Juan, Duraznero and Hoyo Negro – all erupted at the same time and caused a massive fissure to open up on the side of the ridge, almost three kilometres long. It is only a metre wide and two metres deep but, if the volcanoes erupt again, the whole of the west flank could tumble into the sea and generate a massive wave – a mega-tsunami. The scientists say that this wave could be a kilometre high and travel across the Atlantic Ocean causing massive devastation in America.'

The proprietor stopped briefly and slowly shook his head, overcome by the telling of his story.

'Who would have thought,' he finally added, 'that tranquil little La Palma could harbour a sleeping giant that, one day, might reach across the oceans.'

The HR director thought about it and nodded solemnly. He bought himself and the café owner a San Miguel each and, as he sipped his, he absently watched a huge cruise ship sail majestically from around the southern tip of the island and head away into the distance, across the Atlantic. Perhaps, he thought, he might be safer on the boat rather than here, in Puerto de Naos, right beneath the sleeping giant.

John Houston, relaxing on the balcony of his luxurious suite, watched the picturesque little island of La Palma slip into the distance, the distinctive conical shape of the Caldera de Taburiente volcano dominating its profile. The Mid-Ocean Oil CEO would like to have visited the island but, having only joined the cruise at Tenerife at the end of the Canary Islands leg of the cruise, it would have to wait for another time. And if you had told him that he was almost within hailing distance of one of his senior staff, his HR director, he would have shrugged and probably yawned – he neither cared nor found it interesting.

He was, however, looking forward to the forthcoming ten-day luxury cruise of the Azores, an archipelago of nine islands, fifteen hundred kilometres away in the Atlantic Ocean. Especially as his personal assistant, Anya Petrova – tall, blonde and exceedingly beautiful and whose twenty-eighth birthday was in four days' time – was accompanying him. It was fitting, he thought, that he, her boss, should treat her to a luxurious cruise as a birthday present and even more fitting that he, as a distinguished CEO of a well-known oil company, should be seen with a beautiful blonde on his arm. After all, what was the point of all that money and power, if not to use it?

'John, I am ready,' a soft, heavily accented voice called from the lounge.

The CEO's heart leapt and he felt a tingle of anticipation surge through his body.

'And so am I,' he growled back excitedly, as he turned from the balcony rail and entered the lounge.

But his excitement soon evaporated. Anya, statuesque and displaying her long tanned legs and athletic body, stood in a short white skirt and tight Lycra top.

'What's wrong?' she asked, noticing John's disappointed expression. 'Had you forgotten? You promised me a game of tennis today.'

As the oil executive swallowed his disappointment, the *Venus of the Seas*, the largest, most elegant and stylish cruise liner to grace the seven seas, sailed majestically onwards, into the Atlantic, onwards towards the Azores, fifteen hundred kilometres away.

Heathrow Airport, London, England

Inspector Cassidy was tired. Since the discovery of the bodies at St Francis Hospital he had hardly slept and hadn't seen his wife and children in days. And now, in a crowded operations room at the airport, he was coordinating Operation Spitfire, a carefully planned and rehearsed detailed response to any potential plane hijacking anywhere in the UK. He had established all the emergency services and NBC units at strategic points; he had established a no-go civilian zone around the plane; he had briefed and deployed the Metropolitan Police firearms unit and the anti-terrorist unit; he had kept Superintendent Jamie McDougal informed, who had then briefed the Prime Minister; and he had liaised with a small detachment of the SAS.

But, like many hostage situations, this one had become a nerve-wracking wait-and-see operation. Specialist police negotiators had made contact with the two suspected terrorists but so far, after sixteen long and delicate hours of negotiations, the terrorists had made no demands.

But then, he mused, this was an unusual hijacking. It had obviously not been planned but was the result of desperation by the two terrorists who had realised that they were about to be discovered – they clearly knew no more about their immediate objectives than the inspector. And their hostages were not the normal targets, decadent Christians, but were fellow Muslims, followers and believers of Islam. They were families, relatives and friends returning or visiting from Pakistan and no doubt most would be peace-loving and moderate in their outlook. And now they, rather than the trained policemen, had become the main negotiators with the hijackers, arguing and discussing the complex and delicate nuances of Islamic teachings.

And, at first, Inspector Cassidy had believed that this would be the way to a peaceful conclusion – fellow Muslims persuading the terrorists to see sense and lay down their arms. But secretly sent texts and telephone calls from some of the passengers had begun to paint a different and increasingly worrying picture. Clearly, the young Islamic fundamentalists were so idealistic that black was very black and white was very white and there was no room for even a hint of grey. And through the long night the calm intellectual discussions on the meaning of Mohammed's teachings had given way to erratic and irrational ranting and raving and, recently, to screaming threats to blow up the plane.

Inspector Cassidy had no reason to doubt them. They could have sarin and they could have a Semtex bomb. And, who knows, there could be a third or a fourth terrorist waiting patiently among the passengers. And with all those passengers and nine crew on board, he couldn't afford to take the chance – he would have to continue the nerve-wracking wait-and-see game.

Suddenly, his earpiece crackled into life.

'Sir, its Alpha One,' the chief negotiator said, 'we've had a breakthrough – they've made some demands.'

'Good,' Cassidy replied, relief clearly evident in his voice, 'now we have some bargaining power. What do they want?'

'They apparently need a doctor because their wounds are still bleeding where they ripped them open to get at the bombs. They want them stitched back up again.'

Inspector Cassidy nodded and smiled to himself. That was an easy demand to meet and was an excellent opportunity for planting a policeman on board.

'And the second demand?'

'They want the plane refuelled and prepared for take-off,' Alpha One replied.

'Damn!' Inspector Cassidy cursed. 'We can't let that happen. Have they said where they want to go?'

'Yes, but you won't believe it,' Alpha One replied. 'They want to go to Iceland.'

For a moment there was silence.

'Did you say, Iceland?' the inspector asked incredulously.

'Yes, Sir – Iceland.'

'That's weird,' Inspector Cassidy said, as much to himself as the chief negotiator. 'Why Iceland? It's cold, it's dark, it's not a Muslim country and, apart from the credit crunch, it's not involved in world affairs. It's bizarre.'

An hour later, after being briefed and provided with a paramedic's overalls and a medical bag, 'Doctor' Cassidy nervously climbed the stairs that had been pushed against the side of the Boeing 777. As he entered the plane his first impression was that it was cold – in late December and with no heating, the plane was like a fridge. His second impression was the palpable atmosphere of fear and dread. His third impression was that the two terrorists were remarkably young and that they were very close to breaking point – their eyes were panic-stricken, their faces were pale and clammy, their clothes were soaked with blood and they exuded fear, exhaustion and abject loneliness. They could easily break and give in or, God forbid, detonate their bombs.

'I'm a doctor,' he said calmly. 'I'm here to stitch your wounds.'

The two young men, still holding their packages together, looked at him, then at each other and nodded. One of them undid his jacket and lifted a bloody shirt, revealing a suppurating open wound, oozing blood, pus and a foul stench. Inspector Cassidy almost gagged but managed to contain it, instead concentrating on rummaging in the medical bag.

'We'll need to clean the wound and give you an antibiotic

injection,' he said, hoping to buy some time.

'No!' the patient suddenly barked. 'You stitch only. Stop the bleeding.'

The policeman looked at him and nodded. He was weighing up the chances of making a grab for the bomb, hoping that a hypodermic syringe in his hand would give him an edge. He had reasoned that, if he could do that, then the breast implant presumably full of sarin would be difficult to disperse and it would give him, the passengers or the SAS time to pounce. But clearly the hijackers were nervous and the one with the bomb was constantly fiddling with it.

Trying to look as professional as possible, he selected a sterile stitching needle and tried to thread it but his hands shook so much that it was impossible. Sweat began to bead on his forehead and he silently cursed himself for not getting the real medics to have already done it for him.

Suddenly, as the two hijackers watched him closely and his trembling hands fumbled with the needle, a mobile phone rang and his patient took one from his pocket.

For a brief moment, the policeman wondered what Alpha One was doing phoning the terrorists at this crucial moment, before realising that instead a text had been received.

The terrorist looked at the message and then showed it to his colleague. Inspector Cassidy noticed a subtle change in their expressions – their eyes narrowed and a grim determination and a religious zeal replaced the fear and exhaustion. In that brief moment, he instantly knew that he and all the passengers were doomed.

Three seconds later, the bomb exploded, blasting the two terrorists and the policeman to smithereens and sending a fine mist of deadly sarin molecules throughout the plane.

Alpha One, standing just outside the aircraft, had microseconds to register an exploding hole in the fuselage before being covered in debris and sarin toxin. Thirty seconds later, he collapsed to the ground, gasping for breath, vomiting and his body shuddering in violent spasms. Thirty seconds later, he was dead.

New York City, USA

Joanna Turnbull liked New York's Columbia University. Not only because it was originally called King's College when it was founded in 1754, the name of her college at Cambridge University, but mainly because it had a brilliant, exciting and active research department – the Geophysics and Tectonic Plate Division. And, of course, because it was headed by Professor Nathaniel Conrad.

The lecture was already nearing the end and by the time her taxi had managed to struggle through New York's congested traffic from the airport, and she had dithered at the entrance, wondering whether to wait or go in or not, it was almost over.

She read the display notice and chuckled.

NEW YORK–A CITY WAITING TO TREMBLE?
EARTHQUAKES BENEATH MANHATTAN!
A lecture by Professor N Conrad

Typical of the professor, she thought – he had a knack for making even tectonic plate physics sound interesting. She decided she'd like to hear him lecture once again and quietly slipped into the back of the packed auditorium.

'. . . So, in conclusion, what do we have?' Professor Conrad was saying. 'We've shown that Manhattan sits on a deep layer of soft Ice Age sediment over hard igneous rock and that it is criss-crossed by earthquake faults. We have seen that there has been quite a bit of seismic activity in and around the New York area and even some, fairly recently, beneath Manhattan itself. We have further seen that the majority of these earthquakes are relatively mild, mainly in the 2 to 5 magnitude range, and have caused little if any damage.

'However, we cannot rule out the possibility that a more serious earthquake may occur. But even a 6.8 quake, like the one in Kobe in Japan, would not be as devastating as one might expect because, as we have shown, modern buildings, even skyscrapers, are designed to withstand such tremors.

'So, is New York a city waiting to tremble? Yes, I think that it is. But should New Yorkers quake in their boots? No, I don't think that they should.'

Professor Conrad sat down and there was a round of applause – like all his lectures, this one had been energetically delivered and warmly received.

'If there are any questions,' he added when the applause had died down, 'I should be only too pleased to answer them.'

Next to Joanna, a kindly-looking gentleman fidgeted nervously but eventually held up his hand and stood up.

'Er, hello, Professor Conrad,' he said timidly, 'I'm Jacob Goldstein of the Mayor's Office. Thank you for such an excellent talk and it's gratifying to know that we New Yorkers can sleep soundly in our beds. I was just wondering – have any of these earthquakes happened under the sea off New York? You know – did they cause a tsunami?'

Professor Conrad stood up again and walked to the front of the podium.

'Excellent question, Jacob,' he replied, 'and the answer is yes, some of the earthquakes have been offshore, but no, tsunamis were not caused. To be honest, I think it is highly unlikely that a tsunami could be produced here because you would need a massive offshore earthquake, 8 to 9 on the Richter scale, near a steep-sided rift valley, that then triggered an underwater landslide and a resulting tsunami.

'Of course, that doesn't rule out tsunamis arriving from elsewhere. As New Yorkers, you've all no doubt heard about the death and destruction waiting to be unleashed from a volcano on La Palma, in the Canary Islands, off the west coast of Africa. Well, I can categorically tell you now that there are very few scientists that support that sensational speculation and you have as much chance of drowning in a Spanish monster wave as you have of getting an enormous tax rebate from the IRS.'

There was a round of laughter and Professor Conrad sat down.

'That's all very well, Professor Conrad,' someone shouted from the audience, 'but you haven't explained the Mohorovicic Discontinuity and its reflective influence on the seismic waves. Thermal inversions are common in the atmosphere, but couldn't a similar one in the Earth's mantle deflect and concentrate tectonic seismic activity, creating a hotspot sufficient to generate a Richter 9 earthquake?'

Professor Conrad frowned, stood up again and peered into the far recesses of the audience.

'Yes, er, good question,' he eventually managed to say lamely. 'If you could just stand up and repeat the question – that might help.'

Joanna stood up and most of the audience turned round to look at her.

'Yes, Professor, the Mohorovicic Disc . . .'

'Joanna!' Professor Conrad suddenly shouted, laughing. 'Dr Joanna Turnbull! You are a wicked student. I should have known it was you. We can leave Mohorovicic and his Discontinuity in peace now. Thank you, everyone. And, Dr Turnbull – I'd like to see you in my office. Right now!'

'You haven't changed a bit,' Professor Conrad said, kissing her on both cheeks and ushering her into his laboratory. 'You're still beautiful and still asking awkward questions to which you already know the answers.'

She laughed. He had been her favourite lecturer at Cambridge and his infectious enthusiasm had ensnared her into the dynamic world of geological and environmental physics and plate tectonics. And now, she had become the teacher at his old university.

'Yes, sorry about that disgraceful showing off,' she replied. 'But actually, I do have one question on your lecture.'

Professor Conrad laughed.

'Only one? That's a relief.'

'Yes, and I'm sure that there's a good reason,' she continued, 'but when you were talking about offshore earthquakes and tsunamis, you didn't mention the Hudson Canyon. After all, it is the size of the Grand Canyon and one of the largest submarine canyons in the world – and it's just on New York's doorstep. If the canyon sides collapsed, couldn't it trigger a huge tidal wave?'

Professor Conrad considered for a moment and then nodded slowly.

'Yes, it's true,' he admitted. 'In fact, as you know, something similar happened in the Grand Banks in 1929. The resulting tsunami even killed twenty-eight people on the Newfoundland coast. Yes, Joanna, a collapse of the Hudson Canyon would unleash devastation on the city. Computer models predict a tsunami several metres high, similar to the potential storm surge from a Category 3 hurricane. But why terrify the poor New Yorkers any more? After all, it's not their fault that the Federal Government has neglected sea defences for so long.'

'Hmm, you're probably right,' she admitted. 'Sometimes it's best to live in peaceful ignorance. After all, there could be an offshore earthquake tomorrow or it could be in five hundred years' time.'

'Why don't you leave stuffy old Cambridge and come to Columbia,' he continued. 'We have some exciting research projects going on at the moment. We could do with your analytical mind and healthy scepticism.'

'Well, actually, that's sort of why I'm here,' she replied seriously, 'to talk about one of your research projects. There's something I'm worried about.'

'Go on,' he prompted, sitting down at his desk.

'Well, it's about your semi-submersible survey of the Gakkel Ridge,' she started, sitting down opposite him, digging out her laptop and switching it on. 'You discovered that there had been quite a bit of volcanic activity in the past and that there were still a few smokers emitting clouds of gas and debris. At

Cambridge, we've been monitoring the Gakkel Ridge for seismic activity for the last couple of years and, all of a sudden, in the last few months, it's gone wild. For some reason it's become hyperactive, with a constant series of deep-crust earthquakes, many in the 6 to 8 Richter magnitude range but a few, recently, at 9.2 and 9.3.

'Yesterday, a friend of mine at the Danish Geological Society told me about multiple violent tremors stretching in a line from northern Greenland to south-eastern Greenland. Worryingly, in the last few days, they've increased from magnitude 7, through 8, to 9.3. What worries me is that no one really knows what's beneath the ice cap – is it land sunken under the immense weight of the ice; is it a circular archipelago of mountainous islands forming a ring around the ice cap; or . . .' She paused, loading a detailed map of the Arctic sea floor topography onto her laptop screen. '. . . an extension of the Gakkel Ridge that cuts through Greenland and joins the Mid-Atlantic Ridge at Iceland?'

Professor Conrad slowly nodded his head – it was a theory that he had heard before but there was no evidence to support it.

'Go on,' he prompted again.

'My contact at the Danish Geological Society,' Joanna continued, 'told me that their research teams on the ice cap report that the ice has lifted by at least three kilometres. And, what with the devastating and abnormal glacial flood they had recently, I seriously think that something major is brewing. We don't have the funding at Cambridge but you do. Couldn't you organise a research team to fly up to the ice cap? We have to find out what's happening up there.'

The professor looked at her, smiled and then burst out laughing.

Joanna's jaw dropped and her face reddened. She started to speak but was lost for words, which made him laugh even more.

Eventually, he held up his hand and apologised.

'Sorry, Joanna, but I couldn't help it. I'm not trying to get my own back it's just that you materialise all of a sudden, out of the blue, and just at the most appropriate time. It's fate.'

Joanna frowned, confused.

'I don't understand,' she mumbled.

'Yesterday,' the professor explained, 'we heard that a USS nuclear submarine, a USAF AWACS and a British icebreaker had all disappeared in the Arctic near the Gakkel Ridge. Before the plane went down it reported seeing a huge string of geysers bursting from the sea. That seems impossible – the sea is meant to be three kilometres deep in that area. But it's true – satellite images have confirmed that a line of geysers and plumes of smoke stretch hundreds of kilometres along the Gakkel Ridge from the North Pole to northern Greenland. And look . . .'

He turned his computer monitor round and Joanna gasped – in glorious colour, an infrared satellite image showed a red streak cutting through a blue wasteland.

'Is that a river of lava flowing through ice?' she asked, her eyes wide with astonishment.

Professor Conrad nodded.

'Is it Greenland?'

'Yes, it's a close-up of northern Greenland,' he said. 'The normal images didn't show anything and we think steam from melting ice has hidden this huge gash in the ice cap. But with infrared, we can clearly see the molten lava. And you could be right – the Gakkel Ridge could be a spur of the North Atlantic Ridge, joining it near Iceland, which, as you know, is volcanically very active. But what's just as amazing is that you've arrived just as my senior seismologist has taken ill and he can't go.'

'Can't go?' Joanna asked, confused.

Professor Conrad smiled again.

'Yes, Joanna, don't unpack your bags. We're on a flight to Baffin Island this afternoon and in the morning we fly to the ice cap. My research team is ready and waiting. We have to find out what's going on up there.'

Joanna jumped up and grabbed him and kissed him on the cheek.

Blackpool, England

For a fleeting moment, Susan felt the overpowering weight of depression and despair lift and a glimmer of a smile crossed her face. Her sister, Sarah, had come over to stay and support her and she had driven Susan to a giant electrical store on the outskirts of Blackpool to find a birthday present for Lucy. Susan had just seen some portable DVD players for sale. Looking at them, she was comparing the quality of the pictures when, without realising it, her mind lost itself in one of the films, Disney's *Return to Neverland*, and she thought how wonderful and magical it was.

It had been six days since Craig had vanished and she was struggling to cope. All hope was disappearing fast and news reports had said that air and sea searches, hampered by storms and fog, were being scaled down. After all, even with survival immersion suits no one could survive more than several hours in those frigid waters.

She had phoned Mid-Ocean Oil that very morning to speak to the HR director but she had been told that he had suddenly gone sick and all his assistant could say was that there was no further news. Frustrated, she had insisted on speaking to the CEO but when she was told that he was on holiday she had slammed the phone down and burst into tears.

Her doctor had suggested a course of anti-depressants but what good would they do? True, she was desperately unhappy, frantic with worry, achingly sad and depressed, but hey, who wouldn't be. But she still had a glimmer of hope and had to remain strong for Lucy, so she refused to succumb to the false soporific of drugs.

'Susan?' Sarah said softly, 'are you all right?'

Susan looked up and stared at her sister. For a brief moment she was confused – what was she doing and why was her sister here? But then she snapped out of it.

'This is a nice DVD player,' she said. 'Lucy will love it. What do you think?'

Sarah nodded her agreement and Susan picked up a box and they headed for the pay desk. On the way they had to pass through the television sales area and on one television Sky News was showing – it stopped Susan in her tracks.

'. . . And, for the first time,' the news presenter was saying, 'we have actual footage of the actual last moments of the oil platform, *Ocean One*, taken a few days ago by one of the support vessels.'

The news presenter vanished and a dark and jerky video film appeared, showing a hostile world of a blazing oil rig being assaulted by wild weather and enormous waves. The support vessel was rising and falling in the swell and, lashed by sea spray and howling wind, the crewman taking the video was obviously struggling to record the dying moments of the giant oil platform. But as he zoomed in it was possible to see the lifeboats being launched, one of them jamming at the stern and hanging dangerously beneath the holocaust, and men desperately jumping or falling into the raging seas.

Mesmerised, Susan watched as the scene from hell unfolded, a scene days ago and thousands of kilometres away and yet so close to her heart – somewhere, among all the horror and mayhem, was her husband.

Suddenly, the cameraman must have spotted two men still on the rig and he zoomed further in until he could make out what they were doing.

'My God!' the cameraman gasped above the howling wind. 'Those two guys are trying to release the lifeboat. I think they've got an oxyacetylene cutter and are trying to free the cable.'

Smoke and flames could clearly be seen around the two men as they frantically fought to save their colleagues and giant yellow and orange fireballs erupted around them as escaping gas and oil ignited and exploded. Suddenly, the jammed cable must have parted because the lifeboat slid into the water and safely away from the rig.

'They've done it!' the cameraman suddenly shouted, his voice elated and emotional. 'Those guys have done it – they've saved all those men. They're heroes. Who are those guys?'

He zoomed in as far as he could and, although the picture was grainy and jerky, you could clearly make out two desperate and smoke-blackened faces.

In the crowded shop, Susan gasped and dropped the portable DVD.

On the television, massive explosions rocked the oil platform and dense smoke and flames surged through the rig – the two heroes vanished.

Susan screamed and collapsed to the ground.

'Susan!' Sarah shouted.

'Oh my God!' the cameraman gasped, his voice trembling and emotional. 'The men have gone. They've been swallowed by the flames. Oh my God!'

As Sarah, shoppers and shop assistants rushed to Susan's aid, and the television showed a massive iceberg suddenly crashing into the platform, the news presenter's voice could clearly be heard again.

'. . . And we believe that these two brave men, operation team leaders and friends, were Craig Macintyre and Sean O'Brian. Sadly, they are believed to have perished in the inferno. John Houston, CEO of Mid-Ocean Oil, has said that these two heroes will be remembered and honoured in the close-knit oil industry. Mid-Ocean Oil sends its deepest and heart-felt condolences and sympathy to all the family and friends of those who perished in this terrible and unpredictable accident. Mr Houston has said that he, personally, will take charge of the containment and clean-up operation.

'And now, to other news. The political situation in . . .'

Nantucket Island, USA

It was just before midnight. The huge rolling surf of the Atlantic crashed into the exposed east coast of Nantucket Island, about four hundred kilometres north-east of New York. At low tide, the waves reared up and collapsed, with a resounding boom onto the beach, sending sand and spray flying into the air. After several days, the dense bank of fog had begun to fade away and a weak silvery moon highlighted the white lines of surf as it rolled into shore, an offshore breeze sending spindrift flying into the air.

Above all this, at the end of a rough track off Surfside Road on the east coast of the island, a lonely campervan stood sentinel, the only witness to the wild and desolate night. Despite the encroaching rust and an endless catalogue of breakdowns, the ancient orange-and-cream, split-screen, Mark 1 campervan was a valuable, loved possession.

Inside, it was warm, cosy and unmistakably smelly. Eternally damp, salty wetsuits mingled with a pungent vegetable vindaloo, jasmine joss sticks and the sweet smell of cannabis. But it was home. Billy Hayes – tall, blond and goateed – had lived in it for eleven years now, touring the surf spots around the east and west coasts of America and occasionally doing manual labour to provide for his meagre existence. At twenty-nine he probably should have gotten a proper job and settled down, done the nine-to-five daily grind and the forty-five-year lifetime grind but, hey, what did that bring you – a robotic and monotonous existence of toiling for a boss at work and a boss at home. No – he needed a mortgage and kids like a hole in the head.

'Pass the joint, dude,' his lithe companion said dreamily, her shaggy mane of blonde hair spilling over her bronzed shoulders.

Candice was her name, Candice Buttercup. Probably not her real name but it suited her, and in the two months that she had shared his bed, his van, his beers, his surfboards and surf, he realised that he was becoming fond of her. Shit! It always happened – soon, it would be time to move on.

But, for now, they stared dreamily out of the windows, watching the waves crash onto the beach and dreaming about another day's glorious surfing in the morning.

'Dude, this is the life,' he said to no one in particular. 'Not a care in the world, just the endless ocean and the freedom to ride the waves. To watch the moon's silver glow and chill the night away.'

Candice giggled and passed the joint back.

'Not too chilled,' she said softly, sensually stroking the inside of his thigh.

Billy took a last deep drag on the joint and slid the window open to flick the stub outside. Immediately, a breeze blew in and he savoured the cool salty air. But then something suddenly caught his attention. Offshore, a white light seemed to blaze briefly in the sky before slowly fading away.

'Did you see that?' he asked, wondering if he had put too much cannabis in the joint.

'Hmm?' Candice mumbled, beginning to undo her blouse.

'Perhaps it was the Great Point lighthouse,' he said, although he was sure that was further north.

But then, suddenly, as the final tendrils of mist lifted, a huge ghostly white shape appeared on the horizon, lit up by the weak moonlight. Far out to sea it was indistinct but was clearly too massive for a cruise liner, but like many of the cruise ships heading towards New York, this, whatever it was, was also heading south. Was it an iceberg? He shivered – he was clearly more spaced out than he thought.

'Come on, surfer boy,' Candice said giggling, her blouse now discarded, 'it's time to get wet and wild.'

That evening the fog had begun to disappear. In the distance, through gaps in the swirling mist, Craig could see the flashing lights of a lighthouse. He thought he could also see a string of lights that could be a coastal town, but he had no idea where he was. For all he knew he could be passing Boston, New York, Atlantic City or even Norfolk.

Fortunately, as fast as his frostbitten limbs had allowed, he had climbed out of the life raft and fired off the emergency flares. Unfortunately, two of them had failed to ignite and only the third had sailed high into the sky and thankfully been blown towards the coast. He could only hope and pray that its brief beacon of distress was seen and acted upon. If not, all he had left was a red smoke flare for daytime use and the orange life raft itself.

At least the air temperature had warmed up a few degrees. It was still freezing at night but it managed to reach two or three degrees during the day so he knew they were still drifting south.

His mind, no longer logical and beginning to play tricks on him, kept seeing huge lumps of ice melting or breaking off from the base and he began to be paranoid about the whole iceberg flipping over and tipping their fragile home into and under the sea.

'We'll be eating steak and chips, tomorrow, Sean,' he mumbled through his ice-coated face mask, 'with mountains of bread and butter and great hot mugs of whisky-laden coffee.'

Sean stared back through lifeless eyes, his face covered in frost and icicles. One of his hands, frozen solid, held up a crumpled piece of paper, an almost illegibly scrawled last will and testament.

'And think of those beautiful nurses,' Craig continued. 'Angels of mercy, pandering to our every whim and administering tender, loving care. Tomorrow, Sean, tomorrow . . .'

But, on shore, in an old campervan that rocked to the rhythm of Candice Buttercup's energetic sex, the only person who had seen the distress flare was otherwise engaged.

Islamabad, Pakistan

Mohammed allowed himself a brief smile of satisfaction. The final piece of the jigsaw had fallen into place and the operation could go ahead. It was strange, he mused, how events unfolded – almost always unexpectedly and almost always due to the vagaries and aberrations of the human character. People were weak, lazy, cowardly, greedy, selfish or just plain stupid – or, in the case of certain individuals like Abdul Hamid, all of those things combined.

After Malik had asked Mohammed to arrange Abdul's 'disposal' because of his greed, laziness and stupidity, Abdul had betrayed the cause again by cowardly refusing to detonate the bomber's suicide vest they had fitted to him. And now, ensconced in the police station in Islamabad, he had apparently betrayed his faith and his friends and told the policemen everything he knew. And now he must die.

Mohammed looked at the three large drums strapped to the top of the van and hoped that they would survive the journey. Rusting, battered and covered in barely legible Russian military writing and hazard warning signs, they were already quite old, fragile and . . . deadly. This was the source of Malik's sarin nerve agent and now Mohammed knew exactly what to do with the rest.

Not that you would have realised that to look at him – a smooth-skinned, middle-aged, well-spoken businessman, he was as respectable as they came. No, it was the three scarred, disabled bomb-makers and terrorists that he had organised and bankrolled who would be taking the risk and the sacrifice – but then, they were the ones who would ascend to heaven in an instant.

'Wahid!' he called out to one of the men who was just getting into the van. 'Take it easy on the journey. These chemical drums are like eggshells and we don't want them breaking prematurely. And we don't want you being pulled over by the police.'

Wahid, a grey-bearded and wizened little man, grinned a toothless grin and then accelerated away. The van, with its three occupants and emblazoned with *CINNAMON BAKERY – SWEETS & DELICACIES* on its side, darted into the heavy traffic.

Mohammed cursed and ran for his black Mercedes car. He

was going to follow somewhere behind to ensure that everything went according to plan, but if he was going to keep up with Wahid then he had better get a move on.

Thirty-five minutes later they were in the quieter and more affluent outskirts of Islamabad and driving down a wide, leafy lane of large white-washed bungalows. Mohammed slowed to allow the van to gain some distance as it sped down the lane towards a large gated house at the end. For some time now they had known that this was a supposedly secret and secure safe house for CIA operatives and they had been watching it for several months. And finally, and fortuitously, the final piece of the jigsaw had been put into place that gave them the opportunity to destroy it and the American spies – Abdul Hamid had apparently been taken there in order to further betray his friends and his faith.

Mohammed watched as the van neared the large gates and the two young passengers jumped out and ran towards them. Simultaneously, they clasped themselves to the metal bars and shouted exhortations to the heavens – and then there were two almighty explosions and fireballs as their suicide vests exploded, sending lumps of metal and flesh flying through the air.

Wahid grinned his toothless grin again and accelerated the bakery van towards the gap. A couple of white-shirted Westerners ran from the side of the house and began opening fire but neither hit Wahid and he managed to run one over before smashing into the front of the house. The three large drums of sarin strapped to the top of the van broke free and smashed against the masonry, crumpling and sending their contents flying through the air.

Just at that moment, Mohammed saw the front door of the house open and there, standing horrified beside a Westerner, was that fat sweaty oaf – Abdul Hamid! As Hamid immediately took in what was happening his face became a sudden mask of fear and panic and he turned to run. But molecules of sarin had already entered his lungs and he began to gasp for breath, sinking to the floor and beginning to drool and vomit. Within moments, his eyes wide with fear and his body shuddering in violent spasms, he released a long and blood-curdling groan. Thirty seconds later, he was dead.

Mohammed smiled and, reversing his car, turned to drive away and back into Islamabad centre. Behind him, he heard a sudden massive explosion as Wahid detonated the explosives in the back of the van. He smiled again – a perfect operation – Malik would have been proud.

Chapter 8

20 December 2012
Reykjavik, Iceland

Dr Hashim's house was a far cry from the squalid surgery and post-operative recovery conditions back in Peshawar, from where these men had started their long and dangerous journey. He was pleased with what he had achieved, surreptitiously and single-handedly turning a detached residential house in the middle of Reykjavik into a state-of-the-art mini hospital. He looked at their faces – the ten young men lined up in the home-made hospital ward were exhausted, lost and scared. They were little more than boys really, aged between eighteen and twenty, and they were in a strange land far away from home and he vowed to look after them the very best he could.

'Abeye,' he said to one of the nurses, 'you and Elli can administer the preoperative sedative injections now. Then bring the first one down for the epidural. I'm going to scrub up – I want to start in thirty minutes.'

Downstairs, waiting patiently in a small room next to the operating theatre, Malik and Patrick O'Keefe carefully unpacked a large timezone electronic world clock, almost a metre long and two-thirds of a metre tall, designed for boardrooms and identical to the one on the wall of Conference Suite 3A at the Hotel Aurora Borealis. Laying it face down on the table, Malik unscrewed the screws holding the back plate in place and, lifting the back off, exposed the inner workings.

'Is there sufficient room in there?' Dr Hashim asked, wandering into the room in surgical gown and nodding towards the time piece.

Malik nodded. After three years of preparations he was not going to leave anything to chance and, although he had already dismantled the clock several months ago to ensure everything would fit, he wanted to give Patrick one final rehearsal.

'Dr Hashim,' one of the nurses suddenly called from the operating theatre, 'the first patient is ready for the epidural anaesthesia.'

Dr Hashim returned to the operating theatre and Malik followed him, covering his face with a surgical mask and standing to one side to watch.

While Abeye Umgalla attached the electrodes for the heart monitor to the patient's chest, Elli Salumptu collected the surgical instruments and stainless-steel trays from the autoclave steriliser. The patient was drowsy but still awake and his eyes flitted nervously around the room.

'Don't worry, Nadeem,' Dr Hashim said soothingly, 'God is with you and he will guide my hand. Once we have the epidural in place, you won't feel a thing.'

While Abeye positioned Nadeem on his side, Dr Hashim cleaned the lower back area with iodine tincture, injected the skin with lidocaine anaesthetic and then very carefully inserted a Tuohy needle between two vertebral lumbar bones and into the epidural space. Once he was happy with the positioning he slid a catheter through the needle, withdrew the needle, secured the catheter to the skin with adhesive tape and then attached the other end to an epidural anaesthetic infusion pump.

While he waited a few moments for the anaesthetic to take effect, Elli gently removed the dressing covering the abdominal wound and cleaned the surrounding area with iodine tincture. When this had been done Dr Hashim wasted no time in snipping the black nylon twine of the sutures. The edges of the wound were still raw but had already begun to fuse and he had to reopen them with a scalpel. Adeptly, he prised open the wound and carefully moved the large intestine to one side and there, nestled among the blood and intestinal coils, was his prize – a very large breast implant. Delicately, he scooped it from the body cavity and placed it in a stainless-steel tray held by Elli.

'*Voilà!*' he announced theatrically. 'The treasure magically re-appears.'

While Abeye cleaned and re-stitched the wound, Elli washed the breast implant and passed it to Malik.

'Excellent,' he said, smiling at Dr Hashim. 'Now, all we have to do is retrieve the other nine packages.'

Einar Sigmundsen, Reykjavik's portly and balding chief of police, was astonished by what he saw. As he crossed the Hringbraut towards the magnificent entrance of the Hotel Aurora Borealis, the full impact of the security measures for the G20 Summit meeting really hit home.

Of course, as chief of police, he had been heavily involved in Operation Icelandic Saga since the very beginning. But formu-lating and drafting the plans on paper for what was easily Iceland's most extensive and expensive security operation ever was one thing but actually seeing it in action was another. Hringbraut, the main road through Reykjavik's city centre and usually a river of traffic throughout the day, was deserted apart from a few pedes-trians – part of a curtain of steel thrown around Hotel Aurora Borealis.

Such a high-profile international meeting could have been sched-uled for any of the major cities anywhere in the world rather than in a remote and sleepy little island on the edge of the Arctic Circle. But its very isolation was its attraction. Recent summits, in Washington, London, Pittsburgh, Toronto and Seoul, had become a magnet for protesters and political activists and the important economic, environmental and poverty agenda had largely been overshadowed. Huge and sometimes violent demonstrations had disrupted the cities whose streets were descended upon by anti-capitalists, anti-war activists, frustrated environmentalists, disaffected youths, the unemployed, trade unionists . . . in fact, anyone who bore a grudge or who had an axe to grind.

With the constant fear of terrorism, the security operations had become huge and extremely costly. Iceland – distant, expensive to travel to and with few local disaffected groups – was a logical choice of venue. After all, the meeting had important things to discuss – key issues affecting the global economy, Third World poverty and global warming – and distractions they could do without.

As he entered the hotel's foyer Sigmundsen was initially greeted by one of his own men but then quickly accosted by plain-clothed, large American-accented men who demanded to see his identification and made him walk through a metal detector and a body scanner. That was fine, he thought – after all, they were only doing their job and there were going to be some very, very important people arriving here later today.

The Hotel Aurora Borealis had six hundred rooms and every one would be taken by G20 Summit diplomats, advisors and security – guests had been excluded since yesterday. Tomorrow, at the nearby airport, flights would be severely restricted; a no-go vehicle zone had been established around the hotel, and police forces, security services, coast guard units and anti-terrorist units from several nations discreetly checked the hotel and neighbourhood or prepared to deploy against protests and marches.

The chief of police was sure that such a massive security operation would not be needed but he agreed that they had to be prepared – just in case. After all, what with the G20's past record of sometimes violent demonstrations and with terrorist attacks currently plaguing London, it paid to be ready – just in case. As he successfully passed through the cordon of security he headed down towards the conference centre. He wanted to make sure that Conference Suite 3A would be as secure as Operation Icelandic Saga had planned.

And then tonight, he thought excitedly, he was having dinner with a rather sensuous and buxom lady whom he had recently met and who, surprisingly, had taken a fancy to him. He needed to buy some champagne and flowers, get home, shaved, show-ered and put on his best suit. After all, the curvaceous Frida Jonsson seemed to have a twinkle in her eye and it paid to be ready – just in case.

To a casual observer, the little family enjoying a shopping trip in the city centre would have made a poignant impression. Holding hands and constantly hugging each other, they looked happy despite their obvious infirmity – the father was weak and pale and had heavily bandaged hands; the mother was haggard and exhausted; the daughter was bent over with a shuffling gait; and their husky puppy walked with a pronounced limp. They looked as though they had only recently survived a major accident or stepped straight out of a disaster movie.

'Daddy,' Nunni pleaded again, 'please can we buy a nice fluffy doggy bed for Miki Nanook? He used to love his old one and with his poorly leg he needs a comfy bed.'

Tukku laughed and Gilda smiled. It was strange – they had lost everything they used to own but they had never been happier. In a matter of days they had been on a shattering emotional rollercoaster ride and now that it was over and all four of them were safe, it was like a new dawn. Nothing else mattered – their house, their car, their possessions, were all gone – but they had themselves. It was like a rebirth, a sudden realisation that their love for each other was all that really mattered. Everything else was just baggage.

'Of course, Nunni,' Tukku said, chuckling. 'Miki's got to have a cosy place to sleep. Let's go and find a pet shop.'

After the devastating glacial flood had wiped away six hundred homes and sixteen hundred inhabitants, the mystical wheels of insurance had slowly and ponderously begun to grind. Unfortunately, and sadly, the friendly insurance broker in Tasiilaq had also been swept away, along with the insurance records of many of the inhabitants. But, ironically, the Nygaards were in a strong position – with few people left alive there was no one else to claim and the loss to the insurers would be negligible. But still, the wheels turned slowly and, if it had not been for the generosity and kindness of Dr Hashim, they would be penniless.

To Tukku, Gilda and Nunni, he was an angel.

Ice cap, central Greenland

Above the enormous pent-up energy of the huge ancient slab of the Earth's crust emerging beneath the Arctic, a solitary figure worked feverishly on the ice. Frustrated that the steam clouds prevented him from recording the spectacle below and claiming a place in geological history, he had laboriously rigged up hundreds of metres of rope in order to abseil down and get closer to the action. It was an arduous task and it was beginning to take a severe toll on his mind and body. He dare not waste time melting ice to cook food or make drinks as he knew that Olaf wasn't far behind and consequently he was low on energy and severely dehydrated. He had removed his face mask, goggles and outer gloves to assemble the satellite transmitter and aerial, video equipment and ropes, and his fingers were now stiff and frostbitten, his eyes were bloodshot and swollen, and his nose had split and blackened. But he ignored all this and hummed happily as he worked – a gaunt and deranged solitary figure.

He looked at the GPS again and giggled – it now showed a height of eight kilometres. Eight kilometres! Three kilometres of ice and five kilometres of . . . something else. This was insane, he thought, absolutely and bloody fantastically insane. No wonder the ice cap continually creaked and groaned and he struggled to breathe – after all, he was almost as high as Mount Everest. A truly remarkable and historic geological event was taking place and only he, Jarvik Petersen, was there to record and preserve it for posterity. A Nobel Peace Prize in the making and glory . . .

Suddenly, the satellite phone crackled into life. He looked at it and cursed – if that was Olaf again, he could go to hell.

'. . . Jarvik,' a faint crackly voice said, 'it's Gunnar. Gunnar Pattersen. Thank God you're still all right.'

Jarvik looked at the phone and wondered whether or not to reply.

'. . . Jarvik, don't do anything rash. Just stay where you are – Olaf's on his way. He's found Runi and Johann and some of his team are helping to get them back to base camp. You can join Olaf's team if you . . .'

Jarvik looked at the phone again and, with a wry smile, lobbed it into space, into the swirling steam cloud and oblivion.

Quickly, he lowered the video camera and a portable transmitter over the edge of the ice and then donned the abseil harness. He looked into the steam cloud and for a few metres he could clearly see how steep and slippery the ice wall was. If this chasm was as large and deep as he suspected, descending three kilometres to the base of the ice, then, unless he found a ledge somewhere, he would come to the end of the rope, dangling a kilometre or more in space. He looked at his stiff crooked hands – it would be impossible to climb back up. He giggled again. This was a one-way ticket – to fame, glory and oblivion.

Humming the Danish national anthem, he stepped over the edge and disappeared.

Prudence Island, New England, USA

Jacob had never been to Prudence Island before. As he stepped off the ferry, he marvelled at its peace and tranquillity – a far cry from the bustle of downtown Manhattan. Apart from an old man fishing from the end of the wharf and his son in a Dodge pickup truck patiently waiting for him, there was no one else around. Only the raucous squawks of the seagulls disturbed the peace and quiet.

But he didn't have long to savour the serenity. The ferry only came once a day and it was due to head back to the mainland in two hours' time. He had to be on it as tomorrow was Martha's day – the anniversary of her arrival in America, sixty-six years earlier, and the day he had promised to realise her dream of paying homage to Lady Liberty.

'Dad!' Joseph suddenly shouted. 'It's great to see you. I didn't really expect you to come all the way over here.'

Jacob laughed.

'It's only a four-hour subway, train, taxi, ferry and now pickup truck journey,' he said jokingly, although knowing that he would have to do it all again in two hours' time.

'Well, now that you're here,' Joseph said, 'you can have a look at our facility. It's taken a lot of work but it should suffice.'

Jacob looked askance at his son – not that old chestnut about the Second Coming of the Messiah and the Apocalypse he hoped.

'Well, if it doesn't,' he said, 'you'd better get a move on. It's the 21st tomorrow.'

Joseph frowned and looked seriously at his father.

'Dad, you should have come and stayed here and brought all the family,' he said. 'They'd be safe here. There's plenty of room.'

'Look, Joseph,' Jacob replied seriously, 'I respect your views but, as you know, I'm not a great believer in the imminent destruction of mankind and the miraculous appearance of the New Dawn. If Yeshua does reappear, I, like everyone else, will be ecstatic, but I don't want to live my life preparing for it. But, if *you* do, I respect your views – just don't waste your life.'

'OK, Dad, so why have you come here?'

Jacob climbed into the truck.

'Let's have a look at your new home. Then I'll tell you.'

The US Navy had been busy on Prudence Island during the Second World War. Not only had they built substantial wharves and harbour facilities but they had also built a network of underground ammunition storage bunkers. Despite being unused for sixty years they were still dry and serviceable.

'This is amazing,' Jacob said, honestly impressed at what had been achieved and the logistics behind it. 'You must have enough provisions here for months.'

'Years!' Joseph said proudly. 'There are nearly a hundred of us here but we think we could survive for almost three years. And we've stockpiled hundreds of different grains and vegetable seeds and bulbs so that when we emerge we can start farming straight away.'

Jacob was taken aback. If only his son had devoted his time and energies to a real job he could already be a qualified attorney or vice-president by now.

'Dad,' Joseph said excitedly, 'come and have a look at the engine room.'

When they arrived, Jacob whistled. The cavernous bunker was packed with gently purring diesel generators, air purification plants, water-filtration units, radio equipment – in fact, everything needed to survive underground.

'These walls are three metres thick', Joseph continued, 'and made of reinforced concrete, and each entrance has a two-metre-thick steel blast door. When these close, just before midnight tonight, we will be self-sufficient and protected from the outside world.'

Jacob nodded slowly. He had known of Joseph's plans and his involvement with the Messianic Jews for some time but it was only now that he realised that they really were serious. And with racks of semi-automatic rifles and revolvers at strategic places throughout the complex, he knew that they really did mean business. Centuries of persecution, especially the horrors of the Holocaust, had been an expensive lesson – unswervingly relying on God's protection was one thing but having an edge, a means to fight back, was another, arguably better, insurance policy.

'Joseph,' he eventually said softly, 'I have something important to tell you.'

Joseph looked at his father and sighed.

'Sorry, Dad, but you know I can't come to the Statue of Liberty tomorrow. I love Grandmother but I have to be here to . . .'

'No, no,' Jacob said quickly, 'it's not that. It's not about Martha.'

Jacob sat down on a crate of supplies, his expression sad and dejected.

'I've not been well,' he began softly. 'I've had some tests and they've diagnosed pancreatic cancer. Apparently, it's already at an advanced stage and has spread to the duodenum.'

Joseph looked at his father, his face shocked. Deflated, he slumped onto a crate next to Jacob.

'They've advised me that there's no point undergoing the discomfort and trauma of chemotherapy,' Jacob continued, 'and it's too invasive for surgery. I've only got a few months left and that's why I'm here . . . to say goodbye.'

New York City, USA

Paul Gates was still struggling to come to terms with what had happened at the isolated shack, high up in the Adirondack Mountains. It had been a massacre, plain and simple – three FBI agents and six National Guardsmen had been slaughtered and a dozen more injured or maimed. He had been over and over the operation in his mind and he couldn't find a fatal flaw. They had been murdered, as simple as that.

And now, two days later, exhausted by twenty-hour working days and lack of sleep, he knew time was running out. Tomorrow was D-Day – 'Desperado Day', he called it. He refused to give it the semi-mystical titles of Armageddon, End of Time, Apocalypse or the Second Coming of Christ. Like the Secretary of State, he thought they were all nuts and losers – people desperate for an opportunity to become worthy, rather than worthless pieces of junk.

His department, like every other police force in America, had been inundated with information on suspicious characters, weird plans, desperate plots and criminal schemes. His men were all exhausted and were looking forward to the Christmas break.

By then, D-Day would be over and things would be back to normal.

But, first, he had to find Mary Dewey-Bell and her terrorist friends.

Mary Dewey-Bell and her terrorist friends were, in fact, not far away from the FBI headquarters in downtown Manhattan and, had Paul Gates found out about it later, he would undoubtedly have cursed and shaken his head in dismay. While he occupied a generously proportioned and finished deputy director's office on the seventh floor, they sat in a cold, cramped and smelly dry cleaning van parked in the street below.

'She's just come out of the Mayor's Office now,' Jakbar Mulla hissed from the driver's seat.

'Make sure it's the right one, this time,' Mary Dewey-Bell growled. 'We don't want to grab another senile old fool.'

From the back, Ali Pasha and Nguyen Phan opened the side door and jumped out, pulling large sacks of dirty linen tumbling onto the sidewalk. Behind them, Granny Dewey-Bell climbed out and unravelled a large map of New York City. Immediately, the chilly wind blowing down the street plucked it away and sent it spinning down the sidewalk.

'I'll get it,' a tall and distinguished old lady shouted, as she speared it with her walking stick. 'Here you go,' she said, handing it over to Granny Dewey-Bell. 'I'm terribly sorry, but I appear to have put a hole . . .'

But she never had chance to finish. Ali and Nguyen grabbed her and threw her into the van, followed quickly by the dirty laundry sacks. Although shocked and winded, she gamely tried to climb to her feet and began screaming for the police before Ali threw one of the heavy sacks at her, knocking her unconscious.

'Right, let's go,' Granny Dewey-Bell ordered, climbing into the back of the van and placing masking tape over the old lady's mouth. 'And don't forget,' she added, laughing, 'you can call me Granny Goldstein now!'

Iqaluit, Baffin Island, Canada

Although Joanna had found New York cold, her brief stay had done little to prepare her for the freezing temperatures in Iqaluit. At minus thirty-six degrees Celsius, with a biting northerly wind blowing straight from the North Pole and an eternal twilight gloom, it was a sudden and brutal introduction to life in the Arctic Circle in winter.

It didn't help that Iqaluit, despite being the capital of Baffin Island, was a treeless and haphazard collection of unremarkable buildings that had started life as a Cold War American airbase. At the head of Frobisher Bay on the south coast of Baffin Island, it was as remote a capital as you could get, with access for most of the year by aircraft only. And it was equally hard to believe that Baffin Island, with only twelve thousand mainly Inuit inhabitants, was the fifth largest island in the world – with every person enjoying an average forty-two square kilometres to themselves.

Fortunately, Joanna had work to do. While the rest of the team unloaded and re-boxed the equipment ready for loading onto a chartered Cessna, she had the portable seismometers to check and recalibrate. She needed somewhere away from traffic, even the spartan Iqaluit traffic, and had chosen the far end of the runway as the best location – but it was bitterly cold, even with thermal underwear, two down jackets and padded salopettes.

But after an hour, with the seismometers spread in a circle around her and connected to a central laptop, she was satisfied that they were working and fully calibrated. Under normal circumstances she would have suspected a malfunction – after all, earthquakes bigger than 8 on the Richter scale generally occurred only about once a year – and that was anywhere in the world. To have several, in the space of sixty minutes, was impossible – yet she already knew that this was happening beneath Greenland and along the Gakkel Ridge. And anything at magnitude 9 or above was frightening – the devastation and loss of life would usually be massive, as had happened following the Indonesian earthquake in 2004.

'Nathanial,' she called over her VHF radio, 'we're still getting huge quakes, some as high as 9.1 and 9.2 somewhere up north. This is terribly worrying. I'm going to leave the equipment here for a couple of hours and come back – I want to speak to Sir David Appleby. If we can convince him that something catastrophic might be building, we may get some more help.'

'OK,' Professor Conrad agreed. 'Come back and let's have a conference call.'

Thirty minutes later, they had managed to prise Sir David from a departmental climate change meeting.

'Dr Turnbull,' the government's Chief Scientific Adviser said, not bothering to hide his obvious irritation, 'I hope it's important.'

'Yes, Sir David, it is,' Joanna responded, ignoring his rudeness. 'I have Professor Nathanial Conrad here from New York's Columbia University. Do you remember the discussion we had in the Prime Minister's office about the volcanic activity on the Gakkel Ridge? Well, we think . . .'

'Not the Gakkel Ridge again!' Sir David snapped. 'I told you then that it's far too deep – the weight and pressure of the water suppresses the volcanic activity. Granted, some gases may escape and find their way into the atmosphere but it's a minimal contribution to the carbon dioxide produced by man's enormous . . .'

'Sir David!' Professor Conrad suddenly interrupted. 'We're not talking about global warming here. We're talking about a dangerous and massive level of seismic activity here in the Arctic Circle and, believe me, the risk it poses could completely overshadow long-term climate change. Who knows what's happening to the tectonic plates but, by God, it frightens the hell out of me.'

For a while there was silence.

'Where actually are you?' Sir David eventually asked. 'I guess you're not actually in Cambridge at the moment, are you, Joanna?'

'No, we're in Iqaluit on Baffin Island,' Joanna replied. 'We're preparing to fly to the Greenland ice cap.'

'Baffin Island?' Sir David asked incredulously. 'You do get around, Joanna. Is Cambridge funding all this?'

'Look, Sir David, there's some very unusual seismic activity up here,' Joanna persevered, ignoring the sarcasm. 'It's unusual because there's not thought to be a subduction zone up here that could cause all these earthquakes. If it was the Ring of Fire in the Pacific then I could understand it, although even there it would frighten me. The 2004 tsunami in Indonesia was caused by a 9.1 magnitude earthquake, and we've being seeing events of that magnitude along the Gakkel Ridge and under Greenland for days now.

'But what's equally odd is that, generally, the first earthquake is usually the biggest, releasing gigatons of pent-up pressure, followed by smaller aftershocks – but here, it's the reverse. For several days now the earthquakes have been building in magnitude and it's really, really scary.'

Again, there was a moment's silence.

'Hmm, Joanna,' Sir David said eventually, 'I grant you that it is somewhat out of the ordinary.'

Professor Conrad laughed.

'Out of the ordinary!' he said, shaking his head in disbelief. 'That must be one of the famous British understatements I've heard so much about.'

'But at least it's sparsely populated up there,' Sir David continued, ignoring the sarcasm. 'So if anything does happen it wouldn't be anything like on the scale of the Indonesian devastation. There might be a few Inuit villages that . . .'

'Sir David!' Joanna snapped. 'With seismic activity on this scale anything could happen. We could see a super-volcano erupting, spewing out so much ash and debris into the upper atmosphere and the jet stream that it plunges the world into darkness and lowers global temperatures by several degrees – you could forget global warming then.

'Or, if a tsunami is triggered, it could sweep across the Arctic Ocean and devastate the coastal communities of northern Canada, Alaska, Siberia and maybe even Norway and Iceland.'

'Hmm, I think that's a bit of an exaggeration, Joanna,' Sir David replied. 'You're hypothesising that an indeterminate catastrophic event might, possibly, maybe, perhaps, happen sometime in the foreseeable future. And what, exactly, do you want me to do about it?'

'Speak to the Prime Minister,' Joanna said without hesitation. 'Persuade him to convince the other leaders that they urgently need to set up monitoring stations around the Arctic Ocean and prepare for immediate evacuation of all coastal communities. I'm sure he would listen to you, Sir . . .'

Sir David laughed.

'You want me to put my reputation on the line for the half-baked hunch of a single, sorry, two scientists who have only a few seismic recordings as evidence. Well, I'm afraid I can't do . . .'

'We also have the infrared images,' Professor Conrad interrupted, 'visual sightings of . . .'

'Look, I don't care,' Sir David snapped angrily, 'the Prime Minister's already left for the G20 Summit in Iceland and I've got a global warming symposium to prepare for. Goodbye.'

The phone went dead and Joanna and Professor Conrad looked at each other in disbelief.

'Don't worry, Joanna,' he said, 'the guy's a jerk. But, I must admit – I forgot that the G20 Summit is in Iceland. In retrospect, that may not be the best place right at this . . .'

Suddenly, Dan Wood, their technician and radio operator, came rushing into the room.

'I've just heard,' he gasped, 'a huge tidal wave is sweeping down Baffin Bay between Baffin Island and Greenland and it could hit Iqaluit in an hour. For Christ's sake,' he shouted, beginning to panic, 'we have to get up to higher ground. Come on!'

North Pole

'There she is!' the young second lieutenant Yuri Dorensko shouted excitedly, pointing into the murky twilight gloom.

He had done a brilliant job – his young eyes, powerful binoculars and long hours of vigilance on the bridge had helped them to find a tiny black speck in a vast black ocean.

It should have been easier. Unexpectedly, their target had moved from its last known position and it was so low in the water that radar had failed to detect it. And they had expected it to be trapped in the ice but, strangely, the ice had vanished.

After steaming from Arkhangelsk five days previously, the *Smolensk*, the newest and largest icebreaker in the Russian navy, had spent three days searching the North Pole for the disabled American submarine. It was a vital mission – to save the men before they perished. And, it was a matter of national pride – to beat the Americans, demonstrate their technical superiority and, above all, demonstrate their altruistic and humanitarian spirit.

'Notify the rescue teams and get ready to launch the boats,' Vladimir Anadyr, the captain of the *Smolensk*, ordered the first lieutenant. 'And see if you can raise the USS *Arizona* on the radio. Yuri, you go with the rescue teams. But be careful – who knows what information the Americans are keeping to themselves.'

As he scanned the submarine with his own binoculars as it lay floodlit by the ship's searchlights, the damage that it had suffered in its collision with the ice became immediately apparent. Bow down and stern in the air indicated flooded forward compartments and the conning tower had taken a hit, losing its radio antennae and air snorkel.

His ship – vast, nuclear-powered and specifically designed for icebreaking, salvage and rescue – was easily capable of the task. But still Captain Anadyr was worried. They had already seen strange, massive geysers spouting from the sea like some mythical monsters and they had given these a wide berth. And, just as bizarrely, all the ice had vanished. In all his years, he had never seen anything like it before.

But what was more worrying were the readings from the depth sounder. It should have been a good three kilometres to the seabed here but instead it showed no more than a kilometre. Either his equipment was malfunctioning, which was highly unlikely given that his ship was the most advanced vessel in the Russian navy, or else, God forbid, the Arctic Ocean was somehow draining away. He shivered. Let's hope the Russian technicians and engineers who built the equipment had got it wrong, he thought.

For the thirty-four survivors and one would-be rescuer, life on board the USS *Arizona* had been tense and unpleasant. Although the nuclear plant was still operational, its power had been restricted for safety reasons. Thankfully, there was sufficient oxygen but the air was becoming hot and fetid. But far worse had been the uncertainty and the long and tense wait. It had been five days now since the accident and the terrible deaths of one hundred and eighteen of their crewmates, including their commander, Commander John Clayton. Whatever was out there, it was a deadly, silent killer and they dared not open the hatches again for fear of allowing it to creep into their sanctuary.

But they were getting desperate. Rescue was taking forever. Although they had rigged up a temporary radio antenna using their emergency breathing apparatus and now knew that rescue was on its way, for Captain Crowder it was even more frustrating. He couldn't understand why a rescue team from the *Polar Explorer* hadn't arrived – after all, he'd been gone for three days now. What were they doing?

'Captain Crowder,' Lieutenant Bradshaw, the acting commander said quietly, ensuring the other men were out of earshot, 'we've just received a message from a Russian icebreaker. They say they are close by and are sending a rescue team over to us.'

'A Russian icebreaker – that's excellent news,' Captain Crowder replied. 'We've got both the American and Russian cavalries coming to our aid. We'll soon be out of here. Can you ask them what the *Polar Explorer*'s doing?'

'Captain, you don't understand,' Lieutenant Bradshaw hissed. 'This is the world's most advanced nuclear submarine, worth three billion dollars. Under international maritime laws they'll be able to claim salvage. As acting commander of this vessel it is my duty to prevent unauthorised access and unwarranted intrusion by foreign countries.'

Captain Crowder's jaw dropped. He was a seasoned ship's captain and yet never had he heard such nationalistic, old-fashioned Cold War paranoia. Admittedly, the Russians probably could claim international salvage rights but he very much doubted that they would. And, after all, technically, it was the British who had found the submarine first.

'If they try to board,' Lieutenant Bradshaw growled, 'I'm going to flood the stern ballast tanks and drop a few metres below the surface.'

'What!' Captain Crowder shouted. 'That's crazy – are you mad? I'm not a submariner but what if you lose buoyancy and we sink like a stone? With the bow already flooded it's too risky – you could kill the rest of the crew. Look, all you've got to do is tell the Russians to hold off for . . .'

Suddenly, there was a loud hammering on the side of the hull and it startled the captain. Before he could say another word, Lieutenant Bradshaw had jumped up and quickly stalked off.

Only eighty-five kilometres separated America from Russia. Had it not been for the Bering Strait, separating the Arctic Ocean from the Bering Sea, the desolate and frozen lands of Alaska would have touched the equally desolate and frozen lands of Siberia. And, in the midst of most winters, a bridge of ice often formed its own entente cordiale.

Little more than fifty metres deep, treacherous currents swing back and forth through the Bering Strait, driven by the daily tidal rhythm, and sudden terrible storms could erupt, sweeping down like screaming banshees from the North Pole. But for the huge American naval icebreaker USS *Northern Star* and its accompanying giant salvage ship, such currents and wild waters should have been inconsequential to the powerful diesel engines and reinforced hulls. But already four days out from Anchorage and they were still struggling to break into the Arctic Ocean.

'This is crazy,' Lawrence Jacksonville, the captain of the *Northern Star*, growled. 'The current should be no more than five knots and it's running at twenty-five knots and strangely there's no ice. And it's not ebbing and flowing as it should do – it's simply pouring out of the Arctic Ocean. It's like we're trying to go uphill!'

Major Brock, the muscular commander of the small marine unit attached to the *Northern Star*, nodded. He appreciated the captain's frustration – they should have already reached the damaged submarine and even now be towing it back to base.

Suddenly, the radio operator came over the loudspeaker.

'Captain, we've just received a message from the USS *Arizona*,' he reported.

'Let's hear it,' the captain replied.

Over the loudspeaker, a faint, crackly and breathless voice sounded.

'. . . They're trying to board,' the voice said. 'I'm going to dive to throw them off . . . Imperative that you get here soonest . . . Don't want the sub to fall into . . .' Suddenly, a klaxon sounded on the submarine and the breathless voice was gone.

Captain Jacksonville looked at the major.

'What the hell?' he growled. 'Who's trying to board?'

'Must be the Russians,' the major growled back. 'But at least it's a rescue – it's more than we can do.'

The captain flicked the intercom.

'Sparks,' he said quickly, 'tell the *Arizona* to abort the dive. I repeat, abort the dive. It could be days before we get there.'

But it wasn't days – it was never.

Arctic Ocean

For millions of years the seabed lying three kilometres below the surface of the Arctic Ocean had remained largely unknown and unexplored. Only recently had its topography been mapped and its surface explored by the occasional remote-controlled deep-sea submersible, sent down to the stygian depths of freezing temperatures and enormous pressures. Black smoky fumaroles and strange blind creatures inhabited this alien world, disturbed only by the occasional whale carcass drifting down or by rising magma along the Mid-Atlantic and Gakkel Ridges.

But below this relatively young fragile layer of oceanic crust, only twenty kilometres thick, the huge slab of ancient crust, returning over aeons from the centre of the Earth, pushed inexorably upwards, lifting and cracking the sea floor.

As the seabed bulged upwards, the icy waters of the Arctic Ocean, almost enclosed in a bowl bordered by the landmasses of Canada, Russia, Alaska and Greenland, poured out, draining southward through the Bering Strait, Baffin Bay and the Norwegian Sea. Trillions of gallons a minute flowed south and, in the narrow straits of Baffin Bay, so much water tried to pour through that tidal bores were created. But in the Atlantic, the rising sea levels were largely unseen – there were no monster waves rearing up on the beaches and surging inland. Instead, the frigid Arctic water sank beneath the warmer Atlantic water and it would only be at high tide that the danger would reveal itself. With trillions of cubic kilometres of Arctic Ocean flowing south, and with high tides falling on a dreary winter's evening, coastal communities were blissfully unaware that disaster was approaching.

But as the massive slab of ancient tectonic plate sought to muscle its way to the surface and to obliterate the Arctic Ocean, it held another, far more frightening and devastating surprise. A few metres of coastal flooding was nothing compared to the cata-clysmic disaster that was about to befall mankind.

Iqaluit, Baffin Bay, Canada

Dan Wood had been right to panic. As they raced out of the airport building they could clearly hear a deep and distant rumble heading their way.

'I've heard that before,' Professor Conrad shouted. 'It sounds like the tidal bores I heard in the Ganges and the Amazon. We have to get to higher ground.'

Iqaluit had been built on a small plain surrounded by hills and mountains and was a sprawling community connected by dirt roads and with virtually no public transport. Many locals stood around listening to the strange distant noise; their hardy Inuit culture and upbringing made them resist the urge to panic. A few more inquisitive souls jumped into four-wheel-drive trucks and headed for the coastal track to get a better view of what was coming.

'I heard on the radio that Pangnirtung on the east coast has been wiped out,' Dan Wood said. 'Apparently, a huge tidal wave swept up Cumberland Sound. A thousand people lived there.'

'Iqaluit could be next,' Joanna said, scanning around for high ground or some transport they could use. 'If it comes shooting up Frobisher Bay, it could be here in an hour.'

'Come on then!' Professor Conrad shouted, beginning to sprint to the airport hangar. 'Only one thing for it . . .'

As they ran towards the hangar, Joanna could see through the partly open door that the rest of their team were carefully loading boxes of equipment into the chartered Cessna, oblivious of the impending doom.

'Where's the pilot?' Professor Conrad shouted.

'He's working,' one of the team replied. 'He's also got a job as a taxi driver – he's got one of those big four-wheel-drive trucks.'

Professor Conrad cursed.

'Dan, try to get him on the radio,' he ordered. 'And everyone else, listen up,' he growled. 'There's a tidal wave heading our way and we need to be airborne as soon as possible. Let's get the hangar doors fully open and get the rest of the boxes loaded. Does anyone know if it's been refuelled?'

Outside, Joanna tried to listen as Dan tried to get hold of the pilot, but she couldn't freeze out the terrifying rumble of sound that was growing louder by the minute. She stared down the runway and out into Frobisher Bay, expecting any moment to see a white wall of water surging towards them. Bizarrely, she remembered that she had left all the seismometers at the end of the runway and that, without them, any scientific work they did would be a waste of time. Without thinking, she began to sprint down the runway.

'Joanna!' Professor Conrad shouted, beginning to trot after her. 'What are you doing? Come back!'

But Joanna ignored him and sprinted even faster. The seismometers were at the end of the kilometre-long runway and she reckoned she could get there, disconnect them all and get back to the hangar in about twenty minutes.

'Professor!' Dan suddenly shouted after him. 'I managed to get through to the pilot and he's on his way.'

'Thank God!' the Professor said, watching Joanna's shrinking form and slowly shaking his head.

'But there's one other thing,' Dan added. 'He's bringing his family.'

'He's bringing his . . .' Professor Conrad started to explode, before realising that it was the natural thing to do and he could neither blame nor stop him. 'Right, get the plane unloaded,' he shouted at his crew. 'Get all the boxes and crates back out again – we've got some more passengers.'

Twenty long and desperate minutes later, a large Toyota Landcruiser screeched to a halt beside the hangar and from its cavernous interior the pilot, seven members of his family, two pet dogs and suitcases full of luggage fell out.

'Jesus!' Professor Conrad cursed. 'That's some family.'

The pilot shepherded his flock onto the Cessna and Professor Conrad looked at the little plane and slowly shook his head.

'What's the carrying capacity?' he asked the pilot as the pilot pushed the two large husky dogs into the cabin.

The pilot shrugged.

'Not really sure,' he said. 'It's a Cessna 208 Caravan and, although it's only a single-engine turboprop, it's meant to carry nine passengers and one crew.'

Professor Conrad did a quick computation.

'But there are eight of you, six of us, two dogs and your entire luggage.'

The pilot shrugged again and climbed into the cockpit.

'Shouldn't be a problem,' he shouted through the cockpit window, 'we've only got about half a tank of fuel so that'll save some weight.'

Professor Conrad and Dan Wood looked at each other and shrugged – what else could they do?

As the pilot started the engine and did a cursory check of the systems, the research team climbed aboard and Professor Conrad pointed down the runway to where Joanna was struggling to carry the seismometers.

The pilot shrugged.

'OK,' he said. 'The prevailing wind is from the north so we need to taxi down there anyway so that we can take off into the wind. Especially,' he added unnecessarily, 'as we're so overweight.'

As the Cessna manoeuvred out of the hangar and began to taxi down the runway, something in the distance caught their attention. Frobisher Bay was a 300-kilometre-long fjord, tapering from one hundred kilometres wide at the southern end to about ten kilometres at the northern end, near Iqaluit. On the horizon, in the gloomy twilight world of late afternoon, a silvery white line appeared and even at that distance they could tell that it was huge.

Joanna, struggling to carry a dozen heavy seismometers and

cables, stopped momentarily to catch her breath and, with a feeling of dread, looked behind her. The deep rumble of fast-moving turbulent water was closing in fast. As a geologist, she knew that it couldn't be a tsunami as the fjord was too deep and, as Professor Conrad had said, it sounded more like a tidal bore. She had only ever seen the River Severn bore but that one only rose to a couple of metres high and was often ridden by intrepid surfers – she knew that tidal bores could be much, much bigger. In China, the Qiantang tidal bore could often be heard two hours before it arrived and that was said to be up to twelve metres high and to travel for hundreds of kilometres at fifty kilometres an hour. If this tidal bore was on that scale then Iqaluit was doomed.

'Come on!' Professor Conrad frantically shouted out of the cockpit window, as much to Joanna as to the pilot. 'We don't have long.'

When the Cessna reached Joanna, Dan Wood grabbed the seismometers and threw them into the cabin. Without stopping, the pilot veered the plane around and began accelerating.

'Jump in!' Dan screamed, as Joanna raced beside the open doorway, but she was exhausted and beginning to slow.

As Dan grabbed her arm he caught sight of a monstrous wall of water, forty metres high and stretching the whole width of the bay. Even over the roar of the Cessna's engine he could hear the deep, powerful rumble as ice and boulders smashed along the fjord walls or churned in the turbulent water.

'Jump!' he shouted again.

With her last reserves of energy she launched herself at the doorway and he managed to grab an arm and yank her inside.

'Let's go!' Professor Conrad shouted unnecessarily as the pilot was already accelerating as hard as he could.

The little Cessna raced down the runway, its single engine roaring with maximum power, and behind it the tidal wave smashed into Iqaluit's coastline and shot a hundred metres into the air with a tremendous boom and an ear-shattering shockwave.

'We're too heavy!' the pilot suddenly shouted. 'We're not going to make it!'

Professor Conrad jumped out of his seat, scrambled into the cabin and began flinging suitcases, bags and boxes out through the open doorway. Some of the pilot's family tried to protest but the scientist's team joined in and any unnecessary junk was unceremoniously discarded. Dan grabbed the seismometers and, apologising to Joanna, tossed them through the doorway.

As the Cessna sped along the runway, back towards the hangar and the airport buildings, the icy waters of Frobisher Bay surged into Iqaluit and raced up the runway after them. Joanna, gasping for breath and staring out of the window, saw a couple of men leave the airport building and desperately race towards the abandoned Toyota Land Cruiser. After what seemed like an eternity, the little plane's wheels eventually left the tarmac and the pilot immediately retracted them and pulled back the controls as hard as he could to climb as fast as he could.

When Joanna looked down she saw the giant boiling maelstrom surge across the airport, smashing into the buildings and hangar, engulfing the speeding Land Cruiser and surging across Baffin Island's largest community.

In a matter of seconds, several thousand people perished.

Reykjavik, Iceland

Unfortunately, only Inspector Cassidy and the Metropolitan Police's chief negotiator had known that the two terrorist hijackers of the Boeing 777 from Islamabad had demanded that the plane be flown to Iceland. And they had been blown to smithereens or covered in deadly sarin mist. Inspector Cassidy hadn't had time to tell Superintendent Jamie McDougall so he had been unable to brief the Prime Minister on the true motives of the two bombers and they could only continue to assume that London was the target of some deadly and devious terrorist plot.

As the Prime Minister looked out of the window of the chartered British Airways Boeing 747, he watched fascinated at the necklaces of red and white lights that clearly showed the main roads of the Icelandic capital, delineating its city centre and residential areas. Normally, when flying into a city at night, ribbons of lights left the central maze and headed off like the rays of a spiders web into the countryside to other towns and cities. But here in Iceland, Reykjavik stood alone, surrounded by the black emptiness that was the desolate volcanic plain and mountains.

It was a relief to be landing. It had been a short journey, but a busy one. He had spent the whole trip discussing the agenda for tomorrow's G20 Summit. For him, the global issues of finance, terrorism and climate change were the most important, and, in terms of immediacy, international terrorism had risen to the top. What appeared to be unfolding in London was a terrifying new development and clear evidence of the depths of depravity that these desperate people would sink to. Surgically implanting bombs and nerve gas into naive and impressionable young men was a barbaric and callous act and, in his mind, the perpetrators were no better than murderers and criminals. He refused to call them even 'fundamentalists'– surely, no religion could be that cruel and filled with such bitter and twisted hatred. But then, he thought sadly, Catholicism and Protestantism had hardly been angels of humanitarian compassion and understanding through Europe's long and bloody history.

While the British Prime Minister mused on religious intolerance, down below Reykjavik's chief of police, Einar Sigmundsen, walked arm in arm with Frida Jonsson. The previous evening she had cooked him a delicious meal and he had promised to reciprocate by treating her to the newly opened Pasta Roma, a new and cosy Italian restaurant, ideal for relaxed and intimate evenings.

Although not a particularly romantic person, the police chief knew he couldn't go far wrong with a pleasant stroll along the marina on the way to the restaurant. The problem was there seemed to be a high tide – an exceptionally high tide. He was anything but a mariner but even he could see that something wasn't quite right. The promenade, normally a delightful floodlit walk from which one could look down on all the fishing boats and leisure cruisers, was almost awash, and they had to dodge wavelets lapping over the edge. It was a bizarre sight with boats appearing to be almost sailing onto the promenade and road, towering over Einar Sigmundsen and his companion.

'Look!' Frida suddenly said. 'Isn't that a boat under the water?'

The police chief peered into the dark murky water and, sure enough, the pale ghostly shape of a small cruiser could be seen a metre below the surface.

'That's odd,' he said. 'It must have sprung a leak. Sorry, Frida, I'll have to report it to the harbour office so they can get someone down here to investigate.'

Later, after a huge meal of vegetable pasta for Frida and a seafood pasta dish for Einar and two bottles of Frascati, conversation flowed easily and Einar Sigmundsen's interest in Frida began to evolve from pure lust to a real romantic attachment. And when he held her hand and she didn't flinch or even attempt to remove it, he began to believe that she felt the same way. For Sigmundsen, at forty-seven, this would be a first.

'Frida,' he said softly, his bleary eyes misting over with emotion, 'you are without doubt a vision of pure loveliness. You are the most beautiful woman I have ever met and I want to shower you with love and attention, gifts and treats.'

Frida beamed with pleasure and, bending over the table and thereby enhancing and displaying her curvaceous charms, she planted a succulent kiss on his cheek.

'You are such a gentleman, Einar,' she cooed. 'You obviously know how to please and look after a girl. I'd love to have lunch with you at the Hotel Aurora Borealis – I've never been there and I've heard it's absolutely sumptuous and the food is out of this world. What about tomorrow?'

'Er . . . ah,' the chief of police stammered, 'the G20 Summit meeting is at the Hotel Aurora Borealis for the next few days. You've got the American President coming, the British Prime Minister, the German Chancellor, the . . .'

'Oh, Einar,' Frida pleaded, her big brown eyes staring lovingly into his and her ample bosom heaving in her low-cut dress, 'couldn't you just sneak me in?'

'I'm sorry, Frida,' Einar said, 'but all the restaurants are closed or out of . . .'

Suddenly, the chief of police felt a hand grasp his leg and gently it began to caress the inside of his thigh. He held his breath, his heart racing and his loins beginning to stir.

'Couldn't you find a room?' she pleaded. 'Just a little room – a little bedroom? We could have lunch in there, with champagne and chocolates and . . . and . . .' She tailed off her sentence, looking deeply and meaningfully into his eyes and caressing his thigh even more firmly.

Einar Sigmundsen swallowed. This was the most exciting offer from a woman, indeed, the only offer he had ever had from a woman, in his entire life.

'Well, er,' he began, 'I probably could get access to a room. I'm sure I could. It would be wonderful to . . .'

Suddenly, his mobile phone rang.

'Chief,' one of his men said, 'I'm down at the marina with the harbour master. You won't believe this but there are several boats beneath the water. The harbour master thinks that they didn't have enough slack on their mooring lines and have tipped over and sunk as the tide came in. But get this – the tide is almost five metres higher than it should be and it's still rising. It's over the promenade now and lapping onto the main road.'

Einar Sigmundsen frowned – that was weird. And it was the last thing he needed during a very romantic dinner and on the eve of the G20 Summit.

'OK,' he said reluctantly, resigned to his fate, 'I'm on my way down.'

Blackpool, England

It was a terrible evening but at least they were on their way home. Susan didn't like driving at night at the best of times but with a force 5 westerly wind, driving rain, and speeding vans and lorries, the A584 from Preston to Blackpool had been turned into a dark and dangerous spray-drenched nightmare. Even with the windscreen wipers working overtime, it was still murky and indistinct.

But at least Bonnie had been to the vet. Susan had decided that she wouldn't be able to cope with an exuberant and randy canine teenager and the poor dog had accordingly been neutered. Now still drowsy he was laid out flat in the back seat, snoring loudly and oblivious to the wild night outside. Lucy, sitting in the front seat, was navigating, despite the fact that it was more or less the same road all the way home.

When the A584 left the dual carriageway and veered left towards the coast and Lytham, the traffic thinned and Susan breathed a sigh of relief. Once through Lytham they had only another five kilometres to go.

But ahead, as the road left Lytham and ran along the coastal dunes, something very strange had happened. For about thirty metres the road dipped and here it was usually only about two metres above the high tide level. But not tonight – tonight, it was more than half a metre *below* high tide.

In the gloom and driving horizontal rain, Susan didn't see it until the very last moment. Frantically, she braked but the car ploughed into the water, swerving to one side and stalling. Lucy screamed and Bonnie looked up and began whimpering. As the headlights dimmed and then went out, they were plunged into pitch blackness and icy-cold sea water began to seep into the foot wells and waves began crashing against the window.

Lucy screamed again.

'Don't worry, darling,' Susan said, as positively and as calmly as she could. 'We'll soon be out of here.'

But as she fumbled for her phone to dial 999, the car began to move. The A584 had been built on a raised embankment and on the landward side the encroaching sea had smashed part of the retaining wall and the road fell away, two metres to a marshy RSPB nature reserve. Sea water poured like a river across the road and down the embankment, dragging the car with it.

'Quickly,' Susan shouted, 'undo you're seat belt. We've got to get out of here.'

'Mummy!' Lucy cried out, terrified and fumbling with her seat belt.

Frantically, Susan managed to undo her and Lucy's seatbelts, but suddenly the car lurched sideways, span round and was dragged through the gap in the wall and down the embankment. Pushed by a torrent of water it sank into the flooded field and flipped over onto its roof. Immediately, they were submerged in the black and icy water and Susan gasped with the shock.

Fighting back the rising panic that threatened to overwhelm her she fumbled for the door handle and managed to yank it open. As the car was swept upside down across the field, with lungs bursting, she managed to grab Lucy's hand and drag her clear and to the surface. Coughing and spluttering, they drifted with the current until its strength eased and they could finally clamber on to higher ground.

Exhausted and shivering wildly, Susan hugged her daughter and thanked God that they had survived. But tears rolled down her face as she realised poor, innocent Bonnie was still trapped in the car. If only she had decided not to have him neutered – he would still be alive. And now she had lost her husband, their loving family pet and they were lost in the middle of nowhere, drenched, freezing cold and at the beginning of a long and cold winter's night. What more could possibly go wrong?

Meteorological Office, London

In his smart black dinner jacket and bowtie, Sir David Appleby was an incongruous addition to the casually dressed scientists at the UK's foremost weather forecasting centre. And his angry scowl didn't help either. As guest speaker at the Institute of Directors annual dinner in Mayfair, he had been looking forward to the prestigious event and an opportunity to introduce to the business world his idea of a new carbon footprint credits system. But, instead, he had been called urgently to the Meteorological Office.

'. . . It's all very well, but I can't see anything unusual,' he was saying, as he looked at the vast wall-mounted screen showing the weather systems in the northern hemisphere. 'It's completely normal for this time of year. There are a few depressions over the western Atlantic and one over the Norwegian Sea but they're not very deep and not abnormally large. There could be some squally rain over the UK and there could be some snow over central Europe but, hey, this is winter after all.'

George Higginbottom, the bluff, scruffy Lancashire chief meteorologist, smiled.

'Exactly,' he said simply.

Sir David Appleby frowned and for a fraction of a second wondered if this was some not very elaborate and not very funny prank.

'Now,' George Higginbottom continued, 'look at the next chart. This shows the tide times and heights around the UK at this time of year. As you know, tomorrow is the winter solstice and a full moon and, although it is not a spring tide, the tides will be quite high.'

'Yes, yes, go on,' Sir David said testily, looking at his watch. 'As global warming and rising sea levels are very close to my heart, I obviously already know all this. What exactly are you getting at?'

The meteorologist nodded to one of his assistants and another chart appeared on screen.

'This is a compilation of data from marine buoys around the UK and it shows the actual heights of the tides at the moment, with high tide around about now. If we superimpose the previous chart, you will see something rather odd.'

The government's Chief Scientific Adviser looked at the superimposed charts and slowly his bored and irritated expression faded away.

'That can't be right,' he said eventually, frowning. 'It appears to be showing actual tides in Scotland three metres higher than it should and, as you move down towards the south coast, it is still one metre above normal. It can't be a storm surge – there are no storms. Is your computer model correct?'

George Higginbottom laughed.

'I knew you'd say that,' he replied, 'but we've double-checked everything. This is real – there's an unprecedented rise in sea levels coming down from the north and no one knows why. Have a look at some of the local television news channels.'

The screen split into several regional programmes and showed adventurous news presenters standing in waders on submerged seaside promenades or sitting in inflatable dinghies, drifting down the high street.

'. . . Is without doubt a heart-rending story of disaster for the poor owners of these properties . . .' the presenter in Lowestoft was saying as his crew filmed tearful housewives desperately trying to salvage precious belongings from the encroaching flood and stoic pensioners being helped into inflatable dinghies. '. . . Although low lying, never before has this residential area been flooded by the sea. Could it be a stark warning for the rest of us and confirmation that man-made global warming really is causing the sea levels to rise? But where were the warnings from the government's Environment Agency? Where were . . .'

The meteorologist turned the sound down and looked at Sir David Appleby.

'Well?' he asked simply.

Sir David Appleby frowned.

'Well, what?' he said.

'You're the expert on global warming,' the meteorologist snapped. 'Explain this.'

The government's Chief Scientific Adviser shook his head.

'It can't be global warming,' he replied, 'it's too sudden. It will be twenty or thirty years before we see anything like this increase in sea levels. It's, er . . . I mean, er . . . I just don't know . . .'

'Well, you're the UK government's Chief Scientific Adviser,' George Higginbottom snapped, 'you'd better work it out soon. The next high tide is due in the morning and the tide charts show that it'll be almost half a metre higher than tonight's tide. You urgently need to call a national flood alert.'

Sir David Appleby looked at the meteorologist and swallowed hard. He had made his career out of dire predictions of future rising sea levels and now, for whatever reason, it had happened. For the first time in his life, he felt out of his depth.

New York City, USA

Jacob was physically and mentally exhausted. It had been a long journey to and from Prudence Island and it had been a short, but emotionally draining, farewell with his son. He didn't blame Joseph – in theory, they could see more of each other before the fateful day when the Grim Reaper called, but if Joseph needed to hide from the Apocalypse then who was Jacob to say otherwise. He could hardly deny the Second Coming of the Messiah any more than he could deny the First Coming of his own Grim Reaper.

Just as the train pulled into Grand Central Station in the early evening and he prepared to dismount, his mobile phone rang.

'Jacob, it's Gino Spinelli,' his deputy at the Coastal Defence Department at City Hall said breathlessly. 'I know it's late, but you'd better get down here right away. Where are you?'

Jacob looked at his watch and cursed – he had been planning to visit Martha before going home and buying a Chinese take-away on the way.

'I'm at Grand Central Station,' he replied. 'I can jump into a taxi. Are you at the office?'

'No, I'm at West Street, Lower Manhattan – by the Holland Tunnel,' his deputy replied. 'We may have a problem.'

Twenty minutes later, when the taxi approached the wharf, something strange appeared to be happening – the road disappeared and Gino Spinelli appeared to be standing up to his knees in the murky waters of the Hudson River.

'What the . . .' Jacob gasped, as he stepped out of the taxi.

Much of West Street was flooded by twenty to thirty centimetres of water but the West Street Service Road beneath it was completely submerged. Gentle wavelets lapped across West Street and trucks and four-wheel-drive cars ploughed through it, giving the surreal impression they were actually driving on the Hudson River.

'It can't be global warming,' Jacob said, shaking his head in disbelief. 'Is it a storm surge? But if so . . . from where?'

Gino Spinelli shook his head.

'There's not even a category 1 hurricane anywhere offshore. In fact, the hurricane season has finished for this year. It might have something to do with those strange events up in the Arctic, I suppose . . . but that's so far away. We're not quite at category 1 flooding but it's close. High tide was thirteen minutes ago so thankfully it's begun to recede.'

Jacob sighed with relief.

'Thank God for that! Otherwise we would have had to instigate the Emergency Management Flood Evacuation Plan. I would hate to do that and then nothing happened. Mobilising thirty thousand city employees to organise the evacuation of millions of residents would be a nightmare. And . . . especially at Christmas time.'

But his deputy wasn't looking quite so relieved.

'There's another high tide tomorrow morning,' he said grimly, 'just as the rush hour starts. And it's almost a metre higher than this one. If that happens, there could be widespread flooding – most of Manhattan is only two metres above sea level. And, if the Holland Tunnel floods then . . .'

Suddenly, Jacob's mobile phone rang. He looked at the number and recognised Martha's mobile phone.

'Hello, Mother,' he said. 'I'm sorry for being so late but . . .'

'Shut up and listen,' a woman's voice growled. 'We've got your mother and unless you cooperate you won't see her again.'

'Martha? You've got my mother?' Jacob mumbled, shocked and dumbstruck. 'Who are you?'

'Listen carefully,' the woman's voice growled again, 'you've got thirty seconds to talk to her. Just to prove that it is her and that we mean business.'

'Martha?'

'Jacob? Is that you?' a tired and frail old voice said. 'I don't know what they want but I'm scared and cold and . . .'

'Where are you, Mother? What have they done to you?'

'They've tied me up in a bath and filled it with some red powder. But it's not in a bathroom, it's . . .'

'Enough!' the woman's voice growled, snatching the phone away. 'Your dear old mother might be cold now but, unless you cooperate, she's going to get much warmer.' Suddenly, there was an insane cackling laugh and two or three male voices joined in. 'We've filled the bath with thermite so, if the police get anywhere near, well . . . Martha will be twenty-five hundred degrees Celsius warmer. There won't be so much as a charcoaled bone left.'

Jacob sank to the floor. It was too much of a shock to bear. His mother, his dear old mother – harmless, innocent and kind – why? She had never hurt so much as a fly in all her life.

'Why?' he mumbled. 'What do you want with Martha? If it's money you want, you can have all I've got. It's not much, but I'll sell everything that . . .'

'Shut up, you old fool!' the hard female voice snapped. 'And listen. We don't want your money – we want you.'

'Me?' Jacob mumbled confused.

'Yes, you,' the harsh voice said. 'And you're going to have a new mother, a new Martha Goldstein. Hello, Son,' she said, bursting into a cackling laugh again. '*I'm* your new mother.'

Jacob looked at Gino Spinelli, his eyes wide and uncomprehending, his mind numb. Gino frowned, equally confused by his boss's behaviour.

'Tomorrow, at 2.15 p.m.' she continued, 'you are to meet me at the ferry terminal at Battery Park, Manhattan. I'll be a little old lady with a walking stick and a fur coat over a red-and-yellow flowery dress. You'll be watched, so if there's any funny business, any unusual police presence, then Martha will roast like a Thanksgiving turkey. But make sure you've got your Mayoral Office badge – you're treating your old mum to a special trip up the Statue of Liberty.'

'The Statue of Liberty?' Jacob mumbled, more confused. This was weird, he thought – he had already promised to take Martha there as a special treat to commemorate the sixty-sixth year of her arriving in the land of freedom and opportunity. Was he going mad?

'But why do you want to do that . . . ?'

But the phone had already gone dead and, although he dialled the number, it had been switched off.

'Jacob?' Gino asked, concerned and confused and still ankle deep in water. 'Are you all right? What about the Emergency Flood Management Plan? Do we instigate it?'

But, although Jacob looked at his deputy, his eyes were moist and his expression was blank. Inside, there was a terrible and very lonely hollow. For him, Armageddon had come early.

Atlantic Ocean, three hundred kilometres north-east of New York

Shrouded in fog, the giant iceberg was an achingly cold, damp and gloomy place. It was as cheerless and uninviting as a grave-yard and during the murky sunless day Craig had drifted in and out of consciousness, barely registering the dull uniformity. Even cocooned in the Inuit furs inside the life raft, he couldn't escape the frigid fingers of raw, numbing cold that seeped relentlessly from the glacial ice and, though at first he had tried to keep moving and keep the circulation flowing, his feet and legs had turned to stone.

But, now that evening had arrived, his mind had sought a better place and a better time. He was back in the warm glow of a sunny summer's evening and the snug cosiness of his family – he was in the garden watching his daughter play.

Lucy Macintyre was happy. What more could a six-year-old want? She would soon be starting the summer holidays and they had just moved home from dull and wet old Birmingham to exciting and sunny Lytham St Anne's – right next to the sea and just down the road from Blackpool. Blackpool! She had always wanted to go to Blackpool and now the beach, the amusements, the illuminations, the Tower – everything was just on their doorstep!

And, she had Bonnie, the best ever present from her dad.

'Now, don't be so naughty or I'll stop your pocket money,' she scolded Bonnie, her three-month-old cream-coloured Labrador puppy named after the Scottish hero Bonnie Prince Charlie, who was sitting quietly watching a worm squirming on the grass and who clearly had no idea what pocket money was.

'I'm fed up of having to run around after you,' she continued, wagging an admonishing finger, 'you horrid little child. You're always getting dirty and leaving all your things lying around. No wonder I'm worn down to the bone, having to clean and wash and shop and cook and . . .'

'Ruff!' Bonnie agreed, wagging his little puppy tail and gazing with soft brown eyes at the wriggling worm.

Lucy pushed her long curly hair out of her eyes and gazed wistfully across the garden towards the sea. If only her father didn't have to go away all the time. Why couldn't they have oil rigs right next to Blackpool instead of that horrible place across the sea? At least, then he could commute every day and she and mum would see a lot more of him and he could play in the garden with her and Bonnie every evening.

She sighed. She was bored playing mummy and, besides, it was hard work pretending to be annoyed all the time.

'Ruff!' Bonnie agreed again, before sniffing the worm and slurping it into his mouth.

'Yuk!' Lucy groaned, pulling a disgusted face and shaking her head. 'That's gross!'

Craig chuckled. He loved watching them play together and grow up to . . .

Suddenly, his delirium deserted him and he woke up with a start – a shooting pain had erupted from his feet. He groaned – partly from the pain and partly from the knowledge that frost-bite and perhaps gangrene had taken hold. And then he began to cry – he would no longer experience the joy of watching his daughter and her puppy play again and watching them grow up together. And his wife would be without a husband and his daughter would be without a father. Slowly, tears ran down his cheeks and slowly they froze in the chill and desolate air.

Chapter 9

21 December 2012
5.15 a.m. – Reykjavik, Iceland

'Matthew, just in time for black coffee, hash browns and eggs sunny side up,' the American President said, greeting the British Prime Minister warmly. 'A perfect way to start an early breakfast meeting, don't you think?'

The PM looked at his watch and then at his Chancellor, who grinned. The President was renowned for his early-morning meetings but 5.15 a.m. was still bedtime for the two British politicians and their still unshaven, haggard appearance contrasted sharply with that of the President and his aides.

'These are nice rooms,' the PM said, looking around at the luxuriously appointed top-floor suites of the Hotel Aurora Borealis.

For security reasons, and because of the size of the American contingent, the top two floors of the hotel had been allocated to the President and his staff. The British were on the next floor down, sharing with the Canadians, the French, the Germans, the United Nations and the International Monetary Fund, with the other eighteen nations and organisations sharing the next three floors. As expected, security was tight and the hotel and surroundings had become a fortress with lifts and stairwells almost becoming like border controls and overhead there was a strict no-fly zone.

'I thought we could chat before the main meetings,' the President began, joining the Prime Minister in the relaxed seating area. 'You know what it's like when these things get going – with twenty heads of state and twenty finance ministers it's more like a social get-together than a coordinated financial strategy discussion. And, as you know, everyone has their own hidden or pet agenda.'

The Prime Minister nodded. Pre-meetings had become an integral part of each G20 Summit, with a lot of posturing, persuasion, strengthening of alliances, brinksmanship and gamesmanship. In fact, he had already been invited to attend a joint German and French meeting the night before.

'As you know, the last few G20 Summits,' the President continued, 'have, by necessity, focused on reviving the global economy, stimulating growth and reforming and regulating the financial sectors. Now that we're emerging from the credit crunch and countries are beginning to see substantial recovery, we're unfortunately starting to see the return of that old bugbear, protectionism.'

The Prime Minister nodded again but said nothing. After the previous evening's meeting with the Germans and French, he could guess where this conversation was going.

'What concerns me', the President went on, 'is that the G20 is more like a G3. Obviously, you have the traditionally strong USA, the increasingly powerful and vociferous Chinese and, of course, the European Union. The problem is, is that there are four European Union member states of the G20 – France, Germany, Italy and the UK – as well as the European Union representing Spain and the Netherlands and all the smaller EU countries.'

'Yes, it's true,' the PM agreed, 'although many other countries are represented at the G20 Summit they do not have such a loud or united a voice.'

'It concerns me,' the President continued, 'that a rift is developing because certain nations in the EU are finding ways to block free trade and to restrict financial investment in foreign funds. They talk of tax transparency and tax parity but clearly it is neither of these. Matthew, if we let them get away with it, America and China will retaliate and in the process London will be destroyed as a world financial centre.'

Unfortunately, the Prime Minister was well aware of what was going on and what could be the consequences for the UK's economy. But, as a member of the EU, his options were restricted.

'Look, Matthew,' the President continued, 'I know that you Brits are very keen on green environmental issues and constantly looking for new ways for reducing carbon emissions by new renewable clean energy sources. And I know that London and the UK are at the forefront of the fight against global terrorism.'

The Prime Minister nodded his head. 'You can say that again,' he growled, 'on both counts.'

'Well,' the President said, 'in the 2009 to 2011 G20 Summits, we only spent about one percent of the four trillion dollars pledged at those meetings on those two issues. I'm sure that this year you would like to see those budgets massively increased.'

'Yes, we certainly would,' the PM agreed. 'On the issue of climate change, Sir David Appleby, my Chief Scientific Adviser, is very worried about rising sea levels and, as you say, for some reason London has become a target for global terrorism. We need an international intelligence service that collects and collates information on potential terrorist activities. At the moment, it is piecemeal and, to be honest, we don't have the resources in the UK and have to rely on your intelligence agencies.'

'And that's why,' the President continued, 'I'm going to recommend that this G20 Summit allocates two hundred billion dollars to each of those programmes and another two hundred billion dollars each at the next G20 Summit meeting.'

'That would be tremendous,' the PM agreed enthusiastically. 'But,' he added after a moment's pause, 'won't the Chinese object?'

The President chuckled.

'No, because if America and the UK join China in voting

against the EU's protectionist policies, then they'll vote for the two programmes you want.'

The Prime Minister's jaw dropped but, instead of saying something, he smiled.

5.35 a.m. – New York City, USA

'. . . So the Big Apple truly has become the city that never sleeps,' the CNN reporter was saying as he stood ankle deep in murky Hudson River water. 'Here we are, at 5.35 in the morning, and the terrifying vulnerability of our city is exposed and residents dare not sleep. No longer the pure domain of Hollywood fantasy films, here we see the dark and icy waters of the Atlantic Ocean creeping inexorably into Lower Manhattan. New York City is the New Orleans of the east coast – a vast defenceless metropolis of nine million people on the very edge of the global warming battlefield.'

Suddenly, the cameras swung round to a tired and haggard middle-aged civil servant waiting nervously beside the reporter.

'Mr Goldstein,' the reporter questioned, 'what do you say to people who accuse City Hall and the Federal Government of mismanagement and neglect? What exactly has the Coastal Defence Department and FEMA done to protect the city, its inhabitants, and its businesses?'

'Well, er, as you know,' the civil servant began uncertainly, 'the Coastal Defence Department has been very busy under the current administration and the protection of the city is paramount. Together with FEMA we have been updating the one-hundred-year-old floodplain maps and developing the emergency evacuation plan. Our civil engineers have been looking at coastal defence systems in other parts of the world, such as the dykes in the Netherlands, England's Thames Barrier, the levees in New Orleans, the . . .'

'Yes,' the presenter suddenly interrupted, 'but isn't all this too little too late?'

'Er, well, as you know,' Jacob continued uncertainly, 'coastal defence is not cheap and New York City's shoreline is almost nine kilometres long. Four of the five boroughs are on islands and you've got the entire interconnecting infrastructure to protect. Do you realise that New York City is the first American city to actually do detailed climate change planning and . . .'

'Yes, yes,' the presenter interrupted again, 'but I repeat – isn't all this too little too late?'

The civil servant swallowed hard, hopped nervously from one foot to the other and looked longingly into the distance.

'Well, maybe,' he admitted, 'but coastal defence costs billions and New York City simply doesn't have the funds. It's a Federal issue but FEMA's budget has been drastically cut back for the last decade. I'm afraid, homeland security, global terrorism and the wars in Iraq and Afghanistan have a higher priority . . .'

'So, there you have it,' the presenter suddenly interrupted, 'a damning admission of failure by one of the Mayor's senior administrators . . .'

8.40 a.m. – Ice cap, central Greenland

Olaf looked at the ropes disappearing into the swirling mist of the chasm and slowly and sadly shook his head.

'Oh, Jarvik,' he sighed, 'what have you done? Literally – physically and mentally – you have gone over the edge.'

'Olaf!' one of his team called out. 'Come and have a look at this.'

He went over to the satellite antenna that Jarvik had laboriously rigged up and looked at the control panel. The lights for receive and record were lit up and flashing but not the one for transmit. In his haste, and with his mind confused by hypothermia and paranoia, Jarvik had forgotten to turn on the send switch. He had sacrificed his life to bring these images to the public but even now, as he filmed the scenes below in the belief that the whole world was witnessing geological history in the making, nobody was watching.

'You fool!' Olaf whispered. 'You complete and utter idiot.'

Grabbing one of the laptops he connected it to the control panel, downloaded the recorded images and then pressed play. At first the video camera lights showed a blurred white mist but then, as it spun round, a shiny and slippery ice wall, cobalt blue in the halogen lights, sprang into view. For a couple of minutes nothing else happened and they began to wonder if that was all there was. But then, suddenly, the camera spun round again and a face came into focus.

'Jesus Christ!' Olaf gasped.

'Shit!' someone else swore. 'Is that Jarvik?'

A white frost-encrusted face stared manically into the camera lens through swollen and bloodshot eyes and icicles hung from a blackened and split nose. A bloody gash ran from his forehead down to his cheek and his frozen lips moved manically, mumbling incoherently and insanely.

A hand, held up to adjust the camera lens, was a gloveless, blackened claw, frozen and lifeless.

'He's lost the plot,' one of them said as the camera swung away, facing back into the mist.

Suddenly, the camera jerked as Jarvik began to abseil further down and several times it crashed into the ice wall and for several minutes they saw nothing apart from blurred mist and blurred ice and guessed that Jarvik must be almost two kilometres below them by now.

And then the swirling mist cleared and a beautiful yet frightening sight met their eyes. A vast expanse of yellow-and-orange lava bubbled and spat, swirled and boiled, casting an eerie glow beneath the steam cloud and hissing violently as it melted the ice. Molten rock, at sixteen hundred degrees Celsius raced through the landscape like a raging river, cutting a swathe through the three-kilometre-thick Greenland ice cap.

'Holy cow!' one of the men gasped. 'That's unbelievable. The crust appears to be breaking open. I think we should get the hell out of here!'

No sooner had he said that than there was a tremendous shockwave beneath them and cracks began to appear by their feet.

'Run!' one of Olaf's men shouted.

But Olaf paused for a moment, disconnected and grabbed the laptop, and then jumped onto one of the skidoos.

'Let's go!' he shouted, clasping the laptop to his chest.

Huge crevasses opened up near the ice wall and, with a battlefield sound of cannon fire, zigzagged towards them. Millions of tonnes of ice along the whole of the cliff face collapsed into the chasm.

As the skidoos accelerated away, crashing and bouncing across the ice, the crevasses chased after them. With screams of terror, first one skidoo and then a second were caught, plunging four of Olaf's men into the abyss.

'Faster!' Olaf screamed. 'Faster!'

9.10 a.m. – Reykjavik, Iceland

Patrick O'Keefe was worried. As the IT and conference suite technical manager for the last couple of years, the hotel receptionists knew him well. But the hard-nosed foreign security staff had only seen him a few times, despite the fact that he'd made every effort over the last few days to use the hotel lobby as often as possible. Indeed, he had fabricated as many reasons for chatting to the receptionists or hotel manager as he could and he hoped that as far as the foreign security staff was concerned he had now become part of the hotel furniture.

It didn't help that his prosthetic leg was hurting like hell. Mangled so badly in Helmand that the surgeons had been forced to remove all his leg apart from a stump, it had taken years for the skin and flesh to thicken and toughen to cope with the weight and rubbing of a false limb. And now Malik had filled it with several kilograms of sarin and Semtex. The breast implants had been a brilliant idea – they easily squashed into his leg – but the sheer volume of liquid was enormous and the Semtex packages and detonators were heavy and awkward.

'Morning, Patrick,' Sven Magnusson, the friendly Reykjavik police constable greeted, patting him down as part of the security search. 'It's your big day today.'

Patrick smiled, trying hard not to break into a cold sweat.

'Never been one for computer stuff myself,' the police constable continued. 'It's like a foreign language to me. I like something that I can just plug in and go. I hope you don't get your wires crossed today,' he said, chuckling, 'otherwise I don't fancy your chances of being IT manager next week.'

Patrick laughed but the damp patches beneath his jacket grew. He stepped through the metal detector and, as he and Malik had expected, nothing happened. It was the body scanner they were worried about – they weren't sure if it could pick up the plastic explosive and detonators.

But, just then, there was a screech of indignation behind him and he looked around.

A plump and very buxom middle-aged lady, wearing high heels and too short a skirt, stood with her arms crossed protectively around her chest, staring angrily at the police constable.

'If you dare to touch me again,' she growled, 'I'll thump you. I'm a lady and you can't just start fondling a lady.'

'I'm, er, sorry, Miss,' poor Sven Magnusson stammered, 'but it's part of the security procedures.'

Clearly, the security had a problem – with no female police officer available and faced with a well-endowed lady who could probably have hidden a couple of AK-47s and grenades in her brassier, they needed to eliminate her assets from their enquiries.

'Miss Frida Jonsson is with me,' a voice suddenly said.

'Er, sorry, Sir,' the constable stammered, 'that's, er, fine then.'

'No, it's not,' a large steely-eyed and American-accented man suddenly said, leaving the scanner and coming over. 'She has to be frisked.'

The constable looked at the American security man aghast.

'B-but, that's Einar Sigmundsen,' he said, 'and he's Reykjavik's chief of police.'

'And Miss Frida Jonsson is my assistant,' the chief of police growled, becoming embarrassed by the attention.

Frida looked indignant and embarrassed but, in reality, she was worried. Always and proudly a voluptuous lady, today she was even more voluptuous than normal. It had been Stephen's idea. Already she loved him and what he stood for. She had never met an undercover Greenpeace activist before and his fervent commitment to the cause, and injuries received for his beliefs, was truly a heart-warming story. Although already a vegetarian herself, his ardent belief had sent her on an emotional roller-coaster ride of soul-searching. Why should all these rich and powerful nations unnecessarily hunt down and cruelly murder the oceans' most majestic mammals? She could under-stand a few remote Inuit communities killing the odd whale or two for survival – but thousands of them, all in the name of scientific research? It was murder, cold and callous. And the G20 nations allowed the main culprits, the Japanese, to get away with it.

Well, as Stephen had said: it was time to stand up and be counted and that is why her bosoms were unusually fulsome that morning – a breast implant bag, full of whale blood, was stuffed into each brassier cup. When Steven set the hotel's fire alarms off, she was going to rush out and, in the panic, squirt whale blood over as many G20 delegates as she could. Outside the hotel Stephen and the other protesters were going to release thousands of helium balloons saying 'Whale murderers!' She was excited about being a real activist – but she was also a little scared.

'I'm sorry,' the American security agent said, 'but if she isn't searched then she can't come into the hotel.'

Einar's face reddened and he fought to control the indignation and humiliation he felt. Frida gently put a hand on his shoulder.

'Einar,' she said, 'you're the chief of police. You do it.'

Einar looked at Frida and swallowed. Not only would it save face but he was being invited to place his hands on the very objects of his desire. The American shrugged and the local police constable smirked. And, in the background, unnoticed and forgotten, an inconspicuous IT manager sidestepped the body scanner and headed for the conference suites.

The diversion had worked and Operation Armageddon was now well underway.

Despite a chill wind blowing from the north and carrying flecks of snow, a solitary figure was sitting on a bench in the gardens of Landspitali University Hospital, just down the road from Hotel Aurora Borealis. He wasn't on the phone; he wasn't reading; he wasn't smoking; and nor was he dressed for the occasion. Instead, he stared forlornly into space.

'Dr Hashim?' Gilda Nygaard asked, as she, Tukku and Nunni took Miki Nanook for a walk. 'Is that you, Dr Hashim?'

The doctor, dressed only in thin blue surgeon's trousers and short-sleeved top, didn't respond.

Gilda looked more closely at him and saw an exhausted, haggard, clearly troubled man. His lips were as blue as his clothes and his body shivered violently.

'Dr Hashim, what are you doing out here?' she asked, desperately concerned for the poor man.

'I think he's been working too hard, Mummy,' Nunni said. 'He's always trying to heal people.'

Suddenly, Dr Hashim began crying, tears rolling silently down his cheeks. But the silent tears turned to sobbing – gasping, uncontrollable weeping – and he held his head in his hands.

Carefully, Gilda sat next to him and, taking her jacket off, put it round his shoulders. Nunni, close to tears herself, gently stroked his head.

'There, there,' she murmured softly.

Suddenly, he began wailing. 'What have I done?' he cried out. 'Oh God, what have I done?'

10.05 a.m. – North Pole

In the wild waters of the Bering Straits, the crew of the USS *Northern Star* were exhausted. For days now they had been battling to punch through the torrential waters flooding out of the Arctic Ocean. But huge standing waves, fifteen metres high, threatened to spin the ship sideways and broach it in the racing turbulent waters. Twice already they had burst through giant waves and become airborne, plunging into a hole on the other side, and each time crashing with a terrifying boom back into the water.

Captain Lawrence Jacksonville peered into the wild twilight world and knew that he was close to making a decision. Already they and the accompanying salvage ship had nine men in the medical bay with suspected fractures or spinal injuries and he knew that he was risking the entire complement of both ships, three hundred and eighty men in all, trying to punch through into the Arctic Ocean. Clearly, they had gone beyond the operational limits of both ships and, any second, a momentary lack of attention or a freakish freak wave would spell disaster and plunge them all beneath the raging waters.

He punched the intercom to speak to the captain of the salvage ship.

'Toby, the *Northern Star* has got an extra five knots speed over you,' he said, 'so I'm going to give it one more effort to try to punch through. You can begin to drift safely back out of this damned maelstrom.'

But, sadly, he wasn't aware that at that very moment his decision was already too late. The titanic battle between the ancient slab of tectonic plate and the younger Eurasian plate had reached a cataclysmic breaking point. Suddenly, earthquakes releasing massive pent-up energy, way beyond the Richter scale, hit the floor of the Arctic Ocean. The bulging crust shattered and the ancient slab burst through.

Already, as the *Northern Star* reached maximum speed in the twilight gloom, racing towards them was a maelstrom of unimaginable size and ferocity. Trillions of gallons of Arctic Ocean sought to escape and in the Bering Strait there was nowhere for it to go.

Captain Jacksonville peered out of the bridge window and willed his ship forward. At their top speed of thirty knots, they had started to creep forward, the GPS showing a headway of three knots. But slowly it fell to two knots, one knot and then stationary. The captain looked at it and frowned – were they losing power or had the current picked up? But it wasn't long before he got his answer. The sea suddenly became even more frenzied and began to boil and quickly the GPS showed that they were going backwards at five knots, ten knots, fifteen knots . . .

'What's happening?' Major Brock asked frantically, totally out of his depth and uncharacteristically beginning to be afraid.

But Captain Jacksonville never had a chance to respond. The *Northern Star*, the largest American naval icebreaker, dug its stern deep into the sea and then reared up vertically before pirouetting, spinning one hundred and eighty degrees, and crashing heavily back into the sea. Now facing the other way, with its engines racing at thirty knots and the current racing at fifty knots, it charged out of control towards the huge salvage vessel.

Out of the gloom, Toby and the officers suddenly saw the *Northern Star*, in a seething maelstrom, racing towards them.

'Hard astern,' the captain shouted frantically.

But as soon as the helmsman swung the wheel round, the vessel broached and the *Northern Star* slammed into its side. At eighty knots, the reinforced bow of the icebreaker cut through the salvage ship's hull like a hot knife through butter and broke her in two. In seconds, the surging sea swept both halves beneath the surface.

On the bridge of the *Northern Star*, the captain watched in horror as their out-of-control ship sunk its sister ship and then plunged beneath the waves, diving like some demonic submarine. He knew that their time had come.

When Yuri Dorensko had banged on the submarine's hull with a large wrench he had been astonished by the response. Naively perhaps, he had expected either a joyous return hammering or else a deathly silence. He certainly had never expected the submarine to blow its ballast tanks and begin diving. Crouched on the conning tower he had had little time to react and the rescue launches had been forced to race away to prevent being overwhelmed. As icy water flooded the conning tower he had clambered over the side and dived into the sea, desperate to avoid being sucked down by the submarine's wake. By the time his crew mates had recovered him and got him back to the *Smolensk* he was shivering uncontrollably and hypothermic.

'Yuri, my little second lieutenant,' Captain Vladimir Anadyr had said, 'you are a brave and proud sailor of the Russian navy. For you, I will recommend the Imperial Red Star, the highest honour a seaman can earn.'

That was yesterday and now they had no idea where the submarine had gone. Assuming it was without power they had let the *Smolensk* drift with the tide, hoping to keep both vessels close together. They weren't sure whether a malfunction, such as leaking ballast tanks, had forced the submarine underwater or whether they had deliberately used an evasive manoeuvre. But, in any event, far more important, and stranger, things had overtaken them.

'It is an impossibility,' Captain Anadyr was saying to the first lieutenant as they both watched the sonar. 'We've stripped and double-checked the equipment and it doesn't appear to be malfunctioning. But it still shows a ridiculous reading. And now, the GPS is playing up.'

The first lieutenant nodded.

'It's bizarre, Captain,' he said frowning, 'in this part of the Arctic Ocean there are very few currents and yet the GPS shows that we are drifting south at twelve knots. And the depth, which is supposed to be three kilometres, was only one kilometre yesterday and today it's barely two hundred metres deep. Are we drifting over an unknown continental shelf or something?'

Captain Vladimir Anadyr slowly shook his head. He had no idea – none of them did. But it made him nervous – very, very nervous. If it wasn't for the submarine he would have given the order to get the hell out of there. They might be the newest and largest and most powerful nuclear icebreaker in the Russian fleet but, compared to the might of Mother Nature, they were little different from the paper boats he used to make as a child. If Poseidon so much as sneezed, they would be crumpled and sodden wreckage.

'Contact command at Arkhangelsk,' he ordered the first lieutenant, 'and tell them what our situation is. Ask them if we should continue the search for the American submarine or come home.'

He frowned and, for a moment, was deep in thought.

'And,' he added as an afterthought, 'I suggest you download the technical data to them. They won't believe us, otherwise.'

10.30 a.m. – Metropolitan Police headquarters, London, England

It had taken two days for the forensic and decontamination units to analyse and clean the wrecked Boeing 777 from Islamabad, sitting forlornly on a remote runway at Heathrow airport. There had been a huge amount of work to do – painstakingly methodical but at the same time deeply emotional. After all, three hundred and forty-one passengers, nine crew, two terrorists and two policemen had died horrible and messy deaths. But only the two terrorists, three passengers and Inspector Cassidy had died instantaneously from the initial explosion and all the rest had succumbed to sarin poisoning – a terrifying death of desperately gasping for breath, drooling, vomiting, violent spasms, loss of all bodily functions, shuddering and death. The final thirty seconds of existence ending in a frighteningly painful and undignified stinking mess.

Superintendent Jamie MacDougal put the fat depressing folder back on his desk and looked out of the window. It was a typical wet and dreary December day, a Friday and only four days before Christmas. Already, the streets and pavements were teeming with shoppers, miserably racing around for last-minute presents and adding to their burgeoning credit card debts. And, also somewhere out there were ten or more terrorists – plotting and planning carnage.

But finding them was a hopeless task. Just obtaining the backgrounds of all the passengers on the plane would take weeks and, although all police leave had been cancelled over the Christmas period, they just did not have enough manpower to investigate and prevent every major terrorist plot on the UK mainland. So, unless they had a lucky break, then the next thing the superintendent expected to hear was of another terrorist atrocity somewhere in London – and what better than a crowded shopping mall during the most important of all Christian religious festivals – Christmas Eve. And who and where was this Malik Husain? The American Secretary of State had said that Malik was on his way from Peshawar to London and that he was a UK citizen. But since leaving the army, nothing, absolutely nothing, had been found on this man, this Caucasian turned Muslim. He was a ghost, an enigma.

Suddenly, the phone rang.

'Sir, it's Bill Hoskins, head of the communications technical division,' the voice said. 'We've recovered the transcript from Alpha One's phone on the day he was negotiating with the Heathrow plane hijackers.'

'Go on,' the superintendent prompted.

'Well, he was in constant touch with Inspector Cassidy,' Bill Hoskins continued, 'relaying the progress of his negotiations with the two terrorists. It followed standard operating procedure and he had naturally asked them what their demands were. Of course, as you know they had asked for a doctor and that's when Inspector Cassidy volunteered. But they had also, apparently, asked for the plane to be refuelled and flown to, of all places, Iceland.'

'Iceland!' Superintendent Jamie MacDougal repeated. 'Why the hell would they want to go . . . Shit!' he suddenly shouted. 'That's where the G20 Summit meeting is being held. It wasn't London all along, it was . . .'

'There's one other thing,' the communication technician interrupted, 'we've analysed all the mobile phone transcripts emanating from or being sent to the plane and one stands out from all the other tearful, panicky chatter between family and friends. It was a text received from a mobile phone in Iceland and we think it went to one of the terrorists. We can't be sure because they were blown to smithereens.'

'What did it say?' the superintendent prompted impatiently.

'All it said,' Bill Hoskins continued, 'was – *Armageddon!*'

'Armageddon!' the superintendent repeated incredulously. 'Hell, they weren't planning on murdering a few civilians out shopping for Christmas. They're planning on killing the heads of state of the twenty most powerful countries from around the world! They'd plunge the world into chaos. It could be anarchy. It could be war!'

Superintendent Jamie McDougal briefly thanked the communications technical chief and slammed the phone down. Ten seconds later, he picked it up again and dialled an unlisted number for 10 Downing Street.

'Get me the Prime Minister,' he growled.

'Er, he's in Iceland,' a tentative voice said.

'I know he's in bloody Iceland,' the policeman growled through gritted teeth. 'This is a national emergency. It's a Code Red Alert of the highest, I repeat, the highest priority. Now, patch me through!'

Chapter 10

21 December 2012
10.35 a.m. – Nuuk, southern Greenland

The previous day had been the scariest in Joanna's life. And it had nearly been her last one. After escaping the tidal wave with only seconds to spare, the pilot had circled around Iqaluit and they had watched, horrified, the terrible destruction of the little community. The huge seething wave had poured over all the buildings, travelling at such tremendous speed and power that it was like watching a model village being cast into the ocean. Pushed from behind by a train of progressively smaller waves, the icy waters of Frobisher Bay swept several kilometres inland and piled up against the surrounding mountains, burying Iqaluit hundreds of metres underwater.

The pilot's family had screamed and wailed but the scientists were too shocked to speak. Eventually, after circling a couple of times and witnessing nature's awful might and fury, the pilot reluctantly spoke.

'We can't stay up here forever,' he said, his voice trembling with emotion, 'so we need to find somewhere to land. The nearest airport is four hundred kilometres away at Cape Dorset but that's on an island and is only forty-eight metres above sea level. Iqaluit was thirty-four metres above so I suggest we find somewhere higher.'

Despite being almost paralysed with shock, Joanna remembered looking at the pilot and suddenly realising that, although they had escaped the maelstrom below, they were by no means safe.

'S-so, what do you suggest?' she asked tentatively.

'Well, there's only one other option,' the pilot continued, 'and that's Greenland.'

'Greenland!' Professor Conrad gasped. 'But isn't that miles away? Have we got enough fuel?'

The pilot tapped the fuel gauge and thought for a moment.

'Hmm, good question,' he said thoughtfully. 'We have about half a tank of fuel, which should, depending on the wind speed and direction, take us a thousand kilometres or so. The nearest airport in Greenland is Nuuk, which fortunately is the capital of Greenland and fortunately about one hundred metres above sea level. Unfortunately, it's also nine hundred and fifty kilometres away so it will be touch and go whether we make it or not. Fasten your seat belts and . . . pray.'

It had been the longest four hours of Joanna's life. Nuuk, on the south-western tip of Greenland, was an interesting place. It was one of the smallest capital cities in the world, a strange mixture of quaint historic buildings and utilitarian modern buildings and with an Inuit and Danish population of eighteen thousand, a third of Greenland's total. But the previous day, all this had been lost on the scientists as they had limped on the last dregs of fuel, exhausted and distraught, into the airport.

The huge ice cap behind Nuuk, stretching far to the north, appeared to be so vast, and so overpowering, that it presented a brooding, sinister appearance.

'I don't like it,' Professor Conrad was saying. 'The locals have told me that from Nuuk you could never really see the ice cap before and it's only in the last few months that it appears to have grown and come closer. And, they've been plagued by small tremors. Some of the older houses have suffered damage and they're worried there might be a glacial flood like the one that hit Tasiilaq.'

Joanna nodded. She didn't know if she was still overly anxious from the day before but she couldn't escape the feeling that there was a brooding and ominous tension in the air – as though something very, very scary was about to happen.

'Yes, I agree,' she said, 'and I think it's a good idea to fly over the ice cap to see exactly what's happening. I'm surprised the pilot agreed so soon after yesterday's nerve-wracking ordeal. Let's hope he remembers to fill it up with . . .'

Suddenly, their satellite phone rang.

'Hello, Professor Conrad here,' the Professor answered.

'Professor, hello, it's David Appleby here,' an unusually harassed voice said. 'Can I speak to Dr Turnbull, please?'

Professor Conrad held his hand over the microphone.

'It's that pompous British government scientist,' he whispered. 'Don't waste too much time on him – the Cessna leaves in an hour.'

'Hello, Sir David,' Joanna said unenthusiastically. 'Have you thought over what we talked about yesterday?'

'Yes, I have and I, er, think you're right,' he agreed. 'We've had unprecedentedly high tides here – three or four metres higher than normal and I've just heard about the awful floods on Baffin Island. It's terrible. Terrible! I've decided to phone the Prime Minister but I wanted to hear what you think is happening. And if something catastrophic is about to happen, how long have we got?'

For a moment, Joanna was silent.

'Frankly, Sir David,' she eventually said, 'it's anyone's guess. What we have been seeing are clearly the results of unprecedented tectonic plate movements. We don't know why but the Earth's crust up here is destabilising. What with the glacial floods, the tidal bore, the sudden increased sea levels, the volcanic activity in northern Greenland and the massive rise in the height of the ice cap, clearly tremendous dynamic forces are at work here and it's frightening that no one has a clue what's causing it. Or what could happen next. But if, as I suggested before, the Gakkel Ridge extends beneath Greenland and joins the North Atlantic Ridge and it's suddenly become very unstable, there is one place I definitely wouldn't want to be right now.'

'Go on,' Sir David prompted.

'Look at the topological maps of the Atlantic and Arctic Oceans and it's obvious where the two ridges could join. And that's where we could be heading for a massive volcanic seismic hotspot.'

'Go on,' Sir David prompted again, unsure of the layout of the ocean floors.

Joanna looked at Professor Conrad and he nodded.

'Iceland!' she said simply.

10.55 a.m. – Danish Geological Society, Copenhagen, Denmark

'Olaf, thank God you're alive,' Gunnar Pattersen said over the satellite link. 'Have you found Jarvik?'

A crackly, exhausted and emotional voice came over the phone.

'Gunnar, listen,' Olaf's tired voice said, 'Jarvik's gone. He's dead, along with four of my men. The situation is . . .'

'Oh my God!' Gunnar gasped. 'Jarvik and your men – dead? How did . . .'

'Look, I don't have much time,' Olaf interrupted. 'We've managed to set up a satellite antenna but I don't know how long it will last. The whole ice cap up here is collapsing into a huge volcanic fissure and we've only just managed to outrun it. But for how long, I don't know.'

'Then get the hell out of there,' Gunnar growled. 'We've already lost enough brave . . .'

'No!' Olaf suddenly shouted. 'You have to see this. It's Jarvik's film – he lost his life to get this and it's vital that you see it. I'm streaming it to the Geological Society's website now.'

Gunnar flicked his computer to their website. It had already begun to play and Gunnar almost fell out of his chair – Jarvik's white, frost-encrusted face stared manically at him, his eyes bloodshot and swollen, his nose blackened and split and a bloody gash down his face. His frozen lips mumbled soundlessly and insanely. Suddenly, the picture jerked and a blurred wall of ice and swirling mist filled the screen.

'He's abseiling further down,' Olaf's voice came over the satellite phone again. 'Won't be a minute.'

And then suddenly, the mist cleared and a vast expanse of yellow-and-orange lava appeared, bubbling and swirling like a raging river through an enormous chasm of ice. Gunnar gasped and stared at the beautiful yet terrifying sight, mesmerised and speechless.

Suddenly, over the phone, there was a tremendous explosion and then a shout.

'Olaf!' a voice screamed. 'The ice is breaking up. We have to . . .'

And then there was silence and the computer screen went blank.

'Olaf?' Gunnar said. 'Olaf?'

11.05 a.m. – Reykjavik, Iceland

In Conference Suite 3A of the Hotel Aurora Borealis, the G20 Summit meeting had already begun. The heads of state, ministers, advisers and aides of twenty countries, together with several financial and environmental organisations, formed a circle of tables around the room – in all, one hundred and sixty-four people. The large timezone electronic world clock on the wall showed a time of 11.05 a.m. in Iceland.

'. . . The world's economies revolve around free trade,' the British Prime Minister was saying, 'and we must ensure that unilateral barriers or artificial constraints are not created that would hamper the movement and flow of goods. International cooperation and understanding is . . .'

Suddenly, his Foreign Secretary interrupted him, leaning over and whispering something urgently in his ear. The Prime Minister listened for a moment and then his eyes widened in horror.

'I'm sorry, but I must interrupt this trade discussion,' he announced. 'I've just heard from London's Metropolitan Police that it is not London that is the target for a terrorist attack but Iceland. It is not unreasonable to assume that they must be planning to attack the G20 Summit.'

There was uproar and pandemonium in the room, with half of the delegates standing up and everyone talking at once or looking around nervously.

Suddenly, the American President tapped the microphone for attention.

'It's shocking news,' he said, 'but no more than one would expect. International terrorism means exactly that and we, the most influential and powerful countries in the world, are obvious targets. G20 Summits have always been obvious targets and that is why we have the largest and most complex security arrangements possible. You are probably safer here than you would be in your own country.'

The President paused for a moment and delegates began to return to their seats and sit down.

'And what are the options?' he continued. 'All jump on planes and fly home like frightened rabbits or continue the summit and discuss the important global matters that we have to. If we run, the terrorists have already won.'

For a moment the room went quiet and the delegates began agreeing and nodding their heads.

'Yes, we must continue,' the Chinese President agreed emphatically. 'We cannot allow a few political or religious zealots to dictate our chosen path. It is we who must decide our destiny, not they.'

There was a round of applause for both Presidents and the delegates continued with their discussions on trade protectionism. But it wasn't long before there was another interruption. There was a sudden commotion among the Russian and American delegates and the Presidents of both these nations and some of their advisers walked to the back of the room for a meeting. At the same time, the British Prime Minister received another urgent call.

'Sir, it's David Appleby here.'

The Prime Minister scowled, annoyed to have been interrupted yet again.

'Sir David,' he snapped impatiently, 'we've not got to the climate change discussions yet. It's on the agenda for tomorrow.'

'Er, yes, I'm sorry sir,' the Chief Scientific Adviser apologised, 'but it's not that. Well, I mean, it's probably not that, unless of course . . .'

'Please, Sir David, get to the point,' the Prime Minister said irritably. 'I do have a G20 Summit meeting going on here, you know.'

'Yes, Prime Minister,' Sir David continued, 'that's why I'm phoning. There's been an unprecedented rise in sea levels, four or five metres and significant coastal flooding in the UK. In Baffin Island, a huge tidal wave has killed thousands and in Greenland . . .'

Several minutes later, the Prime Minister had finally got the message and, frowning, he handed the phone back to his aide. This was definitely a new angle on global warming, he thought. But how seriously should he take it?

'Gentlemen,' the American President suddenly said, after the American and Russian delegates had returned to their seats, 'I've just been speaking to Theodore Jackson-Taylor, my Secretary of State, and he has given me some disturbing news. Several days ago, one of our nuclear submarines was damaged in the Arctic ice and, in our attempts to rescue it, we have lost an AWACS plane, a large naval icebreaker and a large salvage vessel. The Russian President has just told me that their own icebreaker in the region is experiencing some strange, and very disturbing, er, events. In addition, we have heard from one of our top scientists that massive seismic and volcanic activity is taking place at the

North Pole and northern Greenland and that the Earth's crust is destabilising in this area. They understand that . . .'

'Er, sorry, Mr President,' the EU President suddenly interrupted, 'but I believe we have pictures of what is happening in Greenland. I've just had a call from the Danish Geological Society and they think we should urgently see what their scientists filmed yesterday. If we can just log onto their website, please?'

Patrick O'Keefe came and collected the website details and streamed the film onto a large projector screen. Gunnar Pattersen hadn't had time to edit the film and immediately a large gruesome face appeared on the screen. There was a collective gasp throughout the room and, horrified, one hundred and sixty-four people watched Jarvik's terrible visage and insane mumblings. And then, as a vast river of molten lava came onto the screen, there was another gasp.

'I understand', the EU President said, 'that the Greenland ice cap is beginning to break up. And that, sadly, all the Danish scientists died in their attempts to capture these images.'

For a while there was a shocked silence.

'I have also heard from my government's Chief Scientific Adviser,' the British Prime Minister said, breaking the stunned silence, 'and he is very concerned by what is happening in the Arctic. And, waiting on a satellite link from Greenland is another of our scientists, a Dr Joanna Turnbull. She has a rather disturbing hypothesis that I think we should all listen to. If we can connect to her, please?'

Patrick O'Keefe made the connection and Joanna's voice came into the room.

'Thank you for listening to me,' she said over a crackly line. 'I know you've all got important matters to discuss but it's vital that you hear me out.'

'Go on, Joanna,' the British Prime Minister prompted.

'Well, I don't know why it's happening but I believe that the Earth's crust beneath the Arctic and northern Greenland is bulging and this is draining the Arctic Ocean southwards, causing flooding and tidal bores and pushing up the Greenland ice cap. Clearly, if this continues, there's going to be more and worse flooding, but what really worries me is something potentially far more catastrophic. The Greenland ice cap is enormous, comprising about three million cubic kilometres of ice. If this all melted, as predicted by worst-case climate warming scenarios, the global sea levels will rise by seven metres or more. But if there is a catastrophic failure of the ice cap, something entirely different and far more frightening could happen.'

In Conference Suite 3A, one hundred and sixty-four delegates were silent and attentive. But one man, the hotel's technical manager, wasn't bothered and he kept looking at the large electronic world clock. After all, it really was totally irrelevant for the assembled dignitaries.

'The ice cap in the north is now over one hundred kilometres higher than in the south and, if the magma we are seeing seeps below it, then you could get a lubricating layer of steam. If that happens, the ice cap could slide downhill.'

'And how long would that take?' the American President asked.

Joanna was silent for a moment.

'It's impossible to tell,' she eventually said. 'It could migrate south at a few metres an hour and take years or it could speed up to a few kilometres an hour and take a couple of months.'

Throughout the room, there were a few gasps and some of the delegates began heatedly discussing the consequences for their country.

'But,' Joanna continued, 'another scenario is that it may be so catastrophic that the whole ice cap, a trillion tonnes, falls into the deep Atlantic waters of southern Greenland. If that happens, there will be the mother of all mega-tsunamis.'

'What – larger than the one in Indonesia in 2004?' the American President asked.

'Much larger and totally different,' Joanna replied. 'And that was a tsunami. A tsunami is caused by an underwater earthquake displacing a huge body of water. In deep water the wave is hardly noticeable; it's only when it reaches the continental shelf that it rears up and becomes dangerous. But even the 2004 tsunami, which was the result of a large 9.1 magnitude earthquake and equivalent to sixty-seven gigatons of TNT, was only ten to thirty metres tall and yet it killed a quarter of a million people. A mega-tsunami occurs when something falls into a body of water like a landslide or an asteroid and the impact creates huge waves. It is no different from throwing a pebble into a pond. The problem comes when a large volume of material falls at speed into deep water – here massive waves can be formed.'

'How big?' the British Prime Minister asked.

'Well,' Joanna replied, 'the Lituya Bay mega-tsunami in Alaska in 1958 was more than five hundred metres high. And, the Mount St Helens 1980 eruption caused 260-metre-high waves and that was on a lake. And some scientists believe that, if the Cumbre Vieja volcanic ridge on La Palma, Canary Islands, collapses during an eruption, then a mega-tsunami up to one thousand metres high could be produced and it could travel thousands of kilometres to inundate the eastern seaboard of North America. And we are only talking thirty million cubic metres of impact material in the Lituya Bay mega-tsunami and five hundred cubic kilometres in the potential La Palma mega-tsunami. The ice cap comprises three million cubic kilometres.'

There was a stunned silence in the room. After a few moments the American President stood up.

'Dr Turnbull, can you tell us how large your mega-tsunami might be, how far it could go and when it might happen?'

'Well, Sir,' Joanna replied tentatively, 'those are all very good questions and my answers would be speculative. But I would postulate that a wave *at least* one kilometre high would be generated and it will sweep into the Atlantic Ocean. As to when, all I can say is that I'm a methodical, practical scientist and not easily scared, but I am now.'

'Are we safe in Iceland?' one of the delegates asked.

'No,' Joanna replied, a bit more hastily than she meant to. 'I'm afraid Iceland would be devastated in less than an hour.'

Once again there was pandemonium in the room and many delegates stood up.

The American President stood up again and tapped his microphone for attention.

'Before we have a show of hands,' he said, 'whether or not to abandon the summit for another venue and another time, I should tell you what my Secretary of State has just told me. Apparently, if there is a volcanic eruption and this spews clouds of ash into the air, it will be too dangerous for jet planes to fly in the area as ash and particles of volcanic pumice would clog their engines. If that happens, leaving Iceland would no longer be an option.'

But the delegates never got the chance for a show of hands. Instead, they began to vote with their feet.

Patrick O'Keefe looked at the timezone world clock.

'Shit!' he cursed under his breath before frantically racing out of the room, unceremoniously pushing delegates out of the way.

12.15 p.m. – Greenland

As the huge slab of ancient crust continued to force its way upwards, the newer continental and oceanic crusts continued to deform and bulge. Beneath the great ice sheet covering Greenland, the river of magma stretched for a thousand kilometres from the north coast to the south-east coast, cutting the island in two. Massive earthquakes, way beyond Richter's imagination, shattered the landscape and in the north the ice cap rose ever higher, jerking upwards hundreds of metres at a time. Tongues of molten lava ran between the ice and the rock beneath, creating enormous sheets of trapped superheated steam under immense pressure.

The massive ice cap was now perched at a perilously steep angle, sloping from almost two hundred kilometres high in the

north to sea level, two thousand kilometres away in the south. As
the crust beneath it juddered, the layer of steam began to act as
a lubricant and the ice cap, like an immense glacier, began to
slide down the slope. Trillions of tonnes of ice began a noisy and
unstoppable race south, towards the ocean, minute by minute
picking up speed until it became a giant solid avalanche.

In Nuuk, a Cessna Citation was just taxiing for take-off when
someone screamed. Joanna wasn't sure if it was her but it could
have been. Out of the window she had been watching the brooding,
sinister ice cap perched above the capital. She knew it shouldn't
have been there – never before in recorded history had it been
so prominent so far south and so close to the capital. And, as she
had stared at it almost hypnotically, it had begun to pour down
the mountainside.

'Holy shit!' Dan Wood shouted. 'Look at that!'

The pilot, who had been looking down at his instruments,
looked up and gasped. Somewhere in Nuuk his family and relatives were shopping and his immediate response was to warn
them and he slammed the brakes on and grabbed his mobile
phone. But as he started to punch the numbers he saw that
immense blocks of ice, bigger than skyscrapers, were beginning
to roll down the mountain towards Nuuk. In that instant, he froze.

'We need to take off,' Professor Conrad said, as calmly as he
could.

The pilot watched the first block smash into the houses at the
edge of the capital and the houses splintered into matchwood.
The immense blocks didn't even slow, ploughing through the
capital like bowling balls and heading for the sea. Behind them,
creeping over the mountainside, the three-kilometre-thick ice cap
followed.

'I think we should go,' Joanna said, sounding matter of fact
but in reality still mesmerised by the sheer enormity of nature
out of control.

The pilot looked at his phone and slowly and sadly shook his
head.

'Let's go!' Dan screamed. 'Or we'll all be dead.'

The pilot jumped, shocked out of his trance, and began to taxi down the runway again. It was like a re-run of Iqaluit, only this time the monster came from the sky rather than the deep. The little Cessna raced down the runway and, as Joanna watched, she saw a small Air Greenland commercial jet by the terminal scrambling to load passengers, its engines already running.

Even with their own engines gunning at maximum revs, they could hear what sounded like a battlefield or thunder rolling down the mountainside towards them. Suddenly, a giant ice boulder, the size of an iceberg, rolled on a collision course and the pilot frantically had to swerve onto the grass to avoid it. Mesmerized, they watched it thunder past, ploughing into a block of flats and a shopping precinct, smashing them to pieces.

'Oh my God!' Professor Conrad gasped. 'Not again. This is horrible.'

As more giant boulders raced towards them the little Cessna reached take-off speed and the pilot pulled hard on the controls, racing out to sea and climbing as fast as he could.

Behind them, the commercial jet raced on to the runway and began accelerating, its engines screaming and its passengers staring horrified out of the windows. But as it sped down the runway one of the giant blocks of ice crashed into one of its wings and with an almighty bang it exploded into a ball of flame.

12.20 p.m. – Reykjavik, Iceland

In Conference Suite 4A, Patrick O'Keefe frantically unscrewed a large wall-mounted map of Iceland and exposed a large hole in the wall. On the other side was the back of a large piece of electronic equipment – the timezone world clock, mounted in Conference Suite 3A.

Cursing the politicians for trying to leave before the allotted time, he quickly unscrewed the back and removed it, revealing a stash of breast implants and Semtex packages. Grabbing the deto-nator, he closed his eyes and activated the explosives.

In Conference Suite 3A, fifty-three of the one hundred and sixty-four delegates had managed to collect their documents and leave the room, including the American President, whose security services had taken control and who rather unceremoniously had already bundled him out of the room and the other delegates out of the way. The British Prime Minister had decided to wait for the melee to subside and was taking the opportunity to discuss a sensitive arms deal with the Chinese President.

Suddenly, there was a tremendous explosion and a dense cloud of debris and shards of glass shot across the room. And in the cloud, there was a fine mist of deadly nerve agent – sarin, a killer five hundred times more deadly than cyanide. There were screams of agony as delegates close to the explosion were thrown to the floor or sliced with glass shrapnel from the world clock but many stood where they were, momentarily frozen with shock and covered in a layer of brick dust, plaster and glass. The British Prime Minister, his face smothered in debris and mouth still open in mid-sentence, stared at the devastation and carnage, stunned and speechless. But, as he and one hundred and ten other delegates breathed in the molecules of sarin, none of them had long to be shocked. Within seconds, the deadly nerve agent began to attack and paralyse their nervous systems and they frantically began gasping for breath, a giant hand savagely squeezing their chests. Vital organs began shutting down and they began to release horrible groaning and gurgling sounds. Thirty seconds later, after collapsing to the floor, death came as a horrible, ignoble end, the body shuddering in final uncontrollable spasms.

In Conference Suite 4A, Patrick O'Keefe's headless body lay slumped on the floor, his bitter revenge finally and terribly enacted.

In room 12 of the staff quarters, Frida Jonsson was desperately trying to keep Reykjavik's chief of police's hand away from her bosom when the hotel's fire alarm activated. Immediately, her eyes lit up with a zealous fervour and, thrusting her hand into her bosom, she extracted two large breast implants. Einar Sigmundsen's jaw fell open and he stared in shock and disbelief.

Grabbing a fork from their lunch trolley, Frida ran from the room, clutching the breast implants ahead of her and raced down towards reception. Amid the din of the fire alarm, some of the delegates were frantically trying to re-arrange their flights and security staff and police were racing around, guns in hand, shouting orders and adding to the confusion. Into this chaos strode a plump buxom lady who appeared to be desperately stabbing a couple of breast implants with a fork.

'Save the whales!' she shouted. 'Save the whales!'

Squeezing the breast implants she began squirting fluid at anyone and everyone.

'Whale murderers!' she shouted, not even noticing that the fluid couldn't possibly be the whale blood that she thought it was.

The police and security men were taking no chances and without warning they opened fire. For a very brief moment Frida's face registered the shock of being shot for simply being an animal rights activist, before she slumped to the floor, dead.

Einar Sigmundsen, who had chased after her, reached the hotel lobby just as his new-found love was shot. Shocked, he ran over to her and fell distraught to his knees beside her. Thinking that he was another terrorist, the police opened fire again and he was peppered with bullets.

Unnoticed in the panic and mayhem, several of the delegates and security staff whom Frida had managed to spray with sarin had begun to choke and they collapsed to the floor. Writhing in agony and involuntary spasms, they quickly joined the other delegates slaughtered by the terrorists.

Seven floors above and away from the terrible carnage, on the roof of the Hotel Aurora Borealis, the American President was being bundled into a specially armoured helicopter and flown to the President's private plane, *Air Force One*, waiting at Reykjavik's airport.

At that moment, just down the road in the shopping centre, Gilda, Tukku and Nunni were looking for Christmas presents with the little bit of money that Dr Hashim had given them.

'Look, Mummy,' Nunni said excitedly, 'this would be perfect for Dr Hashim.'

She lifted up an Icelandic sweater, warm but brightly coloured and gaudy.

'This will keep him like toast,' she added enthusiastically. 'He obviously doesn't have one otherwise he would have worn it in the hospital gardens this morning. He was so cold that he was like a snowman! Can we buy it, please?'

Gilda and Tukku both laughed and nodded.

'Yes, darling,' Gilda replied, smiling, 'if you think he'll wear it.'

And, at the same moment, at Dr Hashim's house, Malik was waiting for 2 p.m., the appointed hour of Armageddon. Calmly sitting at Dr Hashim's computer, he prepared to send out a message to the news services around the world:

We of the Iron Fist, the brave warriors of the International Islamic Brotherhood, proudly accept responsibility for the just and holy death and destruction of the unholy and evil cabal of the G20 Summit in Iceland. We call on all followers of Islam to rise against the degenerate non-believers and declare war on the unclean and the unworthy. This is the Apocalypse as long foretold and it is our duty and destiny to follow this righteous path. Death to all unbelievers! Long live Islam!

Upstairs, in the bedrooms, Abeye Umgalla and Elli Salumptu tended to the ten young men recovering from their surgery. In the operating theatre, Dr Hashim's lifeless body lay collapsed in a corner, an empty hypodermic needle of morphine still sticking from his arm. Despite all the preparations and planning, he had failed to reconcile the healing of his Hippocratic Oath with the extreme actions of fundamental terrorism. Suicide had been his only option.

12.55 p.m. – North Atlantic Ocean

Just as the American President was being bundled to the top floor of the Hotel Aurora Borealis, Frida Jonsson was naively squirting sarin around the hotel lobby and Malik's fingers were hovering over the computer keyboard, trillions of tonnes of dense and ancient ice was dropping into the sea along the whole of southern Greenland's coast. There was only a small continental shelf in this region, and the massive three-kilometre-thick ice cap surged deep down to the ocean floor, pushed by the enormous weight and energy behind it. As the huge weight of ice left northern Greenland, the crust beneath surged catastrophically upwards, creating the largest mountain range in the world and increasing the angle and speed of the sliding ice cap.

As trillions of tonnes of ice displaced trillions of tonnes of water, a wave of epic proportions rose up from the depths, two kilometres high and a thousand kilometres long. With a shockwave loud enough to wake Poseidon, the wave began to roar south and east, travelling at eight hundred kilometres an hour – a wall of water so monstrous that it dwarfed any other wave seen before on earth.

2.05 p.m. – Reykjavik, Iceland

The crew of *Air Force One* had run all the pre-flight safety checks and the plane was ready for take-off. They were not going to waste any time – who knew what the terrorists would do next and the safest place for them, and the President, was in the air.

The President, recovering from the unceremonious and undignified escape from the hotel, was trying to regain composure and control over the situation.

'. . . I want you, Theodore,' he was saying to the Secretary of State over the secure satellite link, 'to take charge of this. We cannot allow such an outrage to go unpunished and, whoever is responsible, they must be found and brought to justice. And whatever country is behind . . .'

'Sir,' the Secretary of State suddenly interrupted, 'we've just heard that a group calling themselves the Iron Fist of the International Islamic Brotherhood has claimed responsibility and they've declared a holy war against the, er, unclean and unworthy. That's presumably America and its allies. They're previously unknown to us but they appear to be trying to bring about the Apocalypse.'

'The Apocalypse!' the President spat. 'When I find out who did this atrocity, I'll unleash Armageddon on them! But what I don't understand,' he added, as *Air Force One* began to accelerate down the runway, 'is what was all that about the Greenland ice cap falling into the sea and creating a huge tidal wave? Was that some sort of diversion? To cause panic and mayhem before the bombs went off? Theodore, find out which leaders have been . . .'

The President, absently looking out of the window, suddenly stopped talking. As *Air Force One* had left the ground and was banking hard over Reykjavik, he got a glimpse of an enormous and terrifying sight. From horizon to horizon, a huge wall of water, dark and sinister, appeared to be surging towards them. The plane's engines suddenly began to scream as the pilot had also seen the wave and frantically tried to accelerate and gain height.

'Sir?' Theodore said. 'Mr President, is everything all right? I can hear the plane's . . .'

'Theodore,' the President's voice, calm but insistent, suddenly interrupted, 'call the Vice-President and put him on notice. And call my wife and . . .'

Behind the President's plane, the massive tidal wave, still two kilometres high, surged across Iceland, obliterating and drowning everything in its path. Nobody had a chance as buildings were smashed and everything destroyed and swept away. At eight hundred kilometres an hour, the roaring monster quickly gained on *Air Force One* and the President's voice tailed off as the plane was engulfed.

In Washington, the American Secretary of State stared at the telephone. One moment he had been speaking to the President, the next, screaming jet engines and then – nothing. He tapped the White House telephone operator's number and asked to be reconnected.

After a few moments, he heard the voice of the operator.

'I'm sorry, Sir, but we've lost all contact with *Air Force One*.'

He stared at the phone for a long time, deep in thought.

'Sir?' the operator said. 'Sir, what do you want me to do?'

'Get me the Vice-President,' Theodore eventually said. 'I think we've lost the President.'

2.25 p.m. – New York City, USA

Jacob was cold, wet, miserable and nervous. A light drifting of sleet covered his shoes as he stood shivering beneath an umbrella outside the ferry terminal at Battery Park. He looked at his watch for the tenth time – it was now 2.25 p.m. There was only five minutes to go and there was still no sign of a little old lady with a walking stick and a fur coat.

Perhaps something had happened? Or perhaps it had been a hoax? He daren't miss them in case they thought he hadn't turned up and they harmed Martha. He watched as a miserable and wet old man trudged past, bearing an A-frame proclaiming 'GOD IS RIGHTEOUS' on one side and 'THE END IS NIGH!' on the other. He had forgotten that today was the day of the Apocalypse . . . the End of Time . . . the Day of Reckoning. Frankly, he couldn't give a damn.

Suddenly, a dry cleaning van pulled over beside the entrance to the ferry building, waited a moment and then drove away.

Standing there, looking directly at him, was a little old lady with a walking stick and a fur coat. For some reason, Jacob had been expecting to see an angry, snarling, evil-looking woman instead of a sweet old lady and momentarily he was taken aback. Full of dread, he forced himself to cross the road.

'What do you want?' he growled, bending down so that only she could hear.

The old lady kissed him on the cheek.

'Jacob, what a good boy you are,' she said sweetly and loudly, 'taking your old mother for a birthday treat. Take my arm, dear, and let's get tickets.'

At this time of year the ferry terminal was not too busy and the 2.35 p.m. ferry was only half full. Since the 9/11 attack in 2001, security had been massively increased, which, for what the Statue of Liberty represented – freedom – was something of a paradox. Airport-style metal detectors, body scanners and bag searches were required before boarding the ferry and round-the-clock patrols of the United States Park Police Marine units patrolled Liberty Island. But for the little old lady and her 'son', a walking stick and a small handbag didn't take long to clear.

'Where's Martha?' Jacob growled through gritted teeth as they took their seats on the ferry. 'What have you done to my mother?'

The little old lady turned to look at him and he looked into her cold and grey eyes – a callous, angry, bitter and twisted soul lay within. He shivered. For the first time, he realised he might never see his mother again.

2.30 p.m. – New York City, USA

NYPD, like all the police forces throughout America, were working to a strict holiday ban on this particular tinderbox of a day. So far, apart from the usual homicides, suicides, robberies, muggings, shoplifting, violent assaults, traffic accidents, drug wars, gang wars, arson attacks and occasional helping of old ladies across the street, it had been fairly uneventful. The only noticeable difference was the unusually high number of losers, freaks and weirdoes who had crawled out of some gutter or other and who were desperately waiting for Armageddon to commence.

FBI director Paul Gates, sitting in his office sipping yet another black coffee, looked at the four NYPD reports on his desk. He was a great believer in hunches and, deep down, he felt there was a certain connection, a rapport, between the reported incidents.

Two were brief reports on suspected kidnappings yesterday and the day before in Lower Manhattan, close to his office. On both occasions, eyewitnesses had phoned NYPD after seeing an old lady apparently being dragged into an old truck and a dry cleaning van by a couple of oriental- or Asian-looking men. The third report was from the docks yesterday and was from a night watchman who had seen the unusual sight of bags of dry cleaning being loaded from a van into an old fishing boat. It was apparently too dark to tell if the men were oriental or not, but dry cleaning vans rarely turned up in police reports and the three incidents together were too unusual to be coincidental. Normally, this was police business and the FBI would not get involved, but it was the fourth, and most bizarre, report that had caught the FBI director's eye and somehow glued the three other incidents together.

Early this morning, in a large crate labelled 'Linen' which was waiting to be loaded onto the *Star Princess*, one of the sleek modern cruise liners that sailed between New York and London, a gruesome discovery had been made. An old lady, unconscious and barely alive, had been found in a metal Victorian bath filled with a reddish-brown powder. An electric timer, attached to a thermal lance, sat on top of the powder – it was timed to go off at 3 p.m. later that day – an hour after the *Star Princess* would have set sail.

The FBI director, slowly and sadly, shook his head. These people were pure evil, with a total disregard for the death and misery they would cause. NYPD had ignited a sample of the powder and it had blazed ferociously with a yellow and white radiance – thermite. The terrorists' plan had been simple and ruthless – once loaded on the cruise liner, it would have ignited and, burning at sixteen hundred degrees Celsius, would have destroyed the old lady, burnt through the bottom of the bath and sent the whole fiery magma to burn holes through the decks of the ship. Clearly, they hoped to breach the hull and sink the ship into Hudson Bay, together with as many passengers as possible.

Paul Gates knew immediately that this must be connected to the terrorists who had murdered his men in the Adirondack Mountains. Now he knew why they had been stockpiling thermite. He picked up the phone.

'Mike, get the helicopter ready,' he ordered his deputy. 'We're going to the docks and the Hudson River. And get the NYPD river police to meet us there. But make sure', he added fiercely, 'that everyone is well armed.'

2.45 p.m. – Prudence Island, USA

Old Man Williams banged the handle of his fishing rod against the huge steel door. He had a beautiful haul of fish and it seemed a shame to see it all go to waste. Why not let the strange subterranean folk have some?

Inside the bunker, in a world of their own, the subterranean folk were unaware of the almost biblical offering of fish outside. The steel door was two metres thick and Old Man William's puny knocking went unheard. And, besides, they had more important things on their minds.

The entire complement, ninety-three Messianic Jews, were gathered in the main control room, avidly watching a bank of huge television screens. Each television showed a different news channel, beamed in by satellite from around the world. Nothing unusual had happened so far but there was a tense, and building, expectation that somewhere, something cataclysmic was about to happen. After all, there were only nine hours left.

Suddenly, there was a shout and someone pointed to one of the screens. CNN had flashed up a 'breaking news' message:

TERRORISTS ATTACK G20 SUMMIT IN ICELAND – HUNDREDS FEARED DEAD, INCLUDING WORLD LEADERS – AMERICAN PRESIDENT IS MISSING . . .

'It's started!' Joseph shouted, his voice tinged with awe, fear and a hint of jubilation. 'The Apocalypse has started. Soon, we will witness the Second Coming of the Messiah. Let us pray. And let us prepare.'

Outside, unaware that a cataclysmic battle with Satan was about to commence, an old man shrugged and, not wanting to lug several kilograms of fish any further, tied them to the steel door handle and ambled off. It was a strange world, he thought. Whatever next?

2.50 p.m. – London, England

In central London, a battered old Renault van darted and swerved through the busy mid-afternoon traffic. On top, a large Christmas tree was strapped horizontally, a brilliant camouflage for the two-hundred-kilogram Semtex bomb sat beneath, primed and ready. But the otherwise well-laid plan had hit a snag – they were lost.

'I told you to turn right at Victoria Street,' Ishmail shouted. 'You never listen to what I say.'

'But there was a "No Entry" sign,' Rashid, his younger brother and driver, shouted back. And if you hadn't got us lost in the first place then we wouldn't have been anywhere near Victoria Street.'

'It's not my fault,' Ishmail spat. 'I didn't expect a diversion. It wasn't there when I did a reconnaissance the day before yesterday. If you hadn't been so stoned yesterday you'd have done another reconnoitre as planned.'

'Oh, so it's my fault, as always,' Rashid scoffed. 'You always manage to turn it around. It's never your fault, is it? It was exactly the same when . . .'

'Look, shut up!' Ismail growled. 'We've only got ten minutes and this whole van is going to explode into kingdom come. We'll never find the Houses of Parliament and Big Ben now – so what are we going to do?'

Ahead, down the end of a long, straight and wide road, lay a huge and magnificent building, surrounded by tall iron railings and crowds of tourists.

'What's that?' Rashid asked, pointing and jabbing the horn at the same time.

Ishmail quickly looked down at the map.

'It's Buckingham Palace,' he said, 'where the Queen of England lives. That'll do – we can simply smash through the gates.'

Rashid put his foot down and floored the accelerator. The decrepit old van lurched forward and accelerated to its top speed of ninety kilometres an hour. Jabbing the horn and shouting Islamic curses, he swerved between the busy mid-afternoon traffic, zigzagging down The Mall towards the beautiful edifice of Buckingham Palace.

'Only four minutes to go!' Ishmail shouted excitedly. 'Welcome to Armageddon and death to all non-believers!'

Cars and buses angrily sounded their horns or frantically darted out of the way and tourists and sightseers along the tree-lined avenue stopped and stared in amazement. But some quickly realised what might be happening and shouted warnings or dived to the ground.

At the magnificent gateway of the palace, lines of tourists peering eagerly through the wrought-iron gates turned and looked with horror and panic at the rapidly approaching van, its engine screaming and its horn blasting.

'It's a bomb!' someone shouted. 'Run for your lives!'

Women and children screamed and armed police opened fire. Bullets smashed into the Renault's engine and windscreen but it was too late to stop the momentum. Ishmail suddenly cried out and slumped in his seat as bullets smashed into his head, spraying the cab with his blood and brains.

'Death to all the non-believing decadent pigs!' Rashid screamed, his eyes wide and alight with a fanatical zeal.

But suddenly, a bullet hit his shoulder, smashing the bone and rendering his arm useless. As the van reached the roundabout of the Queen Victoria Memorial, he tried to steer round it but, at ninety kilometres an hour and with only one hand, he lost control. The van swerved and screeching on two wheels careered into one of the huge gate pillars at the front of the Palace. Two hundred kilograms of Semtex exploded, sending a huge roaring fireball into the sky and a deadly hail of shrapnel and mortar across the parade ground, shattering all the windows at the front of the building.

Inside the Palace, panic and pandemonium reigned.

But, suddenly, a calm woman's voice could be heard above the din.

'Settle down, everyone,' she commanded. 'Remember that we are British. And ... you'll frighten the poor dear corgis.'

3.05 p.m. – North Pole

On the *Smolensk*, the warning klaxon was screaming and every-where men were scrambling to reach their emergency posts and to don survival suits and life jackets.

On the bridge, the officers stared out of the window and into the twilight gloom, their expressions a mix of shock and awe. The current had slackened and they were now barely drifting, but around them an unimaginable scene was beginning to unfold. From the surface of the water land had miraculously appeared – rolling hills of mud- and boulder-encrusted ocean floor slowly rising from the sea, draining water and alive with frantically flapping fish and scurrying crabs. In the distance, a huge mountain range had grown, bursting from the sea and spewing enormous columns of ash and red hot magma into the sky – the Gakkel Ridge had risen from its subterranean world. With a crimson sky and belching volcanoes, it was like being in the middle of Dante's Inferno.

Beneath the *Smolensk*, there was barely enough water to float and Captain Vladimir Anadyr steeled himself for a collision. He had considered abandoning ship but reasoned that the sturdy double hull of a large icebreaker was safer than the tiny and fragile life rafts.

Suddenly, there was a shout from one of the officers.

'Captain! Over there – the American submarine!'

As the sea drained away, the conning tower of USS *Arizona* appeared and slowly, as they watched, the hull appeared.

The captain, his eyes wide and his jaw dropped open in astonishment, slowly shook his head in disbelief.

'Amazing!' he growled. 'But clearly the Americans' and our fates are intertwined.'

Suddenly, the *Smolensk* juddered and began to settle on an uneven keel, the decks sloping to the port side at an unnerving angle.

'Hold on!' the captain shouted, wondering if he had made the right decision not to abandon ship.

But after a frightening series of shudders and crashes as loose items fell to the floor and the ship's steel groaned under the strain, the ship's hull settled into the mud of the ocean floor, high and dry – an unlikely and enigmatic sight in a strange and alien landscape.

Suddenly, a man appeared on the conning tower of the submarine, a megaphone in his hand. Captain Anadyr and the officers rushed outside to the wing of the bridge and peered down.

'Good afternoon, *Smolensk*,' a British voice calmly said, 'this is

Captain Crowder, of the British icebreaker the *Polar Explorer*. I'm afraid that I have had to take command of the USS *Arizona* – the commander and most of the crew are dead and the first officer is, er, incapacitated.'

'Good afternoon,' Captain Anadyr called back. 'It is good to see that some of you, at least, are safe. I suggest that you come aboard and we can discuss the extraordinary events and our, er, strange predicament over a bottle or two of vodka.' Certainly, Vladimir Anadyr needed one.

'Thank you, Captain, we will. But have you seen the *Polar Explorer*?'

One hundred and fifty kilometres to the north, another ship lay high and dry, balanced precariously six hundred metres up on the side of the Gakkel Ridge. Fountains of red hot magma and gas violently spewed from a nearby volcanic vent, and a red snaking river of lava flowed past, metres away. And, in this deso-late and incongruous spot, John and Margaret Howard, still lay in their cabin on the *Polar Explorer*, hand in hand and forever together.

3.40 p.m. – Blackpool, England

It was Lucy's seventh birthday but she wasn't celebrating or having a party. Susan had already promised to take her to the Blackpool Tower and, despite what had happened the day before, she still wanted to go. More than a birthday treat, it had become a sort of pilgrimage.

'You're braver than me,' Susan said, as they stepped out of the lift. 'I'm not going on there.'

Briefly, a glimmer of a smile crossed Lucy's face, before her serious, melancholy expression returned.

'That's why they call it the Walk of Faith,' the lift operator said, winking at Lucy. 'Because only the bravest and the most daring people can do it.'

Lucy glanced down and her heart began to beat faster and for a moment she hesitated. She looked round at her mother and then she stepped into the void. The glass floor of the Walk of Faith, one hundred and sixteen metres up Blackpool Tower, gave a terrifying illusion of danger, like walking on thin air, with the roofs of houses and shops a long, long way down and tiny people no bigger than scurrying ants.

Lucy swallowed hard and then walked across the floor and back again.

'Brave girl,' Susan said, giving her a big hug.

Lucy smiled, but again it was only brief.

'Can we find the post-box now?' she said simply.

The post-box was the highest in Britain and was popular with tourists sending holiday postcards. But Lucy didn't want to send a postcard – in her hand she grasped two letters that she had painstakingly written – one addressed to 'My Dad' and the other to 'My Poor Darling Bonnie'. She reasoned that as this was the highest post-box, then it was the nearest to heaven. And that, she was sure, was where her father and Bonnie had gone. As she dropped the letters one after the other into the post-box, tears ran down her cheeks.

Distraught, and to hide her own tears, Susan looked away. The deep and aching emptiness inside her had grown over the last few days and she struggled to contain it. Craig had been taken away from them and now so had Bonnie. Their rescuers had spent two hours searching for the puppy but in the flood and darkness he must have been swept away. Perhaps Lucy was right – perhaps they were now both in heaven.

From the Tower, you could see a long way across the sea, far into the distance. And, just over the horizon, a vast and terrifying wave was surging relentlessly down the Atlantic, heading south, towards them.

3.45 p.m. – New York City, USA

Seventy-eight metres above sea level, Jacob looked out of one of the windows – the jewels in the crown of the Statue of Liberty. He could clearly see the Manhattan skyline and somewhere in there, he guessed, the old woman's accomplices would be holding his mother.

The old woman was standing by another window, peering down towards Hudson Bay. For a fleeting moment he toyed with the idea of grabbing her and dangling her by her feet out of the window – that would make her talk and tell him where they were keeping Martha. But if her accomplices saw, or if he accidentally dropped her, then his mother would be dead.

Suddenly, the old woman took her walking stick and, unscrewing the handle off, took out several tubular lengths, each smaller in diameter than the last. Switching them round, she then screwed each one to the end of another and, after replacing the handle, had a pole six metres long with a hook at the end.

Astonished, Jacob peered out of the window and was amazed to see an old fishing boat tied to the railings that surrounded Liberty Island and three men brandishing guns working on it. As he watched, a couple of security guards ran from the base of the statue and began sprinting towards the old boat and a fast patrol launch from the United States Park Police Marine Unit sped across from Liberty State Park. He watched, amazed, as the men on the fishing boat unwrapped a tarpaulin from the gear in the bow to reveal a huge whaling harpoon gun and pointed it towards the head of the statue.

Suddenly, there were gunshots and he saw the two security guards slump to the ground and he ducked below the window. Seconds later, he heard the report of a much larger gun and out of the corner of his eye he saw a harpoon trailing rope fly in front of the statue. Above his head he heard it crash into the long rays atop the crown, with the rope dangling across the statue's head. Leaning out of the window the little old lady hooked the rope with her extended walking stick and, with a strength belying her age and tiny frame, she dragged a loop of it through the window and into the statue's head. Quickly, as though she had practised it many times, she tied it securely to the spiral staircase.

Below, on the fishing boat, an electric winch had been attached to the rope and this began to climb, pulling a large bag strapped to the rope behind it.

Suddenly, there was more gunfire and Jacob saw the police launch racing forward returning fire. But the three men were heavily armed and one suddenly raised a rocket launcher and sent the rocket hurling into the attacking police boat. There was a tremendous explosion and the bow of the police boat lifted into the air and disintegrated into tiny pieces.

'Shit!' Jacob cursed under his breath. 'This is bad.'

As he frantically wondered what to do he saw the old woman take a camera out of her handbag and with a few deft flicks she turned it into a small radio transmitter.

'This is bad,' he muttered under his breath again. 'Very bad.'

Slowly, he rose to his feet and began backing away from the window, heading for the spiral staircase. The old woman was too preoccupied to pay him any attention and as soon as he reached the staircase he began to run.

Suddenly, from up above, he heard the old woman shouting.

'An eye for an eye!' she screamed. 'An eye for an eye!'

And then, there was a tremendous explosion and he was thrown headlong down the stairs.

A few hundred metres away, in a helicopter racing towards the statue, Paul Gates and an elite FBI unit had been watching the unbelievable attack by the fishing boat and were preparing to intervene. Suddenly, there was a massive explosion near the top of the statue and the enigmatic head of America's most famous national monument was flung into the air, to crash with an enormous splash into Hudson Bay.

'Holy cow!' one of the FBI men said.

The FBI director just stared – speechless. To destroy the Statue of Liberty was a devastating blow, a vile desecration. It was almost as if his grandmother had been killed – it was a personal attack on every American.

Chapter 11

Just under two hours after being created by a cataclysmic failure of the Greenland ice cap, sixteen hundred kilometres away, the mega-tsunami smashed into the west coasts of Ireland and Scotland. Although a mere five hundred metres high by now, the massive wall of water surged over the offshore islands, obliterating the Hebrides, the Shetlands and the Orkneys and crashing into rugged three-hundred-metre-high cliffs. Such was the colossal impact that the ground shook, the spray shot another kilometre into the air and an earth-shattering explosion rolled across the land.

But the deep thunder came just early enough for those in coastal towns and villages to look up and wonder what it was before they were swept away in a roaring maelstrom of water. For a hundred kilometres the wave forged inland, smashing buildings and churning up soil and rocks, becoming a horrible mud- and debris-laden wave. Hundreds of thousands of people, cattle and sheep were drowned in a matter of minutes and, as the wave surged up inlets and valleys, fingers of death and destruction reached the cities of Glasgow, Londonderry and Belfast.

In the narrow northern channel into the Irish Sea, the mega-tsunami was squeezed and blocked, and it was less than two hundred metres high by the time it hit the Isle of Man. It swept

240

across and round the island, destroying Douglas, and headed for the west coast of England.

As Susan and Lucy waited for Blackpool Tower's lift to descend, someone screamed. It was not uncommon and several people had already screamed as they had stepped onto the Walk of Faith. But there was something so bloodcurdling about this scream that Susan looked up. Standing by the railings, a woman was frozen in a tableau of terror, her arm outstretched and pointing out to sea and her eyes wide with shock.

Susan turned to look and an unbelievable sight met her eyes. From horizon to horizon a huge wall of muddy turbulent water and foam surged towards her. Already it had reached the coast in the north, and across Morecambe Bay she could see it surging over Barrow-in-Furness, obliterating the town and heading inland to Morecambe and Lancaster.

Grabbing Lucy's hand, she raced past the gift shop and charged up the first flight of steps towards the top tower. She had no idea how high the monster wave was but she knew that they had to get as high as possible, and at one hundred and thirty-five metres the highest point was another eighteen metres above the Walk of Faith.

Suddenly, there was a massive roaring sound and the tower began to vibrate and hum. As they raced up the stairs she got a glimpse of the wave hitting Blackpool and it almost stopped her in her tracks. Houses, blocks of flats, amusement arcades, the pier, offices, cars, people – everything – simply vanished beneath the surging monster and momentarily she saw a huge oil tanker spinning in the turbulent foam.

Lucy screamed and Susan picked her up and dived up the few remaining steps to the top. And, at that moment, the wave struck the tower. There was a sudden violent gust of wind, a tremendous crash and screech of tortured metal and the tower shuddered violently. She thought it was going to collapse but its lattice structure allowed the water to pass through and it held.

Water rose up and engulfed the lower level, sweeping away the tourists from the gift shop and the Walk of Faith.

'Hold on!' Susan screamed. 'And take a deep breath.'

A gush of water shot up through the stairwell and flowed over them. It seemed like ages but after a few seconds the water began to drain away and Susan and Lucy were left drenched but safe.

After a while, as the roaring of the wave disappeared into the distance, they unsteadily rose to their feet and nervously looked around them. Below, as the water began to drain back into the sea, dragging a jumble of debris and flotsam behind it, there was total desolation.

Blackpool had gone!

4.20 p.m. – North Atlantic Ocean

At the same time that the mega-tsunami was destroying Blackpool, it was sweeping south into the middle of the North Atlantic. For the most part its progress was unseen and unhindered. But rising from the ocean floor and fifteen hundred kilometres from the nearest continent was the Azores archipelago – a string of tranquil tree- and flower-encrusted jewels dotted with whitewashed houses, and blue and green lagoons.

And anchored off the south coast of Terceira, the middle and largest of the nine islands, was a large and luxurious cruise liner. Most of its passengers had already boarded and were relaxing before dinner.

John Houston, sipping a glass of champagne on his balcony, watched the bustle of the little port and mused on how pleasurable the trip had been. He wasn't too bothered with the island hopping and sightseeing or the daily on-board entertainment, but the evening social entertainment was almost the highlight of the day. He revelled in the formal dress code, the cocktail bars, the nightclubs, the casinos and the theatres. And what better way to enjoy it all than in the company of a tall, blonde and stunning

NINE DAYS TO ARMAGEDDON

young lady – they made a distinguished and elegant couple, the envy of many on the *Venus of the Seas*. And afterwards, in their luxurious suite, with the warm exotic scents and sounds wafting through the balcony door, the highlight of each day – the night-time entertainment.

'John,' Anya Petrova called from the lounge, 'I like the Azores. The people are so friendly and the scenery is so beautiful.'

'Like you, my dear,' the Mid-Ocean Oil CEO called back. 'Friendly and beaut . . .'

Suddenly, he stood up and peered across the island. On the other side of the tree-covered lowlands, like Kraken awakening, a huge wave appeared to have risen up and begun surging across the island. Unbelieving, he stared at the 400-metre-high monster as it poured around the extinct volcano, ripping out swathes of trees and crashing into the little town and port. The *Venus of the Seas*, the largest, most elegant and stylish cruise liner to grace the seven seas, was hit sideways by millions of tonnes of water and the whole port side crumpled like a drinks can. The ship was sent tumbling like a toy in the giant turbulent wave.

John Houston, the smooth and distinguished CEO of Mid-Ocean Oil never got to enjoy another night of carnal pleasure.

4.45 p.m. – Prudence Island, New England, USA

On the western side of the North Atlantic, the destructive power of the mega-tsunami ravaged the coast of Labrador, Newfoundland and Nova Scotia and surged down the east coast of Canada and America. With the speed of a cruising commercial jet aircraft, the giant wave swept through the coastal states of New Brunswick, Maine, New Hampshire, Boston, Massachusetts, Rhode Island and Connecticut, wiping away towns and cities and millions of unfortunate people. There was no time for any warning, any evacuation or any preparation. At that time, on a Friday, people were beginning to leave work and head home or to the shops for Christmas shopping.

In the historic city of Boston, the downtown area, sited on a peninsula overlooking the historic harbour, was buzzing with commuters and shoppers. Colonial redbrick buildings mixed with modern office towers, shopping malls and parks, and even in winter it was an attractive place to be. With many people just starting a long Christmas holiday, happy but inevitably stressed from the endless present and food buying, thoughts of Armageddon or the Apocalypse were few and far between.

The first indication that something wasn't quite right would have been a deep and distant roar followed by a shaking of the ground, like a mini earthquake and a violent rush of air. People would have looked up and then at each other – their expressions one of surprise, alertness, shock, fear and, finally, in their last seconds of life, of terror. With darkness surrounding the city, the monster would have swept out of nowhere, two hundred metres high, smashing buildings and people to smithereens. In an instant, the lives, dreams and aspirations of millions of people would have been obliterated and the apocalyptic prophecies become a reality.

Eighty kilometres to the south, and ten minutes away from their own apocalyptic destiny, the inhabitants of Prudence Island were either blissfully unaware or were ready and expectant.

One of the eighty-eight blissfully unaware inhabitants was Old Man Williams who was busily frying fillets of newly caught fish and swigging a mug of homemade beer in his tiny kitchen. His little wooden house, tucked away among stunted pine trees, was little more than a little wooden shack and his pots, pans and cooking utensils had simply been nailed to the walls of the tiny kitchen. It was when these suddenly started rattling and his frying pan began vibrating across the small stove that he got his first inkling of something untoward. Being partially deaf, he only heard the roaring of the mega-tsunami when it had already crossed Narrangansett Bay, wiped out his favourite fishing spots and was virtually knocking on the door. He just had time to look up before being smashed to a pulp by a tidal wave of trees and debris.

In the self-contained subterranean concrete-and-steel world of the only prepared and expectant inhabitants of the island, there was a certain amount of impatience. After all, there was less than eight hours left and there had only been a terrorist attack on the G20 Summit meeting in Iceland. Hardly Armageddon! Where were the Second Coming of Christ and the cataclysmic battle with the demonic forces of Satan? Where were the explosions and brilliant flashes of light as Good fought Evil on the Plains of Megiddo?

Still glued to the bank of television screens, Joseph and the other ninety-two Messianic Jews were not only frustrated but also confused. There had been no more information from Iceland except for confirmation that the American President was now one of the world leaders feared dead. But other than that, there were no more updates from Iceland – it was bizarrely quiet. Perhaps, Joseph thought, a security blanket had been drawn around the terrorist attack or else Satan's cohorts had temporarily won a minor victory.

But it was neither – instead, it was a colossal and devastating tidal wave. And it was about to sweep overhead. As they watched the screens, the ground suddenly began to shake.

'Earthquake!' someone called out.

For a few seconds the vibrations grew and people began to look fearfully around. And then, abruptly, they stopped and all the television screens went blank. There was a collective gasp and then silence.

Eventually, Joseph broke the spell of fearful anticipation.

'Check out the radios,' he ordered.

But like the television screens they were dead apart from an ominous and monotonous hiss.

'Check out the landline telephone and the Internet,' he suggested.

Unknown to the subterranean inhabitants, the satellite dishes and antennae on the roof of their bunker had been swept away and the telephone exchange in the state's capital, Providence, had been demolished along with much of the city.

After desperately trying every link to the outside world for an hour, it was obvious that they were alone. The prophecies had come true – the final battle, the Apocalypse, had begun.

Joseph called everyone together for prayer and for a meeting. They had lived with, and had prepared for, their biblical predictions for years, but when these had come true, it had been something of a shock. Now that it had happened, it was hard to believe.

'Listen up, everyone,' Joseph called out, 'we need to pray and . . .'

4.55 p.m. – New York City, USA

Like Boston at this time of day, New York was alive and teeming with activity – swarms of office workers rushing home or going for a beer, tourists cruising the shops, manic taxis and traffic streaming round and round, power walkers and skateboarders doing their thing . . . New York was a city of endless races, colours, creeds and characters and huge and impressive tower blocks and buildings – the most populous and dynamic city in America, with the best shops, the best restaurants, the best theatres, the best financial centre . . . And in the darkness, just beyond Long Island and Coney Island, the Apocalypse rode the crest of a huge wave almost one hundred metres high, roaring with destructive energy towards the Big Apple. Soon, the geometric streets of Manhattan, Brooklyn and Queens and the winding tunnels and subways, teeming with life, would become raging rivers of death and destruction.

The FBI helicopter pilot was playing a cunning game of cat and mouse with the terrorists in the old fishing boat, hiding behind the Statue of Liberty one moment and the next, easing out sufficiently for the FBI marksmen to open fire. The statue, clad in two-millimetre copper sheeting, provided great cover from the terrorists' bullets, which pierced one side but failed to breach the other. Inside the statue, however, there was very little cover and a still stunned and bleeding Jacob ducked and dived his way down the spiral staircase, the whine and clatter of bullets chasing after him.

But suddenly, there was an enormous rush of air and roaring sound and something massive smashed into the statue. It buckled on one side and creaked and groaned and Jacob's first thought was that a ship or a plane had collided with it.

In the helicopter, the pilot had seen the monstrous wave out of the corner of his eye and instinctively he threw the helicopter into a steep climb. The terrorists' fishing boat was smashed to pieces and Paul Gates couldn't help a moment's feeling of satisfaction and revenge before realising the horror of what he was seeing.

'What the hell is that?' he growled to the pilot. 'Get on to NYPD and City Hall and get an alert . . .'

But as he looked over Hudson Bay towards Queens, Brooklyn and Manhattan, he saw the myriad of glittering lights across a huge expanse of the city disappear in a sweeping wave of blackness – it was like someone was simply flicking the off switch. As the realisation of what was happening sank in, there was a complete and utter stunned silence in the helicopter – family, friends, colleagues and millions of innocent people had simply disappeared.

But inside the submerged statue there was panic and mayhem. Millions of gallons of water were cascading and pouring inside and there were the terrible shouts and screams of hundreds of trapped and panicking tourists in the lower section as they struggled to escape the rising water level.

In the dim emergency lighting of the main body, Jacob had raced down the spiral staircase to escape the evil old woman and the hail of bullets but realised with horror that the exit was blocked and the statue was rapidly filling up – he was trapped.

'Please God,' he pleaded softly, exhaustion and panic beginning to overcome him, 'please help me. Please God, show me the way.'

Suddenly, from up above a bright light shone through the open neck, down into the statue and onto Jacob.

'Nothing we can do here,' Paul Gates shouted to the pilot as he desperately watched the helicopter's search light scan the statue and water. 'I can't see anyone – they must have all perished in there. Let's get back to the city. We might be able to do something useful there.'

Jacob looked up and saw the light. He knew immediately what to do and started to race back up the stairs, drenched and buffeted by the icy waterfall. Behind him the water rose quickly and he struggled to keep ahead, his lungs bursting and his heart pounding frantically. When he neared the top of the spiral staircase towards where the head would have been, he took a detour towards the statue's right arm – the one famously holding the golden torch aloft. Opening a small door, he climbed through and found a steep ladder for use by maintenance men. It was claustrophobic and almost pitch black inside the arm but frantically he began to climb. Suddenly, he burst out into the open, onto the circular platform surrounding the torch, just as a huge whoosh of trapped air and water shot into the night sky.

As he gasped for breath and thanked God for delivering him to safety, he looked down at the statue. Black and turbulent water flowed a few metres below him – Lady Liberty was gone.

5.05 p.m. – La Palma, Canary Islands

Although David Evans was exhausted, he was pleased with himself.

He had accomplished what was, for him, an epic walk along the Cumbre Vieja ridge, eighteen kilometres long and almost two thousand metres high.

It was only two days since he had come to the momentous realisation that he, and his life, were a mess. After ditching his appalling diet, the gallons of beer and the sedentary lifestyle, he already felt better – physically and mentally. He would get fit and return home to find a new job, a job that helped people and brought happiness into this world – he would be a new man.

They had climbed up most of the volcanic peaks along the ridge but, as it was getting late, the guide had decided not to climb the last one but instead to rest, take photographs of the setting sun and then descend. But as the HR director peered into the distance, he suddenly spotted a white line in the north, extending from horizon to horizon. For a moment, he assumed it was an unusual reflection of the sun but, as he watched, it grew larger.

'Miguel,' he called to the guide, 'what is that on the horizon?'

The guide looked where he was pointing and frowned. David got his camera out and started taking pictures. But when he zoomed in on the strange apparition, he gasped.

'It's a wave,' he said simply, 'a giant wave. It must be a tsunami or something.'

It didn't take long for the mega-tsunami, now reduced to less than two hundred metres tall and travelling at five hundred kilometres per hour, to hit the north and west shores of La Palma. The wave tore into the coastal towns, swept over the banana plantations and Canary pine forests and surged up the flanks of the volcanic ridge.

Suddenly, there was a shudder and violent trembling beneath their feet and the HR director looked fearfully at the ground and then at the guide.

'W-what was that?' he gasped.

The guide's eyes were wide with fear and his expression mirrored his feelings – sheer terror.

'The Cumbre Vieja monster has stirred,' he whispered. 'Run!'

Chapter 12

22 December 2012
9.15 a.m. – New York City, USA

'Oh my God!' William Jefferson, the Vice-President gasped, as he stared out of the helicopter's window at the devastation below. 'This is catastrophic – it is by far the worst national emergency this country has ever faced. It will test our resolve and it will test our resourcefulness. But we must overcome this disaster and we must rescue those poor souls trapped by the flood. We have lost many but history must record that we saved many, many more. We cannot, and will not, allow a natural disaster, even one on this scale, to become a national disaster. We cannot fail and whatever it takes will be done.'

In the helicopter, accompanied by Secretary of State Theodore Jackson-Taylor and state department officials from Washington, they were getting their first glimpse of a truly ravaged city. They had no idea how many had died but even conservative estimates put it in the tens of millions. Although most of the water had drained back into the sea, it had left a gruesome legacy – tens of metres deep of mud, debris, timber, vehicles and bodies. In the Manhattan, Queens and Bronx districts, most of the larger buildings had survived but from their roofs and upper windows hundreds of thousands of survivors waved or cried for help, trapped in office blocks and shopping malls.

'This is a huge undertaking,' the Vice-President continued, 'and we have to prioritise. Rescue the wounded and infirm first;

then all these trapped people; and then we must clear the streets, otherwise we will have every disease and contagion known to man. Theodore,' he growled, 'you will need to mobilise the entire country and declare a state of emergency. I will give a Presidential address to the nation at noon.'

The Secretary of State nodded, his face a mask of grim determination.

'And not a stone shall remain unturned,' the Vice-President continued, his voice becoming stern, 'in seeking out those responsible for the terrorist atrocity in Iceland. Be they Islamic fundamentalists, global extremists or plain old-fashioned disaffected crazies – they shall be found and they shall be punished. But we must be mindful of not igniting a tinderbox of repressed hatred – we don't want to see the so-called End of Days prophecies . . .'

'Sir,' one of the state department officials interrupted, 'we're beginning to get information in on the damage to the populated areas in the northern states. I'm afraid New Brunswick, Maine, New Hampshire, Boston, Massachusetts, Rhode Island and Connecticut have all been badly affected. In the older colonial towns, wooden houses and buildings have been turned to matchwood and there has been enormous loss of life. I'm getting provisional estimates of one hundred thousand in New Brunswick; three hundred thousand in Maine; half a million in Boston; sixty thousand in . . .'

As they sped away from Manhattan down the Hudson River listening to the awful litany of destruction, the Vice-President had a brief glimmer of hope – the Statue of Liberty, strangely battered and headless, was still standing – America's symbol of freedom had survived.

But his attention was soon diverted by a frightening and paradoxical sight ahead. Straddling the river and extending from Staten Island to Brooklyn was a huge iceberg, towering over the houses and the buildings it had crushed and standing there as a stark reminder of the enormous and terrifying power of Mother Nature.

'Look, Sir,' one of the FEMA officials suddenly shouted out, 'there appears to be a life raft on it.'

The helicopter flew closer and they could see a man hanging out of the life raft's canopy.

'I think he's alive,' the Secretary of State gasped. 'That's amazing. Where the hell has he come from?'

'Go down and pick him up,' the Vice-President ordered the pilot.

'But, Sir,' the Secretary of State growled, 'we cannot risk you – it looks like a dangerous landing. And, you are the President-elect now.'

The Vice-President looked round at everyone in the helicopter.

'That man might die before we get a rescue chopper over here,' he said, 'and, if I can help it, no one else is going to die in this catastrophe. Take us down.'

Craig Macintyre, frozen, hypothermic, dehydrated, starving and barely conscious, heard a strange noise and thought he was on his way to heaven and they were angel's wings that he could hear. He almost smiled but his frostbitten face wouldn't respond.

'It's all right, Son,' the Vice-President said gently, 'you're safe now.'

'Are you God?' Craig's blackened lips croaked hoarsely. 'Is my journey finally over?'

The Vice-President looked closely at the wreck before him and in his eyes he could see for himself the deep and terrible trauma and suffering that he had endured.

William Jefferson, President-elect, almost broke into tears.

Flying back along the Hudson River they again passed the battered Statue of Liberty. This time, as the Vice-President looked at the iconic monument, he suddenly spotted movement on the top of the outstretched arm and ordered the helicopter pilot to fly closer – an injured and bedraggled man waved frantically at them and the Vice-President waved back to show that he had been seen.

'Get a rescue chopper out here,' he ordered. 'He'll survive but we need to get this man to hospital as soon as possible.'

On the statue, drenched and shivering, Jacob sighed with relief. Soon rescue would come – he would be one of the lucky ones.

'Thank you, God,' he called out, before realising the paradox of thanking a deity who had allowed his survival yet who had unleashed such enormous death and destruction at the same time. 'You are a cruel and strange God and who works in mysterious ways,' he whispered to himself. 'Amen.'

10.55 a.m. – Churchill Falls airport, Labrador

It was shocking news. The worst global disaster since the floods in Pakistan in 2010, the 2004 Indonesian tsunami, the Great Flood in China in 1931, the influenza pandemic of 1918 and the numerous bubonic plague outbreaks around the world. Conservative estimates of the number of people killed ranged from six to twenty-six million. But not only had whole communities been wiped out but whole countries had been obliterated – Greenland and Iceland were unrecognisable, swept clean by ice and water and left virtually uninhabited desolate islands.

'God, it's awful,' Joanna groaned, as they sat in the little lounge of Churchill Falls airport watching appalling images of devastated cities along the east coast of America and the west coast of England. 'I just can't believe it. It's too vast and horrible to take in.'

Professor Conrad shook his head slowly and sadly in disbelief.

'All those poor innocent people,' Joanna added, sighing, 'their lives taken away so suddenly and so horribly.'

She looked over at their pilot, whose face said it all – the shock of losing his family was so unimaginable and traumatic that he stared unblinking at the images, his eyes red with weeping, his mind numb.

'I'm so, so sorry,' she said gently, knowing that whatever she said would be inadequate, but putting her arm round his shoulders for comfort.

The pilot slowly looked round at her and she saw the depths of despair and pain that he was suffering. As he began crying again, tears welled up in Joanna's eyes and rolled down her cheeks.

Later that day, Professor Conrad took Joanna to one side and gently hugged her.

'I'm proud of you, Joanna,' he said softly. 'You are a brave, caring and clever girl. And you have always been the daughter that I never had.'

She looked at him and smiled.

'I have asked you before to come and work with me,' he continued, smiling back, 'and I am going to ask you again. There's a great deal of work to be done – who knows what distortions and pent-up pressures have been created in the Earth's crust after this massive disaster. Who knows what aftershocks and mega-tsunamis are building up. We have to find out and we have to make people listen. Joanna, we need you.'

Joanna looked at him and smiled again. He was right, of course – if the Earth was destabilised, millions more lives could be in jeopardy. It was vital to investigate the trigger for the mega-tsunami and examine the huge forces at work. After all, the Earth's crust was as thin and fragile as an eggshell and mankind lived precariously on it.

Yes, she thought, there was a lot of work to be done.

'We should start right away,' she finally replied. 'There's no time to lose.'

Chapter 13

25 December 2012
12.45 p.m. – Evacuation centre, Manchester, England

Suddenly, the loudspeaker in the huge dining room stopped playing Christmas carols and one of the rescue coordinators spoke.

'Mrs Macintyre, Mrs Susan Macintyre,' he said. 'I have a telephone call for you. Please can you come to the main office?'

Susan put her food down and frowned. She had arranged to stay with her sister in the New Year but wasn't expecting to hear from her yet.

'You stay here, sweetheart,' she said gently to Lucy. 'I won't be long.'

This time it was Lucy's turn to frown.

'No, Mummy,' she said emphatically, 'we're not going to be separated now. I'm coming with you.'

In the main office Susan took the telephone from the rescue coordinator and failed to notice several people watching her.

'Hello,' she said uncertainly. 'This is Susan Macintyre.'

'Hello, Susan,' a voice said. 'This is William Jefferson – the President of the United States.'

Susan looked at the phone, confused.

'The President?' she mumbled.

'Yes, and I wanted to tell you personally,' he continued, 'that we have found your husband, Craig. He's alive and in hospital although he's suffering from . . .'

'Craig?' Susan mumbled, confused and shocked.

'Yes, Susan,' the President said gently, 'he's alive. He must be a very strong and courageous man to survive such a terrible journey and I am proud to have found him and . . .'

But Susan wasn't listening any more. She had slumped to the floor in a heap, tears rolling down her cheeks and sobbing with joy and happiness.

Lucy picked up the phone.

'My daddy's alive!' she gasped, her eyes wide with excitement and elation. 'Oh, thank you, Mr President,' she almost shouted. 'Thank you for finding my daddy.'

'You must be Lucy,' the President said, chuckling. 'Your father has told me all about you. And when he's a little bit better, I'm personally going to see that he returns home safely to you. Goodbye, Lucy, and have a very Happy Christmas.'

'Goodbye, Mr President.'

Lucy hugged her mother and both of them cried unashamedly, surrounded by all the people in the office.

'Lucy,' one of the rescue coordinators said softly, 'we have a little Christmas present for you.'

Lucy and Susan looked up, tears still streaming down their eyes.

'We heard about the sad loss of your puppy,' the rescue coordinator continued, 'and we thought we'd get you one of these.'

Someone passed him a cardboard box and he opened it and pulled out a little, soft and cream-coloured bundle – a young Labrador puppy, all big brown eyes and wagging tail.

Lucy gasped when she saw the tiny bundle, a huge grin spreading across her face and her eyes wide with disbelief and happiness.

'Ooh,' she cooed, cuddling and kissing the little puppy, 'he's so cute. I'm going to call him Bonnie because he's come back to me. My letters have been answered. You're a good Bonnie, but no more eating worms – it's gross!'

Epilogue

21 December 2013
Prudence Island, New England, USA

On a cold and blustery day, one year later, reconstruction work had begun on Prudence Island. A new complex of smart wooden holiday homes was already taking shape and, amid the hubbub of building work, couples and families were excitedly inspecting plots, measuring verandas, planning kitchen and bathroom layouts, frantically calculating their finances or listening to the imaginative sales patter from the marketing executives.

Very few had given much thought to the huge steel doors of an underground concrete bunker set into the low hillside opposite and those who had queried them had been easily pacified by the sales executives. It was only when they noisily began to rumble slowly open did they look up and stare – astonished and a little frightened.

From inside, escaping with a waft of warm, stale air, pale and weak figures emerged, shuffling out from their subterranean home and shielding their eyes from the daylight. Apart from the cries of new-born babies, they were silent and timid, unsure of the post-apocalyptic world they would find.

Were they the only survivors?

Had Satan been finally destroyed?

Was the End of Days truly over?

And was this truly the New Dawn?